Alan Titchmarsh

Only Dad

POCKET
BOOKS

LONDON • NEW YORK • SYDNEY • TORONTO

For Minna and Pops with all my love

First published in Great Britian by Simon & Schuster UK Ltd, 2001
First published by Pocket Books, 2002
This edition published by Pocket Books, 2004
An imprint of Simon & Schuster UK Ltd
A CBS COMPANY

7 9 10 8 6

Simon & Schuster UK Ltd
Africa House
64–78 Kingsway
London WC2B 6AH

www.simonsays.co.uk

Simon & Schuster Australia
Sydney

A CIP catalogue for this book is available
from the British Library.

ISBN-10: 0-7434-7846-0
ISBN-13: 978-0-7434-7846-5

Typeset in Goudy by SX Composing DTP, Rayleigh, Essex
Printed and bound in Great Britain by
Cox & Wyman Ltd, Reading, Berkshire

Acknowledgements

When a father of two daughters writes a book about a father and a daughter, questions are bound to be asked. Mainly by the daughters. But it is an author's privilege not to answer such questions, which means that the reader will have to decide where the truth ends and the story begins.

I owe tremendous thanks to Clare Ledingham who remains a constant source of encouragement and solace, to Suzanne Baboneau for her generosity of spirit, to Amanda Harris for her boundless energy, wicked sense of humour and knowledge of British geography, to Luigi Bonomi who keeps bolstering my confidence and to Hazel Orme whose mastery of the English language is second only to the refinement of her sensibilities.

And I must also thank my two daughters, reminding

them of the legal disclaimer on the title-verso: 'Names, characters, places and incidents are either a product of the author's imagination or are used fictitiously.' You never know; they might just believe it. But then I have always been a dreamer.

Oh, life is a glorious cycle of song,
A medley of extemporanea;
And love is a thing that can never go wrong;
And I am Marie of Roumania.

Dorothy Parker

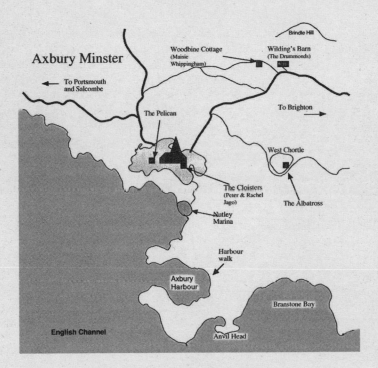

Chapter 1

There are things you ought to know about Tom Drummond. For a start, he never intended to own a restaurant. Well, half of one. Not that there's anything wrong with owning half a restaurant, but it would be a mistake to assume that he had either an obsessive interest in nutrition or a burning desire to entertain. He had neither. He became the owner of half a restaurant entirely by accident. He'd intended to be a farmer. Or, more accurately, his mother had intended him to be one. Tom himself had long harboured dreams of being a writer, but it's difficult to persuade your single parent that you are working when all you do is gaze out of the window wearing a vacant expression. So partly to please his mother and partly because no other job held any particular appeal, Tom became a farmer. It surprised his mother, and it surprised Tom by being particularly enjoyable.

Now you could argue that looking after sheep on the Sussex Downs isn't exactly on a par with crofting in the Cairngorms, but in spite of their supposedly soft location in the southern half of the country, the rolling slopes above Axbury Minster are often blasted by biting winds in winter. Tom and old Bill Wilding would regularly feel the bite of the baler twine on their knuckles as they doled out the summer-scented hay to the obliged Southdown sheep, and the ice on the duck pond would crack like a pistol shot when broken with the heel of a well-placed welly. But on a good day in June or July the smooth, soft slopes were framed by a fuzz of deep green woodland and clear blue sky, and from dawn till dusk Tom shepherded the sheep, cleared the ditches, made the hay and worked the land with a song in his heart and a spring in his step.

Friends asked him why he did it. Why commit yourself to slave labour for peanuts, you, with your nine O levels and three A levels? He knew why: because it gave him thinking time, dreaming time, time to write in his head. So in spite of the long hours and paltry wages, he was, to use an agricultural term, as happy as a pig in muck.

But the happiness was short-lived. Old Bill Wilding

popped his clogs in the dead of winter and the farm came up for sale in spring. After just two years Tom was out of a job and his mother was out of sorts. They took her into a nursing home. For months she deteriorated slowly but steadily and the following summer she departed this life quietly, leaving Tom with a small terraced house, a smaller legacy, a heavy heart and a clean slate.

It was time to write. Unfortunately, as it turned out, it was not the time to publish. After a year of setting down his finely crafted prose on paper only two short stories had appeared in print – one in a regional newspaper and the other in the *Lady*. It was a fair way short of the stuff dreams are made of. Tom conceded that it was time to knuckle down. But to what? Over a bowl of soup in a local bistro he scanned the sits-vac column. Its offerings were not immediately attractive: 'Household insurance: experience essential for liaison and telephone support role' or 'Expanding estate agent requires trainee negotiators'. Difficult to work yourself up into a lather about those. He was beginning to consider seriously how he could fulfil the role of 'Deputy matron required for full-time day duty' when he fell into conversation with the chef – a fair-haired, fresh-faced youth called Peter Jago. Together they bemoaned their respective fates: Tom at a loose end with the remains of a modest legacy, and Peter, with a refreshing lack of anything approaching modesty, desperate to strike out on his own. It was foolhardy, really – they didn't know one another – but they pooled their resources and opened a bistro, the Pelican, with Tom running front-of-house and Peter slaving away in his whites over a hot stove.

To everyone's surprise, except Peter's, the venture took off. But then Peter knew his gnocchi from his goulash and Tom, with his easy-going nature, turned out to be a natural host.

So that's how it started. And it didn't end there. Success encouraged the pair to open another bistro, the Albatross, in a nearby village. But with a twist of irony as bitter as an underripe kumquat, it proved to be more appropriately named than either of them could have foreseen. Although they struggled for the best part of five years to make it pay, in the end the seasonality of the business forced them to cut their losses and sell up.

Not that the Albatross was a total failure on other counts: Peter could bestow his culinary expertise on only one establishment so he had taken on a young cook, a dark-haired girl with a lively wit, a quick mind and a smile that could melt a disgruntled diner three tables away.

It melted Tom, too. They had married within the year and Pippa told him, with a warning flash of her nut-brown eyes, that if he thought he was marrying her just for her cooking he had another thing coming. Tom had not taken the plunge on account of his gastronomic predilections; he had married her because he had never been so totally, irrationally and ridiculously in love in his entire life.

Another thing you ought to know is that Tom Drummond had not given much thought to becoming a father, so it came as a bit of a surprise when a few months after they were married Pippa broke it to him that the patter of tiny feet was a short time away. Over the following months, he accustomed himself to the imminent arrival of their offspring.

Tom was not lacking in the intelligence department, being as quick on the uptake as any other average male. Neither was he ignorant of the probable genetic permutations that might befall, so when Natalie Daisy Drummond – Tally for short – came into his life on 5 May 1985, it took him just seconds to realize that he had become the father of a daughter, and that from now on his life would not be his own.

Partly funded by the sale of the Albatross and partly by Pippa's late parents' legacy, the Drummond family moved from Tom's mother's tiny terraced house in the centre of town to a converted barn that had been one of Bill Wilding's outbuildings. With an acre of land, it suited them down to the ground. Tally grew up among the buttercups and daisies while her mother raised herbs to supply the bistro and a couple of other local businesses.

If you eavesdropped on conversations at the local shops you would discover the general opinion was that the Drummonds had the perfect lifestyle – a view tainted with the merest tincture of envy but not an ounce of ill-will.

The Drummonds have lived at Wilding's Barn for sixteen years now, with never a cross word. Well, that's if you don't count the daily spats about the school run, Tom's exasperated complaints about Tally's loud music when he's making yet another attempt at the now legendary first novel, Pippa's regular complaints about the low prices she's paid for fresh herbs, and Tom's occasional questioning of Tally about the men – or, rather, boys – in her life.

He tries to keep out of her hair as much as he can, but he does find it difficult.

Chapter 2

Any father who wants to survive the role learns very quickly to recognize the different tones of voice in his offspring. It's probably a throw-back to a time when we were on all fours and needed a language less subtle and more succinct in its vocabulary than our present sophisticated *lingua franca*. Tom Drummond had learned to read Tally's minimalist expressions, subtle key changes and vocal inflections after the fashion of a wildebeest at the water-hole responding to the grunts, sighs and gurgles of its progeny.

This morning, it was the tone of voice that indicated the need of a favour – always requested in what Tom had come to think of as 'the three-note "Dad"' – the middle note being a semitone lower than the first and last.

'Da-a-ad?'

Tom sighed and stuck his head round the corner of Tally's bedroom door. 'Mmm?'

'Are you busy?'

'Do I look busy?'

Tally sized up the fraught, preoccupied expression and worked out, in an instant, that the best approach would be one of hurt bewilderment. 'It's just that Mum said she'd drop me off in town and she's gone without me.'

He looked at her as she zipped up the sides of her short, brown, high-heeled boots, the slender legs encased in white jeans, and wondered, as he did almost every time he looked at her, where the years had gone. Clichéd though it might be, it really did seem like only yesterday that she had been knee high and pudgy, clasping his finger in her own plump fist and wrapping her arm around his leg at the approach of any stranger. Now she was sixteen, airily confident yet plagued by insecurities, pretty as a picture yet worried about her spots, trim of figure but fearful of the onset of orange-peel thighs.

Her head was on one side now and she was running a brush through her fine, fair hair in swift, repetitive strokes. Her face, free of make-up except for the mascara on her lashes, and free of spots, if you didn't count the three at her right temple, wore a troubled expression that only her father could lift. She knew the challenge would be irresistible.

'Well, why has she gone without you?'

Tally shrugged and looked blank. 'Don't know.'

'She's gone without you because it's half past ten. She had to be in Axbury at ten o'clock to drop off some herbs. She told you that yesterday.'

Tally looked suitably contrite. 'Slept in.'

'I'm not surprised. What time did you get home last night?'

'Just after eleven.' She said the words lightly, endeavouring to give them little importance.

Tom lowered his head and looked at her from under his frowning brow. 'A quarter past twelve.'

'Was it?' She tried to looked shocked.

Her father nodded.

'Well, you should have been asleep.'

'I'd like to have been. But I wanted to know you were home.'

'But you knew I was with Emma.'

'It doesn't stop me worrying . . .'

She came up to him and smiled, then laid her head on his chest and hugged him. 'You are sweet.'

'Stop trying to butter me up.' He kissed the top of her head. 'If you're ready in two minutes I'll take you. But I'm off then, whether you're ready or not. I want to meet your mum for a coffee.'

She stood upright and looked up at him. He was grateful she was still shorter than he was. Just.

'Thanks, Dad, you're a gem.'

He turned for the stairs. 'Mug, more like.'

While Tally undertook the finishing touches so vital before the rest of the world could be allowed to see her, Tom locked the back door of the house and grabbed his car keys from the hook in the kitchen. He left by the front door and crossed the cobbled yard towards the open end of the barn where the Land Rover stood under a mossy pantiled roof. He was fumbling with the keys when the familiar 'Ooo-ooh!' pierced the clear morning air.

Tom's spirits sank, not so much because of the noise but because of its timing. Maisie Whippingham was a good soul, but in the comprehensive list of her personal deficiencies the inability to choose the right moment to do anything was the most well developed. Among her other shortcomings were a dress sense that made Alexander McQueen seem reserved, and a scant understanding of the sun's relationship with the earth. It wasn't that Maisie was always running late, it was that she failed to recognize that time could be measured on an hourly basis. She acknowledged the days, weeks, months and years, but any further subdivisions were of little account. She ate when she was hungry and she slept when it got dark; her activity in summer was prodigious and in winter minimal. Now, in June, she was at her most industrious.

She waved from behind the hedge of Woodbine Cottage, just across the lane from Wilding's Barn, and beckoned Tom.

'I can't stop, Maisie. I have to take Tally into town then meet up with Pippa and I'm running late already.'

'Yes. Of course. Sorry. It's just that I wanted you to know that I've a load of manure coming.'

'When?' Tom realized the futility of the question the moment he had asked it.

'Sometime.'

'Today?'

'Probably.' Maisie smiled vaguely from beneath the explosion of salt-and-pepper hair restrained under her turban.

Tom put his hands on his hips. 'What do you want manure for, Maisie?'

Maisie's garden was not so much a garden as a conservation area. Mother Nature had long since gained the upper hand and, aside from an annual summer foray with a machete to carve a hole in the brambles for an old pine chair and an easel, Maisie regarded the patch of ground around Woodbine Cottage as a safe haven for birds, hedgehogs and other forms of wildlife that she hoped one day to commit to canvas. Painting was her passion, and however

11

unrecognizable her subjects might be once they had been immortalized within the frame, she loved the idea of being an artist, and read about painting, sculpting and other forms of ornamental creativity – from origami to macramé – in every spare moment. There were a lot of them. Until she was fifty-five she had worked in a bank in London. Then she had retired, sold her London flat, disposed of every form of timepiece that had hitherto ruled her life, bought Woodbine Cottage and set about being a countrywoman – or her idea of a countrywoman.

She went to auctions, when she got the day right, bought strange *objets d'art* to furnish the cottage and dressed like a cross between Edith Sitwell and Vita Sackville-West. Today's turban was multicoloured and sparkled with gold thread, and she wore a navy blue fisherman's smock topped off with a purple chenille scarf and a pair of brown corduroy trousers tucked into knee-high boots. She was clearly in outdoor mode.

'Want to have a bash at the herb garden,' she said.

'But you haven't got a herb garden.' Tom tried not to sound too scathing.

'Not yet. Want soups and things. Like Pippa's.'

Tom cast an eye over the low hawthorn hedge that surrounded Pippa's orderly herb garden, where serried ranks of fennel and coriander were surrounded by borders of parsley and chives. Rocket and salad burnet jostled for light and air between orange marigolds and wigwams of sweet peas. It was Pippa's passion and her pleasure, and Maisie had clearly been bitten by the bug.

'You've a bit of a job on, then?' Tom nodded at the head-high mattress of brambles and thistles that sprang from Maisie's local landscape.

'Getting help. Mr Poling. Coming soon.'

'Well, good luck. Let us know if you want a hand. Later, anyway. Bit pushed now.'

Maisie nodded a mixture of gratitude and understanding – a visual aid intended to complement her conversation, which came out in staccato bursts. 'Tell Pippa – speak later. Need information. Chervil and stuff.' She waved again before ducking back inside Woodbine Cottage, squeezing past the pile of old newspapers that grew ever taller and threatened, one day, to engulf the little porch and its spiralling honeysuckle vine. That was the other thing about Maisie: she never threw anything away. Everything might come in handy. One day.

Tom looked at his watch. There was no sign of Tally. He opened the door of the Land Rover, started it up and sounded the horn, then drove out on to the cobbled yard to wait for his daughter. Still no sign. 'I'm going!' he shouted up at her bedroom window, and gave a couple of revs on the accelerator. Tally flew out of the front door, a jacket on one arm and a bag over the other. 'Sorry! I forgot my mobile.'

Tom shook his head as she climbed up on to the seat beside him. 'Have you locked the door?'

'Oh! Sorry!' Her face contorted and she scrabbled for her keys in her bag.

Tom sighed, switched off the engine and withdrew his own keys from the ignition. 'I'll go,' he muttered resignedly. 'I sometimes wonder if you were born in a barn,' he said, when he got back.

'No. I just live in one.'

He looked at her with a mock scowl, then drove off in the direction of Axbury Minster. As always, with her beside him, he felt like a million dollars.

Chapter 3

Axbury Minster was the kind of town that Anthony Trollope wrote about, a sort of pocket-sized Oxford with muddy feet. It had once been a market town – still was if you counted the farmers' market on the first Monday of every month – but its days of livestock auctions had ceased a good twenty years ago and the sheep pens were now a smart pedestrian precinct coping with well-heeled rather than cloven feet.

The Minster itself wasn't Sussex's finest example of Early Perpendicular, but Betjeman had been complimentary about it even if Pevsner was a bit sniffy.

For the locals it was still the heart of the community, whatever any outsider thought, and held the town together, architecturally if not spiritually.

The Pelican occupied the ground floor and basement in part of a Georgian terrace, which makes it sound grander than it was. It was listed, but it was also listing – to the north-east. At the moment of its creation in 1730 the architect had been having an off-day and his proportions, although generous on a vertical scale, five floors, were economical on width, twenty feet, and niggardly on foundations. But the building had a quaint charm, and the Minster was just a stone's throw away so some of its influence and atmosphere rubbed off on its lesser relations.

Having dropped off Tally outside the Axbury Tearooms where she fell into the arms of her friend Emma with hugs and girly shrieks, Tom parked the Land Rover in the narrow yard to the rear of the restaurant and let himself in through the kitchen door. The usual scenes of lunchtime mayhem – clouds of steam and harassed mutterings from the kitchen staff working their magic over the flames and hotplates of a furnace – had yet to materialize. It was a quarter to eleven on a Saturday morning, the calm before the storm – they opened at noon. Ellen, a plump old dear from the estate on the far side of town, whose arms were a rich shade of rose pink from having been immersed in washing-up liquid continuously for ten years, was sweeping the kitchen floor in readiness for the onslaught.

'Mornin'. Nice one.' She squeezed out a smile and revealed her shortcomings in the dental department.

'Lovely.'

'Thought you were off this lunchtime?'

'I am. I've just parked up here. Peter about?'

Ellen nodded in the direction of the restaurant, and wiped a drip off the end of her nose with practised dexterity and the back of her hand.

Tom pushed open the swing door of the kitchen and walked through to the front of the bistro. He wove his way between scrubbed pine tables and bentwood chairs, past framed opera posters and gesso-edged mirrors, towards the bar that ran down one side of the dining area. The Pelican comprised two long narrow dining rooms on the ground floor, plus the kitchen at the back. The cellar ran the entire depth of the building and was packed most mealtimes, Fridays and Saturdays in particular. On Sundays they closed and got their breath back.

Peter was behind the bar restocking cool cabinets with bottles of lager. He looked up as the kitchen door swung open. 'Can't keep away?'

'Just parked here. Everything all right?'

'Funny you should ask.'

'What do you mean?

'Sam's handed in his notice.'

'What?'

'Says he's found a new job. In Brighton. A partnership. Bastard.'

Tom grimaced. 'Well, you can't blame him. That's what you did.'

'I know, but his timing's not exactly brilliant, is it? Summer is a-coming in and all that. All sing cuckoo!'

Sam had been working at the Pelican for the best part of three years. Peter had taken him on as his junior and trained him up. He'd caught on quickly, not only learning fast but also developing his own creative style, which meant that Peter could have an occasional weekday off – something Tom managed too on account of the growing skills of Sally, the head waitress. Between them Sam and Sally had given Tom and Peter's lives some semblance of normality.

Sam also took the reins when Peter had one of his 'moments'. All chefs have them: they occur when the relentless provision of finely crafted fodder is at an apparent imbalance with the appreciation of the diners. In other words, he got the hump when he thought he was being taken for granted.

These occasional wobblies blew over quickly. He'd return the following day as though nothing had happened, and Tom had learned to cope with the creative temperament – wondering, sometimes, if his

18

own literary capabilities might be improved by the occasional tantrum.

Sam's departure was bad news. It looked as though they would be plunged back into the dark ages – in the kitchen at least.

Peter stretched his hands above his head, then ran them through his fair curly hair. 'It's a bugger. Rachel's going to be delirious.'

Rachel Jago was Peter's driving force, or so she liked to think, not that she'd been in the driving seat for very long. They'd married just two years previously – it was Rachel's third attempt. Her first husband had run off with his secretary, and her second husband had just run off. Peter had resisted a long-term relationship for fifteen years or more but buckled under the onslaught of Rachel's determination. She was the only person he'd met whose will overpowered his own and he seemed constantly in awe of her. The fact that Peter had his own restaurant was convenient from Rachel's point of view and she dined at the Pelican most days with a girlfriend or two in tow. It still rankled when Tom presented her with a bill at the end of the meal, not that she let it show: she would smile broadly and murmur to her guest, 'Have to keep the books in order. No freebies here,' before slipping her gold card on to the saucer and replenishing her scarlet lipstick.

Rachel would have liked Peter to run a chain of restaurants – Le Caprice and the Ivy preferably. She saw him as a sort of Terence Conran on speed and tried her best to persuade him to give up cooking to become more entrepreneurial. The Albatross disaster had happened long before her time. 'The climate's different now. People want variety – they don't want to go to the same restaurant week in, week out. Open another. I'd come, and so would all my friends. You're too talented to put all your eggs in one omelette.'

Having listened to her argument almost daily for the best part of two years, Peter was beginning to think there was sense in what she said – what Rachel lacked in the intellectual approach to an argument she made up for in dogged persistence. So far, Tom was unaware of her apparent progress, but he had detected a certain tension when he was in her presence. The truth was that, for once in her life, Rachel had met her match: Tom Drummond might appear gentle and calm on the outside, but she knew that underneath he was a man of steel. It unsettled her.

Pippa missed nothing. She read Rachel like a book and teased Tom, suggesting that the real reason Rachel appeared nervous with him was that she fancied him. Tom would shudder and give his wife a reassuring hug. Rachel, with her extravagant ambitions, short auburn hair, sharp features and wardrobe expenditure roughly comparable with the Vatican's bill for vestments, was not Tom's type.

What was his type? He had married Pippa seventeen years ago when he was twenty-two and she was twenty, and had known from their first meeting that there would never be anyone else for him. Which was odd: until then he hadn't even been able to decide if he took sugar in his tea.

Now Tom left the Pelican, and a cursing Peter, and walked down the narrow street towards the Minster. Through the window of the Parson's Pantry he saw her, waiting patiently while the prim proprietress wrapped a loaf in a paper bag and pushed it into her basket. As she came through the doorway she saw him and her face lit up. 'I thought you were writing.'

'Taxi driving.'

'She should have caught the bus.'

'Well . . .'

'You're such a soft touch.'

Tom grinned. 'Fancy that coffee? No words flowing this morning.'

'Come on, then, my literary genius.'

Tom's book had become something of a family joke. Nobody expected him to finish it, least of all Tom himself, but it was taken every bit as seriously as if it were the Bayeux Tapestry or the Forth Bridge. It was something that had to be done little by little, and it kept Tom sane.

Pippa put her arm through his and they set off in the direction of the glass and chrome café with its alloy chairs and tables on the pavement, just across the road from the Axbury Tea-rooms patronized by Tally and her mates. Pippa glanced at the gloomy exterior of the brown-painted teashop. 'Is she in there?'

'Yes. Dishing the dirt probably. Funny, isn't it? You'd have thought we'd be in there and that she'd be over here. More her age group.'

Pippa laughed. 'No, they love it in there, with all the old dears. Nobody's bothered about eavesdropping. And they do good toasted teacakes.'

As they sat and sipped their coffee he told her about Sam, and about Peter's reaction.

'Well, you can see his point,' Pippa said reasonably. 'What a bummer. What are you going to do?'

'Advertise, I suppose.'

'When's Sam wanting to leave?'

'End of next month.'

'That's a shame, but it's too late to change things now.'

'Too late to change what?' Tom asked.

'The arrangements.'

'What sort of arrangements?'

'Holiday arrangements.'

'Whose holiday arrangements.'

'Ours.'

'We don't have any.'

'We do now.'

Tom eyed her suspiciously.

'Don't look at me like that. When did we last have a holiday – a family holiday?'

'Last year.'

Pippa sighed and rested her head in her hands. 'I don't call a long weekend in Bath a proper holiday.'

'So?'

'You need a holiday. We *all* need a holiday – you said yourself that the words aren't flowing. You need a break, get the creative juices working.'

'Just a minute . . .'

'No buts. It's booked. Two weeks in Tuscany, a little villa in its own vineyard.'

'When?'

'End of the month. Tally will have finished her exams and Peter can cope with the bistro.' He looked at her open-mouthed. 'You're not indispensable, you know. It's only food,' she said gently.

'But what about Sam?'

'Advertise for a replacement. You can have it sorted before we go. And, anyway, you don't cook so the kitchen isn't your province. It's Peter's problem.'

Tom shook his head. 'No. Rachel is Peter's problem.'

'Poor love.'

'But even so . . .'

Pippa drained her cup and smiled. 'Don't you want to come on holiday with two dishy girls, then?'

'Well, yes, but . . .' He tried to cobble together some words that would explain why this was not a good time, but produced no more than a strangled cry of mock anguish.

With suspiciously adept timing, the head of a fair-haired teenage girl popped through the café doorway. 'How did he take it?' she called.

Her mother turned to her and winked. 'Like a lamb.'

Her father took another sip of his now lukewarm coffee. 'I don't know why I bother.'

But he did, really.

Chapter 4

'Do you think I'm too easy-going?'

Pippa surfaced from a deep sleep and turned to face him, her eyes still tight shut, one arm pulling the covers over her shoulders to keep in the warmth. 'Mmm? What?'

'Sorry. I thought you were awake. I was just thinking.'

'Dangerous.' She pushed out a hand from under the sheets and stroked the side of his head. 'Thinking about what?'

'Whether or not I'm a pushover.'

She opened one eye. 'What's brought this on?'

'Dunno.' He was lying on his back gazing at the ceiling. 'Mid-life crisis, I suppose.'

'Bit early, isn't it?'

'I'm thirty-nine.'

She opened the other eye. 'Well, I'm thirty-seven and I don't intend having mine for a good ten years yet.'

'It's just that sometimes I take stock and I wonder what I've achieved. Where has it all gone?'

They were lying in bed on a Sunday morning, the sun slanting through a chink in the curtains. The house was silent, but the air outside was filled with birdsong and country sounds – the distant bleating of sheep, a breeze rustling through the leaves of a towering sycamore, the low, throaty growl of a tractor coming and going.

'So why do you think you haven't achieved anything?'

'Well, I just wonder if I should have taken charge more, instead of being pushed around by . . . you know . . .'

'"The slings and arrows of outrageous fortune"?' Pippa stifled a yawn.

'Something like that. Fate.'

'You? Pushed around? Fat chance.' She snuggled up to him and put an arm around his waist.

'Well, it took you to organize this holiday we're going on.'

'That's because you hadn't time.'

'It's just that I sometimes wonder how I've ended up

26

where I've ended up. I mean, I never intended to be like this.'

'Thanks very much!'

'I don't mean us. I mean my life. Work. That sort of thing. Why the heck am I running a restaurant? It's ridiculous.'

'It's successful.'

'Yes, but . . . it's not what I intended.'

'So what did you intend?'

'I don't know, really. I don't suppose I ever have. There's writing but maybe I'm not driven enough. I just seem to have these distant dreams of something – I'm not quite sure what.'

'And this isn't it?'

He propped himself up and turned to face her. 'Well, no – yes. I mean, you and me, this is what I wanted, what I *want*, but I'm not sure about the rest.'

'Well, I'm relieved about the first bit.'

'But do you see what I'm trying to say?'

'I see exactly what you're trying to say,' she said. 'We're all conditioned from birth to have some sort of life-plan, a career pattern we follow slavishly until we retire. And after that we have time to do all those things we've had to miss out on between the ages of eighteen and sixty-five, secure in the knowledge that we've achieved our goals.' She kissed his cheek. 'You can't work out why at thirty-nine you're still not in charge of

27

yourself or where you're going. Truth is that nobody is, really. Most people are bored out of their brains.'

'I suppose so.'

'Come on, hun. Who do you know who's really in charge of their lives?'

'Peter is. Rachel is.'

Now it was Pippa's turn to prop herself up. 'And those two are your role models, are they? A temperamental chef and his harpy of a wife.'

'Oh, you know what I mean!'

'I don't know what you mean at all.' There was mischief in her voice. 'Unless you want to throw tantrums every now and again, and have your wife browbeat you into doing things you don't want to do.'

'Well, you do anyway.'

'You . . .!' She pinched him and he let out a yell.

'Don't do that or I'll . . .'

'What? What will you do?' She kept pinching.

'This.' He pushed his naked body on top of hers, then wrapped his arms around her and kissed her. There was a tap at the bedroom door and he rolled away from her swiftly, pulling the sheets up to his neck. The door opened and a tousle-haired teenager walked in, oblivious to the suppressed grins on her parents' faces.

'Can I have the bathroom?'

'All yours.'

'Thanks.' The bleary-eyed vision in an oversized T-shirt bearing the legend 'I am a Natural Blonde, Please Speak Slowly' retreated from the room and closed the door behind her.

'Close!' Pippa giggled.

'Probably doesn't think we do it anyway.' Tom screwed his face up. 'Eugh! How disgusting! People your age!'

'Shouldn't be allowed!'

'It isn't . . . very often,' muttered Tom.

'Are you complaining?'

Tom looked thoughtful. 'Yes, I suppose I am.'

'Well, she's having a bath. How quick can you be?'

'Oh, you know me . . . quick as you like.'

'Sssh! She'll hear you,' Pippa laughed.

They lay in each other's arms, hot and exhausted.

'Bathroom's empty!' came the distant cry.

'Thanks,' Pippa shouted, as she stroked Tom's forehead. 'You're all sweaty,' she remarked.

'Well, I wouldn't like you to think that I was going off at half-cock.'

'Never an accusation I'd level at you.'

He smiled a satisfied smile. 'I'm very glad.'

'Better get up, then.'

'Suppose so. What's Madam doing today?'

'Out on the toot. With one of her fellas, I think.'

'One of? How many's she got?'

'Just the two.'

There was a sardonic note in Tom's voice. 'Can't make up her mind?'

'Doesn't want to. Happy playing the field.'

'That's what blokes are supposed to do. Women are supposed to be faithful. Monogamous.'

'Tom! Welcome to the twenty-first century.'

'Is she still going out with whatsisname – Blob?'

'Blip,' Pippa corrected.

'What sort of a name's that?'

'It's his nickname.'

Tom looked puzzled. 'How does a guy come by a nickname like Blip?'

'His parents already had four children, then he came along. They hadn't intended to have any more. He was a blip in their birth control.'

'Poor little sod. Seems a bit wet to me.'

'Not really. He's sweet, just a bit shy – especially when you're around.'

'But it's not serious?'

'Oh, I think Blip would like it to be, but Tally says he's just a friend.'

Tom looked thoughtful. 'Do you ever wonder what it would have been like if . . . we'd had more?'

'Sometimes. It would have been nice, given her some company. But she seems to have turned out all right. And you can't fight nature, can you?'

Tom leaned forward and kissed her. 'It couldn't have been any better, could it?' He saw that her eyes were glistening with tears, and changed the subject. 'So who's the other hunk?'

'Ask her yourself.'

Tom looked hurt. 'I don't like to pry.'

'But you're dying to know!'

'Yes. And I don't want to be one of those interfering dads who disapproves of his daughter's boyfriends.'

'But you will be.'

Tom smiled unwillingly. 'I know.'

'Well, you needn't worry too much. I told you, she's into friendships rather than romance. Doesn't want to get bogged down.'

'That won't last.'

'No, but I think we should be grateful while it does.' Pippa slid out of bed and walked over to the window, throwing back the curtains to let in the Sunday-morning sun. 'Nice day.' She turned round to face him.

Tom looked at her, framed by the morning light. Her dark brown hair lightly brushed her shoulders, her breasts were round and firm, her waist was still a waist, and her legs, though short, were shapely, taut and lightly tanned. 'You look lovely.'

'I wish I could say the same for you.'

Tom threw back the sheets and got out of bed. He

was taller and broader than she was and he fixed her with a wicked grin. 'Right! That's it!' He advanced on her slowly.

'Tom! Stop it! You'll wake Tally!'

'She's awake.'

'You know what I mean!' She dodged around the bed as he stalked her, like a wolf with its prey. 'I'm warning you! I'll scream!'

'Screams will get you nowhere, little girl! When I've finished with you, you won't be able to scream.'

'Dad, are you being stupid again?' The voice came from the landing outside their bedroom. 'Put your clothes on and be your age. I've made some tea.'

They froze and looked at each other wide-eyed, then collapsed in fits of laughter.

'So, er, what are you doing today?' Tom tried to sound casual as he munched toast and marmalade.

'Going out.' As he had expected, Tally's reply was non-committal.

'Anyone I know?'

'Dad! Don't be ridiculous.'

Tom coughed as a crumb went down the wrong way, then took a sip of coffee to wash it down. 'Only curious.'

Pippa sat down opposite him at the kitchen table, and turned to Tally. 'You know what dads are like, anxious about their children's welfare.'

Tally raised her eyes heavenward. 'And you know what daughters are like,' she said. 'Irresponsible and flighty. Especially after exams when all they want to do is . . . let their hair down!' She smiled at her father. 'Don't worry, Dad. I'm not a slapper.'

Tom choked on his coffee, then recovered himself. 'I should hope not.'

'You're quite safe,' Tally went on. 'As far as I can see the only things that guys are interested in are sleeping, drinking and farting.'

Tom paused, mid-chew, surprised first by his daughter's candour, and second by her accuracy.

Tally warmed to her subject. 'It's true. They're children, basically. I'm not ready for children yet.'

'That's a relief.'

'I think she's trying to reassure you,' Pippa put in.

'I'll try to be reassured.' He drained his cup. 'So where are you wanting a lift to today?'

'I'm being picked up.'

'Thank heavens for that. At last, a friend with his own car.' Then the other side of the coin showed its face and concern set in. 'Is he a good driver?'

'Dad! Stop worrying!' She laid a hand on his. 'He's very careful and he knows I won't even get into the car if he drinks. OK?' She looked at her father's furrowed brow.

Tom sighed. 'Sorry.'

'Oh, it's very flattering, really. I rather like a protective dad. Up to a point.'

'And no further?'

Tally smiled. The sound of tyres crunching on gravel and two short blasts of a horn signalled the arrival of the beau of the day. The object of his affections got up from the table and took her leave. 'I won't be late. Alex has to go out with his parents tonight so I should be back about six. OK? 'Bye.' She kissed her mother's cheek, patted her father's head as though he were a favourite dog, and ran out of the front door, leaving behind her the heady fragrance of a scent that her father wished he were young enough to recognize.

'Well, that's that, then.' Pippa began to clear the table.

Tom gazed out of the window. Then, he asked casually, 'Who's Alex?'

It was Rachel and Peter's day off, too, but it would not be spent, *ad hoc*, as the Drummonds intended. Life at No. 1 The Cloisters – an elegant, white-fronted townhouse in the shadow of the Minster – was planned with precision. Sundays began with a late breakfast, cooked by Peter, and ended with dinner for friends, Rachel's in particular, which she insisted, was a joint effort. This meant that Peter cooked it and she laid the table. The time between might allow Peter to escape for half an hour to walk Delia, his Jack Russell, but was occupied mainly with projects of Rachel's devising. Today they were visiting Payne, Ward and Hatherley, a firm of estate agents. It was a stroke of luck that they were open all day on Sunday.

Rachel had found just the place for Peter's new restaurant – another Georgian townhouse but of far greater elegance than the tottering pile that was the Pelican. Peter's resistance was crumbling: all he needed now was the final push. She would sort out Tom later, once the deal had been finalized. Quite how she imagined Peter would be able to keep secret its existence from his partner, or would even want to, is difficult to understand, but Rachel Jago was a woman with a mission, and nothing would prevent her getting her own way, not even Tom Drummond. The prospect of persuading him gave her a sharp thrill. And what about Pippa? She would need careful handling – but she'd come round: all that was needed was the right approach.

Everyone makes mistakes in their lives, mis-calculations, and Rachel was about to do so. Again.

Chapter 5

'Like the car?'

''S all right. Not much room for bales of hay.'

Alex Blane-Pfitzer turned to Tally with a look of incomprehension. Then he saw the joke. 'Oh, very funny. Bit faster than a horsebox, though.'

'Mmm.' Tally was determined to seem unimpressed with the black Mazda MX5. After all, people shouldn't be given cars like this on their eighteenth birthday. Even if they were second-hand.

'So where to?'

'Thought you'd have decided.'

Alex put a brave face on it. 'The Marina or the Old Harbour?'

'The Old Harbour. It's prettier.'

'OK.' He put his foot down and roared off down the lane. Tally coughed politely and nodded at the 30 m.p.h. sign at the side of the road. If anyone else had done so, Alex would have raised a brace of digits. In this case, he slowed down.

Tally seemed to be enjoying the rush of the wind through her hair, even at the relatively modest speed, and breathed in the fresh early-summer fragrance. Alex kept glancing at her, hoping she wouldn't notice since he was wearing a pair of Storm shades.

'Do you like it around here?' he asked.

She nodded. 'It's the best.'

'Better than London?'

'Much. Can't stand the smell. Or the people. They seem so miserable all the time – walking around with long faces.'

'But London's cool.'

'Who cares about cool?'

Alex turned to her and laughed. 'You're funny.'

Tally shrugged and looked sideways at the hedgerow, filled with foxgloves and stitchwort, cow parsley and campion. 'Maybe,' she muttered.

Alex squeezed into a parking space alongside the Old Harbour, got out and went round to Tally's side to open her door. He offered her a hand, which she took, then pulled her up. They stood facing each other for a moment, and he pushed his shades on to the top of his head. Then she smiled and said, 'Better lock it. Don't want it pinched.'

'No.' The moment had passed. Alex came to and clipped on the hood, then locked the doors.

'They're the easiest cars to break into, you know,' said Tally, matter-of-factly.

'Sorry?'

'Sports cars. I read it somewhere. It takes a burglar three seconds to get inside.'

Alex looked at her, puzzled. 'Oh?'

'Just thought you'd like to know.'

'Thanks.'

He held out his hand, she took it and they began to walk along the path that led from the harbour round the mouth of the estuary. She was a strange girl. He tried to impress her but every time it seemed he failed. Other girls would be excited by his lifestyle, grateful to share it, even, but not Tally Drummond. And yet right now there was no one in whose company he would rather be. She was . . . well . . . a challenge.

It was the perfect June morning – a gentle warmth from the sun, the air still now that the early-morning breeze had dropped. From the winding estuary path – really just dried and flattened mud between rough tussocks of grass – they could see small boats cruising down the Channel. They rounded a small copse, deep green in its summer livery, and a blackbird belted out its alarm call as it fluttered from an overstuffed mattress of brambles. They sat down on a peeling bench to look at the view. Alex slipped his arm around her shoulder and leaned back.

Tally spoke first. 'You'd rather have London than this?'

'Oh, I like it here at weekends, but I miss the action and the company. No mates down here, really – well, one or two, I suppose.'

She seemed not to hear him, not from lack of interest but from being absorbed in what she saw in front of her. The sun glinted on the ebbing tidal waters of the Axe, and they could hear the faint voices of yacht crews as they hauled up sails and pulled in fenders. Gulls and oyster-catchers perforated the air with their shrill calls, and she wondered how anyone could prefer the bustle of a city to this.

Alex saw that he was not getting through. He tried harder. 'Maybe it's because you were born here.'

Tally felt suddenly embarrassed at her apparent rudeness. 'I suppose so. I just the love the sounds and the smells.' She turned to face him. 'How long have you been coming here?'

'A couple of years – ever since my parents bought a house down here. Dad works all the hours God sends. We live in Holland Park, but he wanted somewhere to switch off at weekends. A bolt-hole. That's why he bought The Lodge.'

'He must be doing well.'

'Never thought about it. Don't really see a lot of him. Except at weekends.' He poked around at the smooth pebbles with his toe, looking for a suitable one to skim. 'What about your dad? What does he do?'

'He runs a restaurant. I see him every day.'

'Lucky you.'

'Yes.' She said it lightly but meaningfully.

'You must know him better than I know mine.'

'I've never really thought about it. He's just there.'

'Do you get on?'

She looked thoughtful. 'Yes, I suppose we do. He's irritating and a bit vague sometimes – as though he's not really there – but he's always there . . . if you see what I mean.'

'Can you talk to him?' Alex sat quite still, gazing out across the water.

Tally nodded. 'Always. Sometimes I don't want to, but I know I can if I do want to. He's just . . . well, Dad. How about you?'

'Oh, you know.'

'No, I don't.'

Alex hesitated, unwilling to be disloyal. 'We haven't seen much of each other because I went away to school and Dad works in the City.'

'Did he buy you the car?'

'Yes.'

'The insurance must be huge.'

Her practicality surprised him. 'I suppose so.'

'But you don't really know him?'

Alex shrugged. 'Sometimes I think he'd like to talk more but it's a bit difficult, so I stay out of his way most of the time. Holidays are about the only time we see one another. We go to Salcombe every August, and sometimes earlier in the summer for an odd week. We've a cottage there. Dad likes to sail.'

'And you?'

'Yeah, I like it, too. Till he starts shouting!' He grinned. 'Mum won't sail with him any more. He gets a bit worked up.'

Tally smiled sympathetically. 'I don't remember my dad shouting. He just goes quiet.' She got up and walked to the water's edge, then turned and looked back at him. 'So what about you? What are you going to do with your life?'

'Depends on my As. I've got a place at Edinburgh if I get my grades.'

'To do what?'

'Economics.'

'Yuk!'

He picked up a stone and skimmed it across the rippling water. 'What about you?'

41

'Oh, I want to do what everybody else seems to be doing. Marine biology. But I've only just done my GCSEs so I'm two years behind you.'

'The perfect age gap.' He saw her colour and now it was her turn to pick up a stone and throw it into the limpid water.

Tally looked at his reflection in the shimmering surface, watched his arms flex and extend as he skimmed more pebbles. She walked up the bank a little and sat down on the grassy edge of the path, drawing her knees up under her chin, running her hands over the soft denim and watching him throw stones. Emma was right, he *was* fit, not the spoiled brat Tally had assumed he would be. To be truthful, she had only agreed to go out with him because she was flattered he'd asked her rather than Emma when he saw them in the tea shop. He was tall – a good six feet – and had short fair hair, turned up at the front into that quiff they all seemed to have right now. He wore sturdy deck shoes, jeans that showed off his neat bum, and a baggy pale pink shirt worn outside his trousers. His face, often frowning, was square-jawed, his eyes pale blue. And he had nice hands. She had noticed those straight away. But it was clear that he was indulged by his parents. She was too, but it seemed different somehow.

He turned from the water's edge and came up to where she sat. She shivered slightly, then smiled at him almost apologetically. He sat down beside her, leaned towards her and kissed her. She felt her face moving towards his with a naturalness that surprised her. She closed her eyes as his warm lips pressed against hers. They were softer than she'd imagined. And he smelt of soap. It was a nice kiss.

She pulled away from him and looked out across the water again. She felt a strange kind of anxiety that she had not felt before. She could not work out why.

They sat quietly for a while. Then he asked, 'Are you going out with anybody?'

'Not really.'

'Can I see you again?'

She paused and smiled shyly. 'If you like.'

They got up and walked further along the estuary path, he with his arm around her shoulder, and she with her hands in her pockets.

'We have a problem.' Tom was standing in the kitchen doorway, jangling his car keys and looking mildly irritated.

'What sort of problem?' Pippa looked up from the basket she was filling with sandwiches and crisps, a bottle of wine and two glasses.

'Where did you fancy going for this picnic?'

'Don't mind. Why?'

'How about the back of the barn?'

'Well, I'd thought we might go a bit further than that. Down to the coast? Up on to the Downs?'

'Could be tricky.'

'Why?'

'Maisie's manure has arrived.'

'What's that got to do with it?' Pippa looked puzzled.

'It's right in the middle of the lane. I know I have a Land Rover with four-wheel drive, but I don't really fancy driving it over a mountain of muck.'

Pippa grinned. 'Looks like the back of the barn, then.'

'What a bugger!' Tom hung the keys back on the hook. 'I don't know about getting away for a fortnight's holiday – it seems to me we can't even get away for half a day.'

Pippa craned her neck to see out of the doorway. 'Why she thinks she needs that amount of manure to grow herbs I've no idea. They'll be six feet tall with no flavour at all. Is she moving it?'

'Oh, she's got Mr Poling beavering away with a barrow but it'll take him a couple of hours to get anywhere and then we'll have lost the best part of the day.'

'Does he want a hand?'

'Won't hear of it. Says he doesn't want to spoil our Sunday. I didn't feel I could tell him he'd done that already.'

'What about Maisie?'

'Not up yet. Clearly thinks it's still the middle of the night.'

'Come on, then.'

'Where?'

'Looks like we're in for a bit of a hike. Exercise will do us good. Last one up Brindle Hill's a cissy.'

Tom raised his eyebrows. 'Brindle Hill? With that lot? Are you feeling all right?'

'Never better. Mind you, I suppose you're a bit tired after your early-morning exertions.' She smirked. 'A man of your age and all that.'

Tom picked up the picnic basket from the table, drew himself up to his full height, flexed his muscles and said, in a voice a good octave deeper than normal, 'I'll do it again when I've got you up there, madam.'

'What is it with you this morning? Must be something in the water.'

'No, it's not.'

'What, then?'

Tom beamed from ear to ear. 'I'm going on holiday.'

They edged their way around the pile of stable manure, ducking down below the overgrown hawthorn hedge as Maisie's voice boomed from a bedroom window, 'I'll be down in a minute, Mr Poling. Slept in, I'm afraid. Terrible dreams.'

Like schoolchildren playing truant, they chuckled,

and continued along the lane and over the stile to the right of the cart track, then began the ascent of Brindle Hill across the sheep-dotted meadows.

Soon Wilding's Barn was no more than a matchbox below them, and the sky grew – pale blue and bordered by clouds stained with primrose. Tom powered his way up the grassy slope, drawing the rich, clean air into his lungs and changing hands with the basket at regular intervals. Pippa endeavoured to keep up but finally stopped to catch her breath by a stile, holding her side. 'All right, all right, I give in. You might be old but you're fit.'

Tom turned and looked down at her. 'You all right?'

She nodded, breathless, her cheeks flushed.

His heart swelled at the sight of her – hair held back in a ponytail, brown legs showing below her dark blue shorts, the contours of her body disguised in a baggy rugby shirt of pink and green. He put down the basket on the grass and walked back the few paces to help her, then wrapped his arms around her as she laid her head against his chest, panting.

'Are you sure?'

She laughed through her breathlessness. 'Stitch. That's all.' Then she slapped his bottom and pushed him on. 'Nearly there.'

'No. Let's stop here. No need to go any further.'

They flopped down on the grass and took in the view.

Behind them was an amphitheatre of softly rolling hills where the sheep were grazing, their plaintive bleats floating out and fading to nothing in the warm air. Below them, they could see the snaking Axe, running from the harbour with its flotilla of boats into the widening mud-coloured estuary and the glinting silver sea beyond. The tiny pallid triangles of sail flipped and slid across the water like pond skaters. Around them buttercups wavered in the breeze, and the liquid notes of a soaring skylark floated high above them.

Pippa pulled off her hairband, threw back her head, shook out her hair then fell back into the grass with a sigh. 'Oh, this is the life.'

Tom watched as she closed her eyes, the colour fresh in her cheeks, her hair dark and glossy against the soft green of the downland turf. He picked a long-stemmed buttercup and ran it under her chin and across her cheek. She smiled and murmured, 'What are you doing?'

'Just seeing if you like butter.'

'Bad for you.'

'I suppose everything that's nice is bad for you.'

She opened one eye. 'Not everything.'

He dropped the flower, lifted his hand to her forehead, stroked it gently and ran his fingers through her hair. 'Sorry if I've been a bit of a pain lately.'

She closed her eyes again and he ran his hand down

47

her body then inside her shirt, feeling the delicate ridges of her ribs, the softness of her breasts. She sighed as he stroked her skin, and returned the kiss he planted on her lips.

He lay back on the grass next to her and listened to her breathing – more steadily now, and deeply. He turned to look at her again, his face just a few inches from hers, then began to unbutton her shorts. She opened her eyes. 'Tom!'

'Mmm?'

'What are you doing?'

'What do you think I'm doing?'

'Here?'

He muffled her words with another kiss, deep and longing this time, and she responded, nipping at his lip. The scent of the crushed grass bit into her nostrils, as she felt his hand slide down inside her shorts. She pushed her hands into his shirt, surprised at her willingness to be made love to on top of a hill. Part of her felt she ought at least to glance around to check that they were alone, but the other part did not care. She unbuckled his belt, felt the hardness of his body against hers and her breathing began to quicken. Tom enfolded her in his arms. A few minutes later they were lying panting on the hillside having made love like two anxious teenagers.

With his eyes closed, Tom felt a sense of levitation,

and clenched his fingers around the grass to hold himself steady. 'You OK?'

'Mmm.'

It was some moments before he broke the silence again. 'I do love you,' he said.

They lay there for the best part of half an hour before they got round to eating the picnic. Tom felt the warmth of the sun on his face as he lay back and let his mind wander over holidays, Pippa, work. And Tally, and what she might be doing now.

Chapter 6

Any man who has lived in a household comprised entirely of women will know that there is always conspiracy afoot. It may be spoken, it may even be unconscious, but it is always there.

Over the years Tally and her mother had developed an intuitive shorthand. There were times when they would combine forces to see Tom through difficult patches; there were others when they would present a united front to block some manoeuvre he was intent on performing; there were even moments, rarely it has to be admitted, when they would make a concerted attack on him, and they were certainly not averse to making occasional assaults on his wallet but, more than anything else, they were ever ready to leap to his defence when any outside agency presented a threat.

It was Tuesday morning. The holiday was four days away, exams were over, and Tally had a day off school. She decided that it was time for her and Pippa to go shopping. It was the sort of outing Pippa loved – even though her daughter would persuade her to buy clothes far too young for her. Pippa would try on full cotton skirts that came down to her ankles, and Tally would hold up tiny strappy tops that she considered perfect for Pippa's trim figure. Then garment after unsuitable garment would be held up against Tally's slender frame, and a sort of bargaining ensued, where one unsuitable item of clothing was traded off against something sensible, until, weary yet excited at the prospect of two weeks in Tuscany, the pair flopped down in Tally's favourite teashop and ordered lunch. 'Do you think he'll like them?' asked Pippa, tentatively.

'Course he will. You look gorgeous.'

'I'm not sure about that top.'

'It looks great.'

An anxious look. 'Not too young?'

'Oh, Mum!'

'Well, it's difficult . . .'

'You're not that old . . . Dad is, but you're not.'

'Don't be mean!'

'Is he OK?' Tally asked lightly.

'Yes. Why?'

'Oh, I don't know. He just seems preoccupied.'

'A lot on his mind, with Sam going and everything.'

'Suppose so. Nothing else?'

'I don't think so.' She paused. 'He's been rather thoughtful lately. I think he's feeling a bit restless.'

'Probably just his age.'

Pippa made to reprimand her, but Tally continued, 'No, I don't mean . . . well . . . I mean I'm not being unkind . . . it's just that I suppose Dad's never really done what he wants to do, has he?'

Pippa sighed. 'Not really.'

'Why?'

'Because of us.'

'What do you mean?'

'I think he might have been a bit more adventurous if he didn't have us to look after.'

'But we can look after ourselves.'

There was a conciliatory note in Pippa's voice. 'I know, but your dad doesn't see it like that.'

'What a shame.'

'Not really. I think part of him loves his life, but he doesn't think he's achieved much.'

'And what do you think?'

Pippa looked wistful. 'I think he's achieved a lot, but maybe he feels he hasn't explored his full potential. I also think he's a very good man.'

Tally leaned back in her chair. 'What a lovely thing to say.'

Pippa changed her tone. 'Far too soppy.'

Their conversation was interrupted by a waitress with a flat, cheerless voice: 'Two coffees, one smoked salmon and cream cheese bagel and a cheese and tomato toastie?' She greeted Tally with a nod of recognition and tucked the bill under a saucer.

Tally stirred her coffee. 'Can I ask you something?'

Pippa looked up from her bagel.

'You and Dad. Are you still in love?'

'That's a very personal question.'

'Sorry.'

'Why do you ask?'

'Because Emma says her parents are just staying together for the sake of her and her brother.'

'Oh dear.'

'Do you think that's right?'

'I don't know. I think it's sad.'

'Yes.'

'They must be doing it because they think it's right, though.'

'Would you and Dad stay together for me?'

'What a question.'

'Would you?'

Pippa considered. 'I think we would, but that's not why we have. The answer to your question is yes.'

'Oh good.' Tally beamed and took a bite of her toasted sandwich, then muttered, 'I hope it rains.'

'What?' Pippa frowned.

'Well, there's no point in going away somewhere hot when it's hot here. It's a waste.'

Pippa smiled. 'Don't worry. Storms are on the way. I heard it on the news this morning.'

As if on cue, the door of the teashop opened and Rachel Jago, with a couple of chums in tow, breezed in, pointed at the table in the window where two old dears had barely drained their cups, and chivvied a young waitress into clearing away the crockery. As the two bewildered ladies shuffled out, Rachel set about loudly installing her party, to the irritation of other customers intent on a quiet lunch.

It was some moments before she noticed Pippa and Tally. When she did, she rose from the table with all ceremony, excused herself to her smartly dressed companions, and crossed to where mother and daughter sat. 'Pippa! Tally! How lovely to see you!' She kissed the air to the side of their cheeks, and motored on. 'You must be getting ready for the holiday? Lovely! What a time to go! But I expect we'll cope. The boys are interviewing a new under-chef or whatever today, and I expect Sally will hold the fort. She usually does.'

Under the table Tally slid her hand over her mother's and squeezed it: colour was rising in Pippa's cheeks.

Before either of them could say anything Rachel
continued, 'And I see you've been shopping. In Axbury?
God! I hope you found something. I find it impossible to
shop here. Peter's very sweet and lets me go up to
London once a month. Bless him! Don't know what I'd
do if I couldn't. Still, holiday shopping's different, I
suppose. Doesn't really matter who sees you in holiday
wear, does it? Anyway, must dash. Just treating a couple
of girlfriends to a coffee before we go and see . . .'
Uncharacteristically, her words petered out. For a
moment she seemed flustered, unsure of what to say,
then recovered herself and went to rejoin her friends.

Pippa darted a look at Tally and murmured, 'Don't
say anything.'

Tally's face was bright pink. 'How do you put up with
it?'

'I think pleasant thoughts.'

'Poor Dad. How does he put up with it?'

'He thinks unpleasant thoughts.'

'She's such a bitch.'

'Sssh! Keep your voice down.'

But there was no danger of Rachel hearing them: she
and her two friends were now screaming with laughter,
and had forgotten they were there.

There had been a time when Peter Jago and the
Drummonds had socialized. Before Rachel's arrival on

the scene, he had regularly called in at Wilding's Barn for a drink or supper. He and Tom were good mates who seldom tired of each other's company. His visits became less frequent when he took up with Rachel. She had her own group of cronies, and seemed uncomfortable with Peter's. Always keen to be the centre of attention, she seemed to wilt when other members of the assembled company had their own history.

Her unease transmitted itself to Tom and Pippa who, after a while, felt it kinder not to put Peter in the situation of having to refuse an invitation. They watched as the balance of power shifted: Peter, always ebullient and forthcoming in company, began to stand in the shadow of his overpowering wife. She embarrassed him in front of strangers with the intimate details of their private life, and Pippa learned quickly to distance herself from Rachel on the rare occasions when they found themselves in the same room.

The friendship between Tom and Peter had changed, too, until it was more of a working relationship. It saddened Tom, but he did his best not to dwell on it.

Today at the Pelican the kitchen was pulsating with life. Pans clattered from hob to hob, Ellen was up to her dimpled elbows in suds, and Peter had extracted an enormous salmon from a fish kettle and was laying pieces of it on plates.

'Table twenty-three!' He banged his hand on the hot cabinet to attract the attention of a young waiter. 'Come on, come on! Twenty-three!' The red-faced youth lifted the plates on to a tray then wove his way back between the ovens and out through the swing door into the restaurant. 'Bloody kids! What's the point in fresh ingredients when food sits here for half the week getting old before they eat it?'

Sam, beavering away at four plates of scallops, kept his head down and dribbled some sauce over them. He slid them on to the hot steel and muttered the table number with less volume than his employer: 'Seven.'

Peter tossed Sam a sideways glance. 'You'll need to shout louder than that if you want to attract piss-quick's attention.'

At this point, Sally's head appeared above the hot cabinet and she took the plates of scallops. 'Seven?' she enquired. Sam nodded. 'All right, Chef?' she asked.

It was a normal day in the kitchen of the Pelican. Out front, Tom, in clean shirt and tie, was meeting and greeting. He seated diners, took their orders, suggested a suitable wine when asked and cleared the tables with a deftness that made the plates seem magnetic, while still finding time to chat to regulars and welcome newcomers. It was, he thought, no job for a grown man. Peter was the important one – he cooked the food. The restaurant rose or fell in people's estimation on account of his culinary skills. But Tom's work was front-of-house – the art of being welcoming and friendly without becoming over-familiar or obsequious.

In truth, the success of the Pelican was just as much down to Tom's easy-going manner as it was to Peter's achievements in the kitchen, and it was that, more than anything else, that kept him going.

It surprised him how, over the years, he had come to enjoy other people's company. He had not expected to. It was the solitude of farming and of writing that most appealed to him – still did – but he did now appreciate, up to a point, the value of his efforts in the restaurant. It was all part of life's confetti, he told himself. Some people were destined to be movers and shakers, surgeons and nurses, teachers and airline pilots, and others, like himself, were suited to work in life's amusement arcade. Dining out was an amusement, and he had an important role in helping people to lead brighter lives. Sometimes he almost believed it.

It was a lunchtime much like other lunchtimes. There were unexpected arrivals, who swore they had booked when they hadn't, there were sixes who turned up where fours had been expected. There were couples who looked furtive, and businessmen who talked loudly and drank too much. There were one or two crossed wires when salmon appeared where steak had been expected. Two glasses were broken, a handbag left behind, and a tablecloth stained with red wine. But as the last diner departed and the blind was pulled down on the door Tom was left with his usual feeling of quiet, if vacant, satisfaction.

He left Sally and the two young waitresses to clear up and sauntered through to the kitchen, slackening his tie and rolling up his sleeves.

Peter was washing his hands. 'All right, squire?' he asked. The pressures of lunchtime had lifted, and the heat of his forehead had cooled in tandem with the heat of the kitchen.

'Fine,' Tom replied. 'One handbag that we didn't have when we started, but Sally's checked the contents and put in a call. Expect a knock at the door in a while.'

Peter dried his hands and unbuttoned his whites. 'So, when's the great white hope coming?'

Tom checked his watch. 'Four o'clock.'

'That gives us under an hour to get our act together.'

Tom demurred. 'It's up to you, really. He won't be in my department.'

Peter turned to Ellen, now wiping her draining board with a J-cloth. 'Any chance of tea?'

She didn't look up. 'Kettle's on,' and added, under her breath, 'like it is every day.'

'Come on, then. Let's get out of this hell-hole.'

The two men walked from the kitchen to a freshly cleaned corner table at the back of the restaurant, and as the girls cleaned away the detritus of the day's luncheon, they studied the letter of the sole respondent to the advert in the *Axbury Gazette*.

It didn't take them long. The letter was short and the stationery gave little away.

Dear Sir,
I am writing in response to the advertisement in the *Axbury Gazette* for a sous-chef. I have had several years' experience in the restaurant trade and would like to apply for the position. I enclose my CV for your consideration and look forward to hearing from you.
Yours sincerely,
K. Lundy

'Keith or Kevin?' asked Peter, scrutinising the letter for clues.

'Doesn't say. Might be Karen.'

'She should say so, then.'

'Not if she thinks she won't get an interview because she's the wrong sex.'

'What about sex discrimination?'

'Might be against the law but it still goes on.'

'Even in kitchens?' asked Peter, with wide eyes.

'Especially in kitchens.'

'And where's the CV? It says, "I enclose my CV"?'

Peter made great play of examining the inside of the empty envelope.

'Must have forgotten to put it in.'

'Pathetic.'

'Oh, you don't know. We all make mistakes.'

Peter shook his head. 'Always ready to think the best of someone . . .'

'Until I know the worst.'

Ellen coughed loudly and pushed two cups of tea on to the table in front of them.

'Thanks,' they said in unison.

'Sugar?' She asked. They nodded.

Ellen lowered her eyes to the cups. 'Stir it, then.' Her daily ritual complete, she shuffled back to the kitchen.

Chapter 7

After one false alarm, when the erstwhile diner came to retrieve her handbag, the two men had worked themselves into a state of immoderate apprehension at the prospect of meeting a potential new member of staff. They had appointed waiters and waitresses with neither difficulty nor fuss, but a sous-chef was a different matter. Peter chewed his nails, Tom drummed his on the table. Four fifteen. Still no sign. Then at twenty past four came the knock they had been expecting. They were alone in the restaurant – the staff on their break between lunch and dinner. Tom looked meaningfully at Peter and, without saying anything, went to open the door.

Standing before him was a slight woman with close-cropped fair hair, aged between thirty-five and forty. Her pale green eyes were glistening with what looked like a mixture of anger and sorrow and she clutched the strap of a canvas bag that hung over her shoulder.

'Mr Jago?' she asked, her voice trembling with suppressed emotion.

'Drummond,' said Tom.

The woman thrust out her hand and Tom took it. The grip was firm, the look was not. 'Kate Lundy. I'm so sorry I'm late. Not a very good start. I'm here about the job.' She tried to smile.

Tom beckoned her in, curious to know why she was so distraught but unable to ask. 'Come in. Tea? Coffee?'

'Water, please. Tap.'

Tom pointed towards the table at which Peter was pulling out a chair. 'You OK?' he asked, puzzled by the appearance of their interviewee.

'Yes. Sorry. I hate being late.' She let her bag slip off her shoulder, shook hands with Peter and sat down.

Tom filled a glass from the tap at the back of the bar. 'It really doesn't matter. It's only fifteen minutes or so. Not a problem. We were winding down anyway.' She smiled gratefully at him and took a sip of water. Peter looked at Tom and raised his eyebrows.

Tom tried to break the ice. 'We weren't sure whether you'd be a Kevin or a Keith.'

She put down the glass. 'Sorry. With some chefs you don't even get an interview if you're female.'

Peter took the bull by the horns. 'Have you had many interviews?'

'Not recently, but in the past it's been a problem.'

'Why, do you think?'

Kate shrugged. 'Some chefs would rather swear at a man than a woman.' She was calming down.

Peter leaned back in his chair. 'Do you mind being sworn at?'

'Used to it.'

Tom butted in, anxious to get the conversation on to a less confrontational footing.

'What sort of experience have you had? Only there was no CV.'

She lowered her head to her hands. 'God! I'm sorry. I thought I'd put it in.'

Tom was conciliatory. 'Easy to forget.'

She delved into the canvas bag and rummaged among the contents, saying, 'One fish restaurant . . .'

'Cod and chips?' Peter asked cuttingly.

'Turbot and rösti.'

Peter tried to look unimpressed. Tom suppressed a smile.

'Here it is.' She handed a folded piece of paper to Peter and continued, 'I did twelve months at Brian Turner's restaurant in Kensington . . .'

Peter scanned the CV. 'That was five years ago.'

'Then six months at Claridge's.'

He tried to keep the upper hand. 'Not long.'

'Long enough to know I preferred small restaurants where the work was more rewarding.'

He cleared his throat. 'You don't seem to have worked for a few years.'

'No.'

The two men looked at her, waiting for an explanation.

'Domestic problems.'

Peter crossed his legs and leaned back. 'What sort of problems?'

Tom butted in, 'Would you be able to work six days a week? We do anything up to a hundred covers every lunch and evening.'

'No problem.'

Peter looked at the floor and folded his arms. 'I'm losing a guy I've been working with for the last three years who knows all my funny little ways.'

'I'll do my best to get used to them,' Kate responded.

Peter stared at her. Tom bit his lip, trying not to smile.

'We haven't offered you the job yet,' Peter said. 'And what I've heard so far isn't exactly encouraging.'

'Peter . . .' Tom sensed unpleasantness brewing, but Kate cut in, 'No. You're right. I turn up late, looking a wreck, I forget my CV, then try to impress you with a couple of flash restaurant names but no references, and tell you I haven't worked for a few years. Why should you take me on?'

'Exactly.'

'I'll tell you why. Because I'm bloody good.' She raised her voice, which took the two men by surprise. 'I'm good under pressure and, in spite of what you might think from my appearance, I'm reliable. I can turn a deaf ear to being sworn at and I'm a fast learner – especially when it comes to Chef's funny little ways.'

Peter's mouth hung open.

'If you want a creative prima donna I'm not your woman. If you want a doormat I'm not your woman. But if you want a reliable sous-chef who knows her stuff and can keep cool under pressure then you're looking at her. I won't cook with poor ingredients and I can't promise not to shout back when I'm shouted at, but I won't let you down.'

The two men sat perfectly still.

Kate picked up her bag from the floor. 'I'm sorry. You've probably got a lot of people to see, and I was late arriving so you'll be running behind. You've got my address on the letter.' She got up, and the two men followed suit. She put out her hand and managed a brief smile. 'Just ring to let me know.' And then, resignedly but with good humour, 'I won't hold my breath.' With that she took her leave, and Tom and Peter stood staring silently at the swinging 'closed' sign on the door.

'We'd be mad to take her on.' Peter was levering the cap off a bottle of Beck's.

'Why?'

'Because whatever she says she's completely unreliable.'

'How do you know?'

He took a gulp from the neck of the condensation-covered bottle, then lowered it to the bar counter. 'You've only got to look at her. If she gets into that sort of state when she's had a bad journey and turns up fifteen minutes late, what the hell's she going to be like in the kitchen? It'll be tears every five minutes.'

'You don't know that.'

'Oh, come on, Tom. We've had enough sous-chefs like her in the past. You know what a bastard I am when I'm working. How's she going to cope with that?'

'I thought she coped quite well, actually.'

'That was nothing.'

'It was the first time she'd met you and she refused to be browbeaten. And you were a bit hard on her.'

'A bit hard?'

'Yes, you miserable sod, you didn't give her a chance.'

'No. But she took it.'

'Exactly.'

'What about references?' Peter said.

'We can ask for some.'

'What's the point?'

'Are you saying you won't work with her?' Tom asked.

'I'm saying we should see some more people before we make up our minds.'

'There *are* no more people. She's the only one who applied,' Tom reminded him.

'So we're going for her by default?'

'That's not what I'm saying. I reckon she's better than she seemed.'

'How can you be so sure?'

Tom shrugged. 'Intuition. There was something about her, a sort of inner strength.'

'Christ! Freudian analysis now.'

'It's not Freudian, and I'm not analysing her – just going on my vibes.'

'Dangerous.'

'What's the alternative?'

'Well, on your head be it. But I'll tell you this for nothing, the first time we have tears in there,' Peter pointed towards the kitchen, 'she's outa here.'

'Up to you. I think you'll be pleasantly surprised.'

Peter drained the bottle and dropped it into a crate. 'Sometimes I don't understand you. You've gone soft.

You used to be dynamic and go-ahead and look at you now.'

Tom was surprised. 'What do you mean?'

'Where's your sense of adventure?'

'It's me who's saying we should take her on. You're playing safe.'

'Oh, I don't mean with her, I mean with the Pelican. Why don't you want to branch out, go for it with another place?'

Tom looked at him steadily. 'We've tried that before. We know it doesn't work.'

'Didn't work. The climate's different now, but here we are, stuck in the same old place with the same old faces.'

He should have sensed that this was coming, Tom thought. He'd realized that Peter had been brooding again, but had put it down to worry over Sam's imminent departure.

'So?'

'Rachel reckons we should have another go.'

'Ah.' Tom nodded slowly. 'I see.'

'I wish you bloody did.'

'So, what's the plan?'

Peter had gone further than he had intended and tried to back down. 'Plan? No plan. I just think we should consider it again, that's all.'

Tom was unwilling to tackle the hoary old chestnut

that had raised its head regularly over the past couple of years – since Rachel had come on the scene. He changed the subject. 'And in the immediate future are we giving Ms Lundy a chance?'

'Sure. Why not? Provided she can come up with some references. She won't last but what have we got to lose?'

'Except face?' Tom looked at him with his head on one side.

'*Touché*, you old bastard. *Touché*.'

Tom made the phone call that evening from the back of the bar. It was a busy night but he felt it best that Kate Lundy was put out of her misery. He also wanted to make her smile. He dialled the number. A soft voice answered the phone, quite different from the one he had heard that afternoon. He could hear music in the background, Sheryl Crow or Reba MacIntyre.

'Can I speak to Kate Lundy, please?'

'Speaking.'

'It's Tom Drummond.'

'Oh, yes.' Apprehension crept into her voice.

'Just to say that we'd be happy to have you in the kitchen if you still want the job.'

Silence.

'Hello?'

Still silence.

'Are you there?'

'Yes. It's just that . . . I thought . . . well . . .'

'Probably not a good start, really.' His tone was friendly. 'We'd had a bit of a day and I guess you had, too.'

'Yes.'

'Well, anyway, there we are. If we could have a couple of references it would be useful.'

'Fine, yes, I'll get it sorted.'

'Can you start on Monday?'

'Of course.' There was disbelief in her voice.

'Ten o'clock, then?'

'Ten o'clock's fine.' She pulled herself together. 'Thank you, Mr Drummond.'

'Tom.'

'Yes. Thank you. Well, I'll see you Monday.'

Then he remembered. 'You won't, actually. I'm on holiday for a couple of weeks. You'll have to cope with Chef on your own. Are you sure you can manage?'

'In at the deep end.'

''Fraid so. But Sam will still be there – he's the guy you're replacing – so you won't be without reinforcements.'

'Thanks.'

'Good luck, then, and I'll see you when I get back.'

Tom put the phone down and returned to the heaving restaurant. What a time to go on holiday. Still, it couldn't be helped. And what could he do if he stayed, other than give Kate Lundy moral support? It was Peter she had to impress. It was all a bit of a gamble but, then, everything was a gamble – even the continued success of the Pelican. You couldn't take anything for granted nowadays, least of all success.

Kate Lundy put down the phone and leaned back on the sofa, clutching a cushion. She closed her eyes and mouthed a 'Thank-you' to whoever was watching over her. Then she got up and looked once more at the official-looking piece of paper on the low, glass-topped table in front of her before folding it and putting it away in a file marked 'Bank – Insurance – Personal'.

She poured herself a glass of chilled white wine, then walked to the window to look out at the street. 'Cheers,' she muttered. 'Here's to the rest of your life. A fresh start.' The wine tasted better than it had a few minutes before and perhaps in a few days the butterflies in her stomach would subside. It was only natural, she told herself. After all, it wasn't every day that you got divorced.

Chapter 8

Pippa barely noticed him slide into bed beside her. He knew that she had become accustomed, out of necessity, to his late return from the restaurant and had learned to greet him almost unconsciously. He cradled her to him, and she gave a slight shudder at the chill of his skin, before sinking back into a deep sleep. He would tell her the news in the morning, when she would be fully receptive to the shades and nuances of the interview, and to Peter's renewed interest in branching out.

Tom was wondering about Kate Lundy: would she turn out to be a good find, or would Peter be proved right? He kissed his wife on the back of her neck, turned over and fell asleep.

*

He woke to find the bed empty – as usual. He was the owl, she the lark. He stumbled across the room for his dressing-gown, went to the window, and threw up the sash. Sooty stormclouds were gathering in the west, and a low rumble of thunder broke the still air. The foliage of the kitchen garden was bathed in a strange and threatening light: the blue-green cabbages seemed almost luminous. Then he saw Pippa, on her hands and knees among the parsley, snipping at stems and putting them in small polythene bags. 'You'll have to hurry,' he called.

She looked up at him. 'I know.'

'Have you nearly finished?'

'I've got the mint and coriander still to do.'

Tom realized that both she and the herbs were in for a soaking. 'I'll be down.'

'Thanks.' She didn't like to get him up early when he had been so late to bed, but today she was glad of his help.

He came out in a pair of jeans and a sweatshirt. She rose and pecked him on the cheek. 'Saviour.'

'That's a bit dramatic.'

'Dramatic weather.'

He worked alongside her between the rows of herbs, slipping them into their bags as she cut, breathing in the fresh scent of the mint as the downy leaves brushed against his skin, and the tang of peppery coriander.

'More to sow?'

'Yes, but they'll have to wait. I've got to get these into town first.'

'Want me to run you in?'

'No. You have your breakfast.' She smiled and piled the bags into a large wooden tray. 'We've beaten the weather and that's the important thing.'

A splat on a rhubarb leaf heralded the start of the downpour. They ran for cover as the heavens opened and stood under a pantiled overhang as the rain pelted down. The aroma of damp earth rose to their nostrils.

He put his arm around her and breathed deeply. 'Lovely smell.'

'The best. You can almost hear things growing.'

He turned to her, then leaned down and kissed her. She looked at him, surprised, then put her arms around his neck and responded hungrily. He ran his hands up under her shirt, stroked her breasts and pulled her towards him. 'I have to go,' she murmured.

'Mmm?' He feathered her mouth with kisses, and she smiled while returning them.

'To the shops.'

'Oh, bugger the shops.' He slid one hand down the back of her shorts and stroked her bottom, but she twisted away.

'Tom!'

'Mmm?'

'I'll be late.'

He withdrew his hand and ruffled her hair. 'No time for me?'

'Lots of time for you, but not now.'

Tom sighed. ''Twas ever thus.'

'Liar.'

He grinned. 'Worth a try.'

She was back within the hour, her rounds completed, and he went out to meet her. He kissed the top of her head, put his arm around her shoulder and they rushed to the barn for shelter, leaning back against the old stone wall as the heavy rain beat down on the herbs, releasing an ever-changing mixture of fragrances – fruity basil, aniseedy fennel, the sweet summer scent of rosemary.

'Be able to smell these in the wild next week,' she said, 'with warm sun on them.'

'Yes.' Tom tried to think of two weeks in Italy, but his mind was still on work. He told Pippa now of the previous day's events.

'What does Peter think?'

'I think he's dying to be proved right, convinced she's a no-hoper.'

'Silly boy. Well, I hope he's wrong.'

'You think I was right to go for her?'

'Yes, I do.'

'She was in a bit of a state.'

'There was probably a reason.'

'She didn't tell us what it was.'

Pippa looked up at him. 'You should be grateful.'

'What do you mean?'

'If she'd given you a long explanation as to why she was in the state she was you'd have known you'd got a moaner on your hands.'

'But *we* tell one another our problems.'

'We're married. It comes with the territory.'

He laughed briefly. 'Yes. I suppose so.' He ruffled her hair. 'Anything you want to get off your chest?'

'Not really. Except that I wish we had more time together.'

'Yes. It's all a bit much, really, isn't it?'

'These past couple of days have been so lovely . . . just made me realize . . . you know . . .' She stopped and he saw that she was fighting back tears.

'Hey!' He put his arms around her as the rain clattered about them. 'What's the matter?'

'Just a bit tired, I suppose. Need a holiday. Like you. Sorry.' He brushed the tears off her cheek with the back of his fingers, then folded her in his arms and began to hum. She began to laugh as she recognized the tune – 'Night and day . . . you are the one . . . Only you beneath the moon and under the sun.'

'Come on,' he pulled a clean handkerchief from his pocket, 'wipe away the tears and show me what you've bought for the trip.'

She blew her nose loudly, then looked at him sideways. 'What do you mean?'

'That shopping trip you had in Axbury yesterday.'

'How do you . . .?'

'I can sniff out a carrier-bag from half a mile away. It comes of culinary training.'

By the time they reached the house she was laughing, and within half an hour she had tried on all that Tally had chosen for her. Tom raised his eyebrows only once, at a skimpy top, which she confessed was Tally's. Panic crossed his face, and Pippa assured him that it would only be worn in and around the villa, not in public.

Over coffee he watched as the Pippa he knew returned – strong-willed and good-humoured, annoyed only when she thought he was selling himself short or allowing himself to be walked over. He waved as she drove off to Axbury once more in the old Volvo estate from which she refused to be parted, and felt a protective surge of love for his wife.

Pippa had offered to return to cooking when Tally had started school, but Tom had discouraged her, partly because they agreed that working together might not be a good idea, and that her working for a rival restaurant might be worse.

They had hoped for more children, but none had arrived. Tests had identified the cause as being on Pippa's side. Their disappointment was profound, but tempered by Tally's sunny disposition and constant ability to surprise them. Only when she reached the age of thirteen did they realize that their problems might just be beginning – not in her disposition, which remained as sunny and uncomplicated as ever – but in her attractiveness to the opposite sex.

The rain had stopped. The birds had started singing again. Tom climbed the stairs and stopped outside his study. He pushed open the door and walked to the table in front of the window. To one side of the laptop sat a red file, marked, in black Dymo tape, 'Making Waves'. He lifted the cover and scanned the opening paragraph: 'I never intended to become involved with Eleanor Norwich. I told myself that it would be quite pointless – that I had neither the stamina nor the good looks that would lead to a lasting relationship. I wish I had listened.'

Eleanor Norwich. He seemed to have grown up with her. Well, he'd written her name on that page so long ago now that he might just as well have done. He felt the thickness of the manuscript – about an inch. One hundred and forty-nine pages. He had intended to write a thriller, but it seemed to be turning into a gentle romance. Life mirrors art. He sighed, and went for a shower.

*

Tally was finding it hard to concentrate on Shakespeare – if this was the English teacher's idea of post-exam fun it wasn't hers and the three-thirty bell came as a welcome respite. She stuffed her books into her bag with more than her usual feeling of relief, and walked into town with Emma for a Coke and a teacake in their favourite haunt.

'Are you seeing him again?'

Tally sipped her drink slowly, keeping Emma waiting for a reply. 'Might do.'

'Did you . . . er . . .' Emma's eyes were wide with anticipation.

'Emma!'

'I'm only curious.'

Tally tutted, then took pity on her friend. 'He's a great kisser.'

''S all right for some.'

Tally frowned as she broke off a piece of teacake and popped it into her mouth. 'Mmm.' She swallowed. 'But what about Blip?'

'What about him? Alex is much better-looking.'

'I'm not going out with Alex because of his looks.'

'Oh! So you *are* going out with him, then?'

'No. Well, yes, but not how you mean.'

'How, then?'

'He's just a friend.'

'That's what you said about Blip.'

'I know. But Alex is fun.'

'And Blip isn't?'

'Yes, of course. Well . . . it's different. Oh, I don't know. Alex is far too spoiled. I mean, look at that car.'

'Chance would be a fine thing.'

'He's everything I hate in a guy – self-assured, too much money, up himself. Except that he's not. I thought he would be but he's sweet. And I enjoyed his company.'

'And his kisses.'

'Sssh!' Tally looked around anxiously in case they were being overheard, but the usual coterie of elderly ladies seemed indifferent to anything but their own ill-health and the weather.

Emma looked at her friend searchingly. 'There's something funny about you.'

Tally stopped chewing. 'What do you mean "funny"?'

Emma leaned back in her chair. 'You look different. Especially when you talk about him.'

Tally blushed. 'Don't be silly.'

'You do. See? You're blushing.'

'If you're going to be like that I'm going.' She made to pick up her bag.

Emma grabbed her wrist. 'Stupid. Only joking. But . . .'

'What?'

'Are you in love?'

'Course not. I've only met him once.'

Emma made a face.

'I just don't want to rush.'

'Miss Self-control.'

'You know what I mean.'

'You might not be able to help yourself.'

'Have you been reading *Sugar* again? Or *19*?'

'*Cosmopolitan.*'

'Thought so. I can always tell.'

Emma grinned, then looked thoughtful. 'Do you think . . .' She tailed off.

Tally watched her for a moment. 'Do I think what?' She took another bite of her teacake.

'Do you think it's OK to do it? I mean if it's serious?'

'Do what?'

'Make love. Have sex. You know.'

Tally stopped chewing. 'Why are you asking?'

'Just wanted to know, you know, what you think.'

'Why?'

Emma fidgeted in her chair. 'Pressure.'

'Where from?'

'Oh . . . you know.'

Tally fixed Emma with an unwavering eye. 'It's up to you.'

'Would you?'

'No. I mean . . . I don't think so. Not just sex.'

'That's what I thought. What about making love?'

Tally looked thoughtful. 'I don't know. Not yet.'

'Mmm.' Emma took an unnatural interest in the crumbs on her plate.

'Does Toby want to?'

Emma nodded silently.

'And . . . have you?'

'Got pretty near it yesterday.'

Tally reached out and held her hand. 'You don't have to, you know.'

Emma nodded. 'I know. It's just that half of me wants to and the other half is scared. I don't want to be a slapper. You know?'

'I didn't know you were that serious.'

'Neither did I.'

'How long?'

'A month.'

'Not long.'

'No.'

'Wait and see. But if you do . . . you will . . . well . . .'

'Take precautions?'

'Yes.'

'Oh, don't worry. Toby was already pulling it on when I backed out last night.'

They stared at each other for a moment before collapsing in a fit of laughter. Their hilarity was short-lived.

'Hi!'

Tally and Emma looked up to see a slender youth with dark, cropped hair. He wore a navy blue school blazer, but his tie had been loosened and his off-white shirt was hanging out of his trousers. A Manchester United bag was slung over one shoulder. Tally coloured. 'Hi, Blip!'

'Do you want another Coke?' he asked.

'No, thanks. I'm fine.'

'Emma?'

Emma shook her head and sucked at her straw, but the can was empty and a slurping sound was the result.

Tally regained her composure. 'Sit down. How've you been?'

'OK.' Blip looked uneasy, but lowered himself into the chair opposite the two girls and dropped his bag on the floor. 'Wondered if you wanted to come and see that new Brad Pitt film tonight. It's had good reviews. Thought we could have a pizza after.'

Emma looked from Blip to Tally, from Tally to Blip, like a Wimbledon spectator watching a rally.

Tally blustered, 'Oh! I'm sorry, I can't tonight. Got to pack.'

'I thought you weren't going until Saturday?'

'I'm not but . . . you know . . . lots to do.'

'I see.' Blip looked crestfallen. 'Perhaps when you get back, then?'

'Yes.'

'I've been looking up the place you're going to – in Tuscany. I couldn't find it on the map.'

'It's very small.'

'Oh.'

Guilt pricked Tally's conscience. 'It's quite near Florence,' she added.

'I see. That's nice.'

Tally offered him a smile, but the conversation ground to a clumsy halt. Blip smiled weakly and stood up. He ran a hand through his spiky hair then picked up his bag. 'Maybe I'll see you before you go?'

'Maybe.' And then, feeling that she was being a little too cool, 'That would be nice.'

He nodded at Emma, waved to Tally, and left the teashop without a backward glance.

'Poor Blip,' said Emma.

'Poor Blip,' echoed Tally.

Chapter 9

In the event Tally did not see Blip before she left. Neither did she see Alex, because he had returned to London and would not be back in Sussex before her departure. Pippa had warned her clients that she would not be delivering her herbs for the next fortnight, and had told Maisie that at this time of year the plants would need little water to keep them ticking over and that she was not to worry about harvesting, except for her own needs. 'Own needs. Yes. Fine. Not much water.'

Tom had left the Pelican to mild irritation from Peter, a wink from Sally, and a grudging, gap-toothed smile from Ellen.

On Friday evening the Drummonds prepared their final supper before departure.

'I still think we could have had it on our own.' Tom was laying the table.

'But we haven't seen her for ages. And she hasn't seen Tally for even longer.'

'I suppose.'

'Don't be Mr Grumpy.' Pippa turned from the kitchen sink, shook the water from a handful of greenery and tossed it to him. 'I'm going to sort you out on this holiday. Even your daughter thinks you're out of sorts.'

'I'm not.'

'Just a bit fraught, then.'

He raised his voice. 'I'm not fraught.'

She cocked an eyebrow.

'Much.' He grinned sheepishly. 'Anyway, when's she coming?'

'Any time now.'

Tally's footsteps came thumping down the stairs. 'She's here, she's here!' Pippa dried her hands, Tom put the last wineglass on the old pine kitchen table and the three went to the door to greet their guest.

The filthy Golf GTi ground to a halt on the gravel across the yard, and the figure inside it waved madly. Janie Giorgioni emerged from the wreckage of her car's interior with a broad grin and her arms widespread. 'Hello, my little blessings! How the hell are you? It's been bloody ages!'

Pippa shot her a warning look.

'Well, it has!' She laughed as Tally ran towards her and gave her a hug.

'It's *sooo* lovely to see you, Janie.'

Janie squeezed her godchild in her arms. 'Oh, and you, my love. How've you been? Any boys? Any decent ones?'

'One or two.'

Janie turned to Pippa – 'Lovely to see you, darling' – and kissed her on both cheeks before rounding on Tom. 'And you, Mr Drummond, are you looking after my girls?'

Tom scowled. 'No. I beat them daily. It's the only way to keep them in check.'

'Bastard!' She grinned and kissed him full on the mouth. 'You don't deserve them.'

'I know. Funny how they keep coming back for more. Must be my natural charm.' He kissed her cheek, and said, 'Nice to see you, Janie, even if we are going on holiday tomorrow.'

'Oh, I'm sorry. But it's the only time I've got before I go back up to the frozen north, and as you're going to God's own country I wanted to send my love with you.'

Janie Giorgioni had an Italian father and a Scottish mother. She was tall, like her mother, and dark, like her father, but in spite of being ravishingly good-looking she had remained steadfastly single, claiming that to marry was folly and that you could keep men on their toes far more easily by never giving them all that they wanted. She regarded Tom and Pippa's happy marriage as a rare aberration, and in spite of a sneaking admiration for their stamina, she told them regularly that they'd only been happy 'so far' and that everything might change.

She and Pippa had met at catering school where Janie, in spite of her Italian background, had been studying English cookery. But then, Janie had always been perverse. Since those days she'd changed jobs a dozen times and was now something in the travel business. She went through men like most women go through tights, and in spite of occasional tearful conversations on the phone with Pippa, she usually came up smiling and calling her latest ex 'a bastard like all the rest'.

Tom gazed at her, standing before him in black trousers and sweater, her thick raven hair brushing her shoulders, with a leopard-print velvet scarf thrown carelessly about her shoulders. He wondered how she'd managed to come this far in life without getting attached, though he couldn't for the life of him imagine the sort of man that would ever be the other half of Janie. And yet he thought he detected, just occasionally, the merest hint of wistfulness, though Janie didn't really do wistful. At least, not in company.

She opened the boot of her car, and threw aside clothes and glossy carrier-bags in a frantic search. 'It's here somewhere.'

'What is?' asked Tally.

'The wine. Couldn't let you go without getting you into the mood. Ah! Here we are.' She pulled out two bottles and thrust them at Tom. 'For you. Open them quickly. I'm gasping!'

Tom read the labels. 'Brunello di Montalcini, 1990. Good God! You've been pushing the boat out.'

'Of course. How long is it since I saw you? Nearly a year. What did you expect? Valpolicella?'

Tom grinned. 'Come on, then, you old dragon. Let me pour you a glass.'

'Less of the old.' She slapped his bottom. 'I can give you a good three years.' She turned back to the car. 'Just a minute. Something else. Yes.' She teased a scarlet designer carrier-bag from its mates and held it out to Tally. 'Here you are, sweetheart. Something for the holiday.' Then, 'But don't let your father see. He'll throw a fit.'

Tally took the gift with wide eyes and peeped inside the bag. 'Wow! Oh, wow!' She lifted out the triangle of black, silky fabric.

'What is it?' asked Tom, screwing up his eyes as if to focus. 'A handkerchief? A headscarf?'

Tally raised her eyes heavenward. 'It's a top!' She

kissed her godmother then whispered, '*Stupendo! Grazie!*'

Janie wrinkled her nose and murmured, '*Prego*. It'll look great with a tan.'

'Mmm? What?' Tom strained to catch the conversation.

'I said I could do with a man, but failing that I'll settle for a glass of wine.'

Tom scowled. 'All right, I can take a hint.'

In the event Janie's company did them all good. Pippa put to one side her fear of flying, Tom forgot his pre-occupations, and Tally found that one glass of rich red Italian vintage wine brought unexpected colour to her cheeks and unexpected words to her lips: only when she had blurted out that Alex Blane-Pfitzer was a good kisser did she realize that it would be a good idea to change the subject, and the contents of her glass.

Janie was only too happy to regale them with the saga of her most recently departed combatant, Jason. 'Completely unreasonable. Expected me to do everything for him – and I do mean everything, washing, ironing, cooking. He couldn't even book a car in for servicing without asking me to look up the phone number. Pathetic.'

'So what made you take up with him?' asked Tom.

'Matchless in bed. Unbelievable staying power.'

Tom choked on his wine.

'Only kidding. Oh, I don't know, he seemed fairly kind. Quite a looker. In the end I just got bored, I suppose. I do like a bit of life in my men. After six months I think I'd squeezed every last drop of it out of Jason.'

Tally was forking down a mixed salad and listening, wide-eyed, to her godmother's exploits.

'I mean, look at you, Pippa. Why haven't you got rid of this drone yet?' She jerked her head in Tom's direction.

'Don't know, really. Never got round to it. But he can get the car in for a service without my help so I suppose that's something.'

Tom helped himself to more of Pippa's fish pie. 'You just can't hack it, can you, Janie? If we were at each other's throats the whole time you'd be happy.'

'Yes. But I wouldn't enjoy coming here so much. Mind you, if you could manage the occasional spat it would make me feel better.'

The hopeless expression on her hosts' faces completed her exasperation. 'I mean, don't you ever fall out?'

Pippa shot a look at Tom. 'Sometimes.'

'About what?' asked Janie.

'Stupid things,' said Tom.

Tally tutted. 'Like whose turn it is to take the bins down to the end of the road.'

'Only because your mother always forgets.'

'I do not forget,' chipped in Pippa. 'It's just that I don't take them down as early as you do.'

'But if you leave it until too late they sail on by and you've missed them for another week.'

'When did I last leave it until . . .?' She stopped, her eyes on Janie, who was beaming broadly.

'How wonderful!' she said. 'At last I think I see signs of a crumbling marriage.'

Dessert was a pre-holiday clearing up of odds and ends, for which Pippa apologized. 'Sorry. Everything must go,' she instructed, as she brought from the fridge bits of cheese, yoghurts teetering on the brink of their use-by dates, and a couple of apples.

'Oh dear!' said Janie. 'Remind me to come here again when I need to build up my antibodies.' She forced a knife through a particularly resistant lump of Cheshire and carved the core from half a wizened apple that Tally had left. 'Anyway,' she said, raising her glass, 'here's to you and your holiday. *Alla salute!*'

It was eleven o'clock before Janie took her leave, with Tom enquiring if she was OK to drive and Janie assuring him that her limit was five glasses and she'd only had three. He looked doubtful. Janie kissed Pippa and Tally then turned to Tom. 'You know, there are times, you old goat, when I really do quite fancy you.' She kissed his cheek.

Tom frowned. 'What are we going to do with you?'

'Find me a decent man. No. Find me an indecent man – they're more fun.' She looked at him with a serious expression. 'Usually.'

As Pippa and Tally cleared up, Tom walked Janie to her car. She paused before climbing in and said, with uncharacteristic tenderness, 'Look after them, Tom. They're very precious.'

'I will.'

'And tell Pippa I'll be in touch as soon as she gets back. We shouldn't leave it so long before we see each other again.'

'OK. You take care too, you old boot.'

'Bastard!' She flashed him a reassuring smile, started up the car and careered off down the rough gravel in pursuit of some other unsuitable male.

Tom stared after her. He wondered what Janie was really looking for in life, and decided that he was unlikely to find out, considering that he couldn't even decide what he wanted for himself. He walked to the five-barred gate that led from the yard into an acre of paddock. The scent of newly dampened meadow filled his nostrils and the sounds of Pippa and Tally talking in the kitchen drifted out on the still night air, punctuated by the chink of glasses and the rattle of cutlery. An owl hooted in an oak above the hedgerow. He turned his back on the gate and leaned against it, looking across the light-stained yard towards the kitchen. He watched them together, easy, relaxed and joking, and realized, in a moment of clarity, that his feelings of futility were, as Pippa had suggested, due to nothing more than tiredness. With a stillness untypical of late, he watched as they laughed at some joke, passed plates and glasses and worked together. At this moment, on this particular evening, he could think of nowhere else he would rather be, and no one else he would rather be with than the two women who, for the last sixteen years, had shared his life. He patted the smooth gatepost and went indoors.

Early Saturday morning at Wilding's Barn found the Drummonds packing clothes into suitcases. Well, Tom was packing: Pippa and Tally had done the majority of theirs before Janie's arrival. Tom, as ever, was hurling in an assortment of whatever he could find at the last moment. Pippa had offered to do it for him but he had thanked her politely and said he would do it himself. He wished now that he had not been so cussed.

With a furrowed brow he was mining the contents of a deep drawer of socks when the two women put their heads around the bedroom door. 'Can we come in?' asked Tally.

'Mmm?'

'What are you wearing to travel?'

'Don't know. Haven't thought.'

Pippa and Tally looked at each other, then Pippa's hand appeared from behind the door with a coat-hanger bearing a white cotton short-sleeved shirt and a pair of navy blue chinos, the labels still attached.

'What's this?' asked Tom, puzzled.

'Couldn't let you go in old clothes, could we?' Pippa grinned.

'Or shoes.' Tally brought into view a pair of suede loafers.

'But I thought . . .'

'That we'd only been shopping for us? Oh, no. Didn't want you letting us down.' Tally tossed the shoes at her father, who caught one in each hand. She came into the room and perched on the bed.

Pippa remained by the door. 'Do you think we might go to any smart restaurants?' she asked.

'Well, I hope so. Rude not to.' Tom was sitting on the bed now, trying on his new shoes.

'Good. This should come in handy, then.' She brought her other arm into view, and another hanger, on which was draped a pale blue linen suit.

'What? That's outrageous!'

'You don't know till you've tried it on.'

'But . . .'

'Come on, Dad. Give us a fashion show.'

'I don't know. I leave you two alone for a day and what happens? You spend all my money on blue suits.'

'Not quite all.' Tally's eyes gleamed. 'We've got a bit left over for treats.'

Five minutes later he was standing in front of them wearing the pale blue suit with a cream polo shirt and his new loafers. 'How do I look?' He glanced sideways at the mirror and ran a hand through his dark hair.

'Scrummy.' Tally was sitting on the bed with her legs curled up underneath her, a baggy T-shirt almost entirely enveloping her.

Pippa looked at him with a critical eye. 'Very smart. Quite fanciable, really.' She went up to him, plucked a piece of white cotton from the shoulder of the pale blue suit and pecked him on the cheek. 'Very fanciable.'

'I'm outa here.' Tally made a beeline for the door, calling, 'How long before we leave?' as she bounded down the stairs.

'An hour,' Pippa shouted after her, then looked up at Tom. 'I've always liked you in blue.'

Tom's hand hurt with the pressure. Pippa had never liked flying, but take-off and landing were particularly nerve-racking for her. He eased her nails out of his skin, and she looked at him apologetically.

Across the aisle, Tally was nodding to the rhythm of something on her Walkman and peering out of the window at a damp Gatwick runway, her hand stretched across the aisle to hold her mother's.

Once the aircraft had levelled out, Pippa relaxed her grip. 'Isn't it ridiculous? I should have had a couple of gins.'

'You always say that.'

'I know. I wish I liked it!'

Tom looked at her sympathetically. 'All right?'

She nodded. 'Better soon.'

The flight from Gatwick to Pisa took two hours and ten minutes. Pippa tried to take an interest in the plastic meal, and Tom forced a glass of champagne down her, but it was only after the wheels had ground to a halt on the Italian tarmac that she leaned back, smiled bravely at Tom and murmured, 'Happy holiday!'

They picked up the hire car at Pisa airport as arranged – a scarlet Seat – and drove north on the A12. Tally had unplugged herself from the Walkman and was peering out of the window. 'It's just like a wonky wedding cake!'

Tom and Pippa glanced at each other, then at the Leaning Tower. It was Tally's first visit to Italy, their third. The first had been their honeymoon in Siena, the second a long weekend in Florence four years ago.

'Wait till we get off this road. It gets even better.' The Leaning Tower waltzed by and the car headed on to the A11 and Lucca, then deeper into Tuscany.

Before they reached Florence, they turned north and drove up into the hills. The road was narrower now and dusty, bordered by slender cypresses of deep, dusky green, and fringed by sturdy pines.

Every so often the undergrowth would clear to reveal a view of a vineyard in a valley, or pale grey and purple hills beyond. The early-evening air smelt of dust and rosemary, as Pippa had known it would, and Tally's 'Wow!' came at increasingly frequent intervals.

'Is that all you can say?'

'What?'

'Wow!'

'No. I can also say, "*Dove la stazione di servizio piu vicina?*"'

Tom swerved to avoid a goat on the road. 'What was that?'

'I said, "Where is the nearest petrol station?"'

Pippa turned to her daughter in the back seat. 'Where on earth . . .?'

'And I can say, "*La doccia non funzionia*" – the shower doesn't work, "*Non c'e carta igiencia in bagno*" – there's no toilet paper in the bathroom, and "*Potrei vedere la listo dei vini?*" – can I see the wine list?'

Tom braked hard and pulled up at the side of the road, then turned round to look at Tally. 'Have you been talking to your godmother?'

Tally grinned. '*Solo un' po.*'

Chapter 10

'Look at the sky – it's pink!' Tally's voice held a note of awe. 'I think I'm going to like Italy.'

Tom smiled to himself. At sixteen Tally could be both the sophisticated young woman and the wide-eyed child. At the moment she was in the second mode and through her eyes he saw Italy as he had first seen it himself, in the company of Pippa. They had honeymooned in Siena at the suggestion of Janie, who had told them there was nowhere more romantic in the world. 'Forget Firenze, forget Venezia, go to Siena,' she'd said. So they had, and they'd loved it – so much that they'd never been back. 'It would never be the same again,' said Pippa. But to come again to the country where their love had blossomed, where they had time only for each other, reminded them both of things that were sometimes too easily forgotten, too readily taken for granted.

Tally leaned forward from the back seat so that her head was between her father's and mother's. Tom felt Pippa's hand slide gently under his thigh as he drove up the track towards the villa that would be their home for the next two weeks. He glanced at her, and saw on her face a look of contentment that he had not seen in a while. Suddenly, home seemed worlds away. They were now in a land of olive groves and citrus trees, vineyards and valleys dotted with pumpkin plants and mulberries. A low, pantiled roof hove into view among a stand of dark cypresses as slender as pencils.

'Is that it?' Tally craned forward.

Pippa looked at the map on her lap. 'It might be. There should be a turning just around this corner. Look for a sign that says, "*incrocio pericoloso*", whatever that means.'

'Dangerous crossroads,' translated Tally.

'That's promising,' said Tom.

'Then there should be a sign saying, "Villa Bartolo".'

'Nothing yet. Are you sure it's—'

'There! There it is!'

Tom turned into a rough gravel drive flanked by two crumbling stone gateposts and rough grass verges.

Pippa wound down the window. 'Slow down. I want to smell it.'

Tom laughed. 'What a funny thing to say!'

'You know what I mean.'

'I know exactly what you mean,' he agreed.

Slowly they drove up the pot-holed drive, turning right and left as instructed by wooden arrows nailed to pines, and to the gnarled trunk of an olive tree.

The roof of the villa was a dusky shade of terracotta, a stout stone chimney stood to one side and a ramshackle framework of timber and wire supported a vine on the other. The evening sun slanted through the pale green leaves on to a stone terrace. The window-frames were of brown-stained timber, the walls washed a dusky ochre, and half a dozen wooden chairs surrounded a plank table on the terrace, the fading dappled light flickering across it.

Tom pulled up alongside the terrace and switched off the engine. An electric chirruping filled the air.

'What's that?' asked Tally.

'Cicadas,' answered Pippa.

'It sounds like millions of grasshoppers.'

'It is.'

'Wow! Can I get out? I want to see. This is just so cool!'

Pippa opened her door, climbed out, stretched her arms above her head then turned and lifted the seat to allow Tally to escape. She squeezed out into the open air and stood for a few moments taking it all in. 'It's so . . . Italian.'

'That's a relief.' Tom was getting out now. 'What does it say about a key?'

Pippa looked at the letter that accompanied the map. 'It's in a wooden box on the terrace.'

'That's trusting.'

She grinned at him. 'Welcome to Tuscany.'

'And you.' He walked around the car, took her in his arms and kissed her forehead. 'Have a lovely time.'

'And you, my love.'

Tally disappeared on the other side of the terrace, but her voice cut through the evening air. 'Oh, wow!'

Tom cast a sideways glance at Pippa. 'Her Italian's impressive, but I wish her English was more ambitious.'

They followed her, crisp vine-leaves crunching under their feet. Where the ground fell away in front of them, a small turquoise pool was cut into the hillside, and beyond it the landscape lay like some vast garden arranged for their pleasure.

Pippa gasped. 'Oh, my goodness. How beautiful.'

Tom was more succinct. 'Good God!' The softly rolling vineyards below them were perforated at intervals by cypresses and isolated farm buildings. Pale grey olive groves encroached on their boundary, and the view was framed by mountains flushed purple, copper and vibrant orange in the dying sun. The echo of goats bleating rang out across the valley. It was as close to perfection as they could have hoped.

The letter instructed them that a maid would appear in the morning, that they would find milk and bread in the fridge and a bottle of wine on the table. A box of basic provisions would be in a cool room just off the kitchen, and the local supermarket was just five kilometres away on the road to Pistoia.

Pippa and Tally hung the contents of the suitcases in tall wardrobes while Tom heated a pizza – in an oven whose controls took a great deal of mastering – and opened the bottle of Chianti that had been left on the table. They found glasses, cut up the pizza and ate it under the stars as darkness fell. Then they slid between cool white sheets and fell asleep to the fading chorus of cicadas and the warm fragrance of the Tuscan night.

Tally woke first. The morning light was so clear and strong that she thought someone was shining car headlights into her face. Then she remembered where she was and sat up in bed. Her watch told her it was a quarter to seven. Far too early. But the light had a coruscating brilliance that defied her attempts at sleep. She looked about her. The walls of her room were whitewashed between the stout and curving beams of ancient timber. The furniture was heavy and dark, the bed had an ornate but crudely carved headboard, and the skylight above her allowed the early-morning sun to slant in on to the floor, which was covered with rush matting. She watched flecks of dust swirl in the morning light for a few minutes, then slipped out of bed and went across to the window. She lifted a metal rod and pushed out the old, brown shutters, which clattered against the walls.

The sights and sounds of an Italian morning greeted her eyes and ears. A distant cock crowed. A lizard scuttled into a crack above her head – she shuddered, then laughed at herself. The tall, slender cypresses, which the night before had seemed such a dark green, were almost lavender blue in the morning light. The sky was clear and pale as a bunch of forget-me-nots, and she could already feel the warmth of the sun on her face.

She washed, cleaned her teeth, slipped out of her pyjamas into shorts and a fresh white T-shirt before tiptoeing out of the house and on to the terrace. She breathed in deeply. She had never smelt anything like it before: the crisp, fresh, fruity air was rich with the scent of rosemary and sage, rosy red earth and vine-leaves, cypress bark and pine needles – she saw them all as she turned her head. The rough sandstone of the terrace was warm beneath her feet. She walked to the low wall that surrounded it and looked again at the view of the Tuscan valley. The clear pool, its surface broken by gentle ripples, glittered and gleamed in the morning sun.

She skirted the edge of the terrace and brushed her hand against the prickly stems of bougainvillaea flanking the steps that led down to the pool. She squinted at the brightness of the cerise bracts, then walked down the steps towards the water. She crouched and dipped in her hand. The water was warm.

Tally looked about her. The landscape was deserted. The world had not yet woken. Italy was hers and hers alone. Almost without thinking she pulled off her T-shirt, dropped it beside her on the cool marble, then stretched her arms above her and felt the gentlest of breezes on her skin. The freedom was liberating. She undid her shorts and stepped out of them. For a moment she stood naked by the water, her head lifted to the sun, her eyes closed. Then she lowered herself into the water and gasped as its freshness took her breath away. She dived beneath the ripples, and surfaced only when she had swum the full length of the pool.

She threw back her head to clear her hair from her eyes, and ran her hands over her face. Then she trod water and looked about her at the landscape through the shimmering haze that made the cypress trees dance. She had never felt so free, so . . . happy.

She swam to the ladder, climbed out and went to her clothes. She slipped them on over her wet skin, climbed the steps to the terrace and sat in the dappled light beneath the vine, staring at the morning and waiting for her parents to come to life.

The maid, Maria, was middle-aged with olive skin and a big bottom encased in a nylon overall of pale green. She turned up mid-morning and said hardly anything, but pointed a lot, and the Drummonds deduced that she would be coming in every day except Thursday – '*no giovedi*'. While Maria swept the terrace, made the beds and checked the towels, the three holidaymakers went shopping. The *supermercato* on the road to Pistoia was much more fun than the one at home. There was a certain thrill in buying *latte* rather than milk, *vino* rather than wine, and *pollo* rather than chicken. Even Pippa, a reluctant shopper most of the time, got a kick out of choosing olives and melon, Parma ham and Italian pasta, clams and giant prawns, while Tom filled a trolley with Chianti and Vino Nobile di Montepulciano, muttering all the time about 'Super-Tuscans', which Tally took to be a local football team.

By early afternoon they were grouped around the table on the terrace, having lunched on bread, cold meat and melon, washed down with bottles of Peroni. 'So what does everybody want to do?' asked Tom.

Pippa and Tally looked at one another then spoke in unison: 'Very little.'

Tom grinned. 'Right answer.' He put his hands behind his head, leaned back in the chair beneath the vine and said, 'I might be ready for a trip out on Thursday or Friday.'

Tally got up and walked to the low wall surrounding the terrace. The sun was high in the sky now and the paving baking beneath her feet. 'I think I'll go for a swim.'

'Not till your lunch has gone down,' her mother said. 'And make sure you've got some sun-block on.'

'Oh, Mum!'

'I'm not nagging, Tal. I just don't want you burning. Skin like yours cooks in this heat.'

Tally frowned. 'What about Dad? It's not fair – he always seems to be brown, even when we haven't had a holiday for ages.' She pointed at Tom, whose limbs, protruding from shorts and T-shirt, were already a soft shade of honey.

'He'll need it, too.'

'OK, Dad, I'll go and get the cooking oil.'

'Don't worry about me. My skin's like leather.'

Pippa threw him a sideways look. 'I've heard that before. Last time you couldn't sleep on your back – remember?'

Tally was inside the house now, as Tom murmured, 'As I recall I didn't need to.'

Pippa tried not to smile. 'Show-off.'

He moved his chair alongside Pippa's, then closed his eyes and enjoyed the warmth of the sun, stretching out his hand to find hers. She linked her fingers through his and sighed contentedly before a sharp click caused them both to open their eyes. Their daughter was standing in front of them, camera in hand. 'Ah! What a sweet picture. Two lovebirds asleep together!'

'We weren't asleep, we were sunbathing.'

'Without these?' She held up a tube of cream and a bottle of lotion. 'You'll burn, you know. And I don't want you coming to me and moaning when you can't lie on your back.'

At which point Tom leaped out of his chair, pulled off his shirt, and chased Tally down the terrace steps. Her screams of terror were short-lived. In a matter of seconds her father had whisked her off her feet, scooped her into his arms, and with a cry of triumph leaped high into the air. They hit the water with an almighty splash and sank from view in a tidal wave of foam that threatened to empty the pool and send its contents spilling down the valley.

Father and daughter splashed their way across the pool as Pippa slipped off her shorts to reveal a bikini and dived silently into the water to surface just feet away from them. She brushed her dark hair away from her eyes and enquired, 'Can anyone join in?'

*

On the evening of their first day, as the sun sank behind the olive grove, the three dined on *spaghetti alle vongole*, and sipped Tom's Gaioli '94 as they chatted in the flickering candlelight on the terrace. Tom saw the new colour in Tally's cheeks and the glow in Pippa's eyes, her dark hair held back in a tortoiseshell clip, her shoulders delicately flushed after their first day in the sun.

'Does the food always taste this good over here?' asked Tally.

'Always,' confirmed Tom. 'Especially when your mum cooks it.'

Pippa protested, 'I think it's the sun. The olives are different, the bread is different, even the pasta tastes better.'

'More of the same tomorrow?' asked Tom.

'Oh, I think so,' she answered.

'By the pool for me. Reading,' said Tally and, seeing that her mother was about to draw breath, 'with sun-block on my nose, factor fifteen on my arms and legs and very little else.'

Tom raised an eyebrow. 'I see the handkerchief has come out.' He nodded at the triangle of black silk that was Tally's top, the gift from Janie, and tried to appear disapproving.

'Good old Janie. I should have waited until I had a tan, really, but it's so cool and comfortable.'

'It looks stunning,' Pippa said. 'Trust Janie.'

'Talking of which,' said Tom, 'when did you learn all this Italian? You haven't seen Janie for nearly a year.'

'We talk on the phone and she writes me letters. I wanted to surprise you, so I learned useful phrases like "Is there a market here?" and "Do you take credit cards?"'

'Oh, very handy. Did you learn how to say "my father wouldn't approve"?'

''Fraid not.'

Shortly after ten Tally got up and cleared away the remnants of supper. Her early morning had caught up with her and her head swam with the effects of the heat and the red wine.

Pippa had seen that her daughter's eyelids were heavy, and said, 'Time for bed, Tal. Go on.'

Tally grinned beatifically, stretched and yawned. She kissed her father then her mother. 'You smell nice,' she said.

'Thank you. Sleep well, sweetheart.'

Tally wove her way across the terrace to bed, leaving Tom and Pippa alone with the sounds of the warm Italian evening filling the air around them.

'Happy?' he asked.

'Very. You?'

'Blissfully.'

'Bed?'

'Bed.'

Tom rose and held out his hand. Pippa took it and he folded his arms around her. 'Seems like yesterday,' she murmured.

'I know.'

'It smells the same and sounds the same.'

'That's because it is the same.'

'Are we, do you think?'

'Oh, yes.'

She eased away from him. 'I'm glad.'

He put his arm around her shoulder and walked her slowly along the length of the warm, dark terrace to their room. Once inside he stared at her for a moment. He could hear nothing but their breathing – slow and rhythmic. Slowly he began to undress her. For a split second she looked apprehensive, then relaxed as he removed the cotton shirt and undid her flimsy swimwear. She was naked now, and he caressed the smooth curves of her waist, his lips on her shoulder. She murmured with relaxed delight as he stroked the inside of her thighs, and ran the backs of his fingers gently over her stomach. Then she watched as he threw off his own clothes, never taking his eyes off her. He held out his hand and drew her towards the bed that stood beneath a pair of gilded cherubs fixed to the white wall. As he lowered her on to the cool white sheets they seemed to be breathing in harmony – slowly at first, but then faster. They lay side by side, and he kissed her gently, then more passionately. He had a need to show her how much he loved her, wanted her. They gasped for air between kisses and she called his name, softly, urgently. She reached down for him and he arched his back with pleasure as she stroked him. Then he took her in his arms once more, and gave himself to her in an outpouring of passion he thought would never end. As they lay together in a warm, tangled heap in the fragrant night air, she whispered, 'I'm so glad I met you, Tom Drummond.' Eight words that would live with him forever.

Half an hour later Tom slipped out of her bed, laid the sheet across her and got into his. That was the only downside to the place: single beds. But she was happy, and he was too. Italy was their place, the place where they had their happiest times.

Chapter 11

The following morning Tom woke first. His and
Pippa's room was darker than Tally's, having no
skylight, but the early-morning sun flooded between the
slats of the shutters, making bright patterns on the wall
opposite. He looked across to where Pippa lay, still
sleeping, then eased himself out of bed. He washed,
dressed and crept quietly from the room and out on to
the terrace, where the sight that had greeted Tally the
previous day worked its magic on him, too.

He went to the kitchen and made coffee, then took
the cafetière and a mug out on to the terrace. There, in
the ripening morning, he sat and waited for the rest of
his family.

Tally emerged first, which surprised him: he'd

expected to have to wake her for lunch, as was the norm after the first day's excitement. She appeared, tousled and frowning in twisted pyjamas, rubbing her eyes and asking what time it was.

'Nine o'clock. Early for you.'

'I was up before seven yesterday,' she murmured, through the yawns.

'I thought you'd be having a lie-in.'

Tally shook her head. 'Couldn't sleep. It's all this light.'

'Don't complain.'

'I'm not.' Tally smiled sleepily.

Tom sipped his coffee. 'Do you want to go and see if your mum's awake? She was fast asleep when I left her. Ask her if she wants a cup of tea or whether she's up to coffee.'

'OK.' Tally tottered off, and Tom heaved a contented sigh as he gazed at the landscape. It was, he thought, a view to die for.

'Dad!'

He looked round. Tally was standing on the terrace. There had been a catch in her voice. 'What is it?'

'It's Mum.' He got up and saw the fear in her eyes. Quickly he turned and ran along the terrace to their bedroom door. He lifted the latch and went in. Pippa was lying where he had left her earlier. Still and silent. He walked across the room and sat on the edge of the bed. Only then did he notice that her eyes were wide open.

Time froze, then moved in stertorous fits and starts. He rushed out on to the terrace, shouting, 'Fetch a doctor!' then realized the impossibility of his request. Tally was shaking.

'Where's Maria?' he bellowed. 'Where does she live?' Tally pointed to a little cottage nestling under an ancient clump of olive trees a few hundred yards along the track. 'Go and get her.'

Tally began to cry.

'Quickly!' He ran back to the bedroom.

Tally, trying to stifle the sobs that were racking her body, ran for all she was worth down the track towards the ramshackle cottage that crouched beneath the olive trees. Was her mother alive? Would she die? How did you ask for a doctor? The Italian phrases she had committed so laboriously to memory had deserted her, and all she wanted to do was shout, 'Save my mummy!'

She lost a flip-flop, then shook off the other and ran barefoot, hardly feeling the sharp flints that dug into her bare feet. After what seemed an age, she rounded the corner of the little shack and found Maria throwing scraps to her chickens. Between panting breaths and blinding tears she muttered then shouted, '*Il dottore! La madre!*' Then, '*Chiami un'ambulanza!*'

*

As the ambulance sped to Pistoia, Tom knew the race was futile. When they arrived, the doctor, who spoke good English, was kind and thoughtful, as well as practical. Then he left them in a waiting room for a while. Tom wrapped his arm around Tally, who leaned into him, trembling. They said little.

When the doctor called for Tom, he refused to leave his daughter, so the doctor explained to the two of them that the likely cause of Pippa's death was heart failure. It was difficult to say for certain. There would have to be a post-mortem. They would endeavour to complete the formalities quickly, but it might take a few days. Would they care to go back home immediately or wait and travel with the body? The word brought Tom up short, but he did not need time to think: they would not leave without her.

The doctor suggested that they return to the villa, and they did, but only to pack. They moved into a hotel in Pistoia – utilitarian but clean. It seemed impossible to stay in what for them had been Paradise without Pippa.

Two days passed in an agonizing haze of visits to the British Consulate and the hospital. Everyone was sympathetic and helpful, the consulate in particular, but the end result was the same: Tom had lost the love of his life, and Tally her mum.

Tom watched Tally carefully. There were moments

of frenzied questioning – Why had it happened? Why could the doctor not be certain? Why had there been no warning signs? He could not answer her, much though he wanted to. Then anger and disbelief were replaced by a quiet reserve. He found it more worrying than if she had continued sobbing uncontrollably – it was as if she didn't want to let him down in his hour of need. All he wanted to do was tell her that everything would be all right, but he knew it would not.

On the flight home, they sat as close together as they could, holding each other's hands tightly where once they would have held Pippa's. Neither could bear to think of her making this journey with them, though she did. In a different part of the plane.

Chapter 12

On their return an eerie silence filled Wilding's Barn; a chill beginning to a wretched life. Tom thanked the taxi driver, who did not speak but nodded uncomfortably before he drove off at a respectful low speed. For a few moments the two stood on the gravel, unable to move. Then Tom touched Tally's shoulder. She swung round and buried her face in his chest. He put down the case he had just picked up, and wrapped his arms around her.

'I know. I know.' He rocked her gently as though she were a baby, and as he did so, the enormity of his loneliness began to dawn, its vastness engulfing him. He felt physically sick, and swallowed hard. 'Come on.' He led her to the door, turned his key in the lock and ushered her into the hollow stillness of the house. The quiet was broken by a soprano note, 'Ooo-ooh!' Maisie's greeting floated towards them on the early morning air.

Tom sat Tally on a kitchen chair. 'I won't be long,' he said. Then he crossed the old farm track and walked up the path to Maisie's front door.

Fifteen minutes later he left Maisie sobbing into the tangled folds of a colourful headscarf. It was all too much for her. 'You poor, poor man! And the child. Oh, poor Tally!' she blurted out, between sobs. Tom found himself comforting her instead of it being the other way round. He watched the ring of kohl around her eyes dissolve and trickle down her cheeks. 'Go!' she instructed. 'Go to Tally. Never mind me. I'm so very sorry, Tom. Oh, if there's anything I can do – I'm so sorry to be like this. I will be strong. I will help. It's just – such a shock.'

He found Tally sitting where he had left her, her gaze unfocused. 'I think you should go and have a shower,' he said. She looked up at him as though he were speaking a foreign language. 'You'll feel better.' She said nothing. He had never seen her looking so desolate, so lost. In that moment, under her uncomprehending eyes, the weight of his burden settled on him. He knew he must find something inside himself to bring her through. Failure was not an option. She was all he had left.

*

He sat on her bed as she showered in the bathroom. He was there, but not there, part of things but strangely detached. He floated in a sea of unreality, but nothing was more real. He listened to the splash of the water, the opening and closing of the shower door. She came into the room in a bathrobe, her hair soaking, and sat beside him. He towelled her hair dry, then ran a comb through it. She turned her face to him and looked into his eyes. 'It's so unfair.'

He nodded. All the words in his head seemed so inadequate. What do you say to a teenage daughter who has just lost her mother? How do you explain that life must go on, when you don't believe it can? How can you think positively when every fibre of your body is screaming in pain and anger? He tried to make some sense of the moment, to say the right thing without being too sentimental or too unfeeling, the whole time trying to understand what had happened and finding it impossible to take in. It was Pippa they were talking about, Pippa – who had been younger than he was. Heart failure was something that affected older people, wasn't it? Panic gripped him, and he had to stifle the disbelieving laugh that sprang to his throat. He wanted to be strong. He wanted to be the best support Tally could have, and at the same time he wanted to scream, 'No! Not me! It's not fair! I need her!'

He sat beside his daughter until the light faded, then

brought her a cup of tea. It stood on her bedside table growing cold. Finally she fell asleep. When he heard her breathing steadily he got to his feet and quietly left her room. He walked along the landing and opened the door to his and Pippa's room. The bed was made, the windows closed, but it smelt as it always had – a mixture of clean linen overlaid with the faint suggestion of her perfume. He felt a pricking at the back of his eyes and went to open a window. The sound of a blackbird's evening song sliced through the air.

He glanced down at the table on Pippa's side of the bed and saw a folded piece of paper lying where she had left it. He stared at it for a few moments, then picked it up and unfolded it. It was the bill for his pale blue suit. He clenched his fingers around it and crumpled it in his fist. Then he sat on the edge of the bed and wept.

The next few days passed like some blurred hallucination. The local vicar had been kind, the undertaker matter-of-fact and the locals as supportive as he could have hoped, though solitude was all he wanted.

He phoned Janie, who sounded angry at first, then disbelieving. When she returned his call she said she was on her way. She would not hear otherwise. She was Tally's godmother, she reminded him, her place was with her. He was half glad: perhaps Janie's irreverence would help them through. He was worried about Tally: over the past few days she had gone deeper inside herself, unable to cry. He worried about everything, even the restaurant.

Peter had been devastated at the news, then supportive, insisting that Tom was not needed, telling him to stay at home where he could do most good. Rachel had not called, and he was grateful for that: facing her in the middle of all this was the last thing he wanted.

Two days after they had got back Janie arrived. He met her at the door and surprised himself by breaking down. They cried openly together, which surprised Janie, too. But she pulled herself together quickly. 'Where am I sleeping?'

Tom blew his nose on a large red-and-white spotted handkerchief. 'Spare bedroom at the end of the landing.'

'Have you eaten?' she asked, as she lugged her case into the hall. Tom pushed his hanky into his pocket then lifted up her case. 'Not since breakfast.' He began to stagger up the stairs. 'What have you got in this? A body?' Then he realized what he had said.

'I should laugh if I were you,' said Janie. 'Otherwise you'll cry again.' She wiped away her tears with the back of her hand. 'Any tissues?'

'In the bathroom.'

'Where's Tal?'

'In the garden, I think.'

When Janie had mopped herself up, she walked through the house and out of the back door. It was a warm afternoon, dull, oppressive, with the scent of herbs hanging on the humid air. She saw Tally sitting on a wooden bench at the far end of the garden alongside a white beehive.

As she approached, she saw the girl's vacant stare. 'Hello,' she said quietly, and dropped a kiss on the top of Tally's head. 'You OK?'

Tally was holding tightly to Janie's waist. 'Just.'

'What an absolute bugger.'

Tally nodded.

'Oh, my love, what are we going to do with you?'

Tally eased away from her. 'Did you know?'

'Know what?'

'That Mum had a weak heart.'

'No.'

'Nor me. Nor Dad.'

Tally sat down on the bench, and the drone of bees among the pale lilac flowers of the mint rose and fell. 'She'd had a few pains. She got a stitch sometimes when she walked. Said it was just being unfit.' She looked questioningly at Janie. 'Perhaps that was something to do with it. What if she was frightened?'

'I don't think your mum was frightened of anything.'

'Not even death?'

The starkness of this took Janie by surprise. 'I suppose we're all frightened of death, if we're honest.'

'Maybe it's better if you don't know when it's going to come.'

'Maybe.' Janie sat beside her. 'But, then, I have had friends who died slowly of cancer, and some who died quickly, of a heart-attack. I can't honestly say that either way was easy. You get a chance to say your goodbyes if death comes slowly, but in a way that makes it all the more difficult to bear. It's hard to watch a friend suffer. But if it comes without warning you feel robbed, cheated, angry.'

Tally nodded. 'And alone.'

'Yes. Always. But you console yourself by saying that at least they didn't suffer.'

'I hope not.'

Janie stroked Tally's arm. 'Are you coping?'

'Not really.' Tally forced a flicker of a smile.

'Get tomorrow out of the way. God! I hate funerals, don't you?'

'Never been to one.'

Janie saw the ineptitude of her remark but soldiered on: 'Look, I'm going to say all the wrong things over the next few days because I'm fucking useless at this sort of thing, OK? But I'll do my best. I loved your mum . . . She was my best friend and I don't know how I'm going to manage without her. But neither does your dad. So you and me, we've got to look after him too.'

Tally's eyes were brimming with tears, and she was biting her lip to stay in control.

'I know I take the piss out of your dad, and I know that he thinks I'm a cynical old cow, but he loves me, really, and I love him. He's that rare thing in life, a good man. There are some people, like me, who pretend there's no such thing as a good man. Show me a good man and I'll show you a wanker. But you dad isn't a wanker. He's a star.' Janie sniffed back the tears. 'You remember that night before the holiday when we had supper and I teased your mum and dad about never arguing?'

Tally nodded.

'Jealousy, that's all.'

'No,' Tally said.

'Oh, they knew it was a joke. Knew it was only envy.' Janie turned to face her. 'And that's the truth of it. And now I've got to sort you two out. Because if I don't, your mum will never forgive me.'

The day of the funeral dawned with a stark inevitability. The sun shone. The birds sang, and a soft breeze rustled the leaves of the sycamore outside her bedroom window. Tally put on a long black skirt and jacket, and pinned back her hair. Janie came along the landing and tapped lightly on her door. 'OK?'

Tally nodded.

'You look . . . beautiful.'

Tom came out of his bedroom and the two women turned towards him. For a few moments they just stared, then he ushered them down to where the hearse was waiting in the drive. They saw Maisie drive off in her Morris Minor, a confection of black chiffon and taffeta strapped to her head, then stepped into the large black limousine that purred outside the house. As they motored slowly down the lane, Tally gripped the hands to either side of her, and never once took her eyes off the coffin with the single spray of summer flowers and herbs that she and her father had made that morning.

The journey to the Minster took less than ten minutes, and as the pale oak coffin was raised to the shoulders of the undertaker's men, Janie slipped aside leaving Tally and her father to walk immediately behind it. As they moved down the path to the old Norman archway, Tally heard beating wings above her head. She looked up to see a flock of doves soaring around the tower, the sun turning their feathers a dazzling white. They circled the tower twice, then flew off in the direction of the sea.

They sang 'Praise My Soul the King of Heaven' and 'Love Divine'. The vicar said some kind words, which were pleasant but lacking real conviction, then Janie stepped up to the lectern.

Tom squeezed Tally's hand. Janie had not said anything about a reading, yet the vicar smiled at her and sat down as she positioned herself behind the massive lectern, which was shaped like a golden eagle. She took out a single sheet of paper, unfolded it, then began, 'It's hard to think of this as a celebration of a life, because it was a life that we wanted to go on celebrating together – all of us who knew and loved Pippa. We thought she'd always be there, because she always was there when we needed her. I first met her at catering college, and I was suspicious of her at first. She was cheerful and outgoing, and good at all the things I wasn't – gardening, cooking and making friends. She proved that by quietly becoming the best friend I ever had.'

Janie paused. 'She was also very good at marriage, which I didn't believe in. I'd seen enough lousy ones to put me off for life. But Tom and Pippa Drummond were the most perfect couple I ever knew. I was with Pippa the week she met Tom. She couldn't stop going on about him. Pippa Drew, the girl who was so hard to please when it came to men. We used to tease her that they had to pass a medical and an intelligence test before she'd even go out with them. I tried to tell her that Tom was too good to be true. But she just smiled. I told her to take her time, that it was stupid to fall in love, that she'd only get hurt. Do you know what she said? "I've no choice." When Pippa met Tom, she

128

became a whole person. She seemed calmer, more fulfilled. She used to argue like mad that black was white but when Tom came along it was as if she didn't need to any more.

'I'm not very good with kids. They're noisy. They ask silly questions, and they spill food and drink on your clothes. Then Tally arrived. She did once dribble Ribena down me, but I've forgiven her for that. I also forgave Pippa for making me her godmother when I discovered what fun she was. Just like her mum.

'We might think that Pippa's gone, but she hasn't. She's still here – in our memories and in our hearts, and as long as she's a part of us she'll be alive.' Janie's voice wavered. 'I hope I can go on being annoyed by bits of her, because that way she'll stay real. Pippa spent her life unconsciously undermining me. But it did me good. It proved I wasn't always right, and discovering that you're not always right reminds you that you still have a lot to learn. But in one particular area I know that I was right and Pippa was wrong. She always thought that she was just an ordinary person, and I knew she was not. She was the kindest, funniest, most loving friend I've ever known. And, like Tom and Tally, I'll miss her so very much.'

Janie slipped the piece of paper into her pocket and went back to her seat. The Minster fell silent. Then the faintest sound of strings swelled from the loudspeakers and the Temptations began singing 'Night And Day'. With tears streaming down their faces, Tally and Tom followed the coffin out into the clear and sunny day.

Beside the Minster steps two old ladies tutted disapprovingly: 'This modern generation. No respect. No manners. Fancy a husband wearing a pale blue suit to his wife's funeral.'

Chapter 13

'Today is the first day of the rest of your life.' He sat looking out of the window, his stomach knotted, musing on the naïveté of the statement. 'What if you don't want it to be? What if you've had enough? What if you don't give a bugger about the rest of your life?'

'Are you going to finish this or not?' It was Janie. She was standing in the doorway of the kitchen, a plate of toast in her hand.

'No, thanks.'

She crossed to where he stood. 'You ought to, you know. You need your strength.'

He looked her in the eyes.

She sighed. 'Yes, all right, I know.' She went back into the kitchen and somewhere, in the depths of himself, he heard dishes being washed up. He wanted to move. No. He did not want to move. What was the point?

Janie glanced over her shoulder at the figure leaning against the window frame, her own grief sidelined by her worry for him and his daughter. She glanced at the clock. A quarter to eleven. Tally had still not emerged, which was hardly surprising considering the events of the previous day. When a child's first funeral was her mother's it wouldn't be unreasonable if she stayed in bed for three days. She left the dishes to drain and climbed the stairs. She tapped on Tally's door. No sound. She tapped again. A low murmur. She opened the door and went in. In the half-light she could see the mound of a small body beneath the bedcovers. She pulled back the curtains and let the daylight flood the room.

A tousled head appeared. 'What time is it?'

'Probably time to get up.'

'Oh.'

Janie perched on the bed. 'Only if you want to.'

'Not really.'

'Mmm . . . We could go out for a spin, though. Give you a change of scene.'

'Don't really feel like a change of scene.'

'You'd rather stay here and fester?'

'Not festering. Sleeping.'

'You can have too much of it, you know.'

'What? Sleep?'

'No. Looking inwards.'

Tally sighed. 'It's hard.'

'I know.'

'I can't believe it, really. I keep thinking of things to tell her. I nearly got out of bed this morning to go and tell her something. Then I remembered. It's horrible.' She clenched her teeth.

'Have you had a good cry?'

'Only in church. When I heard that song. It was their favourite. I don't think I ever want to hear it again.'

'You will, one day.'

'How do you know?'

'Because I lost my dad when I was twenty. I was older than you, but it was just as hard. He was lovely.'

'Did you cry?'

'Buckets.'

'So why can't I? It's wrong. I must be awful.'

'Don't be silly. It takes us all different ways. Some of us can't stop crying, others bottle it up. It doesn't make you any less of a person because you can't let go – it's just your way of getting through it.'

'But what must Dad think?'

'Right now he's still in shock. He doesn't know what to think.'

'That's why I've got to be strong.'

Janie pushed the wayward strands of fair hair from Tally's face. 'Don't take the weight of the world on your shoulders, sweetheart.'

'But Dad needs me to be strong. You can see the state he's in.'

'I know. And it's good of you to care, but you're allowed your own feelings, too.'

'Supposing he can't cope?'

'He will. Eventually. He's just got to work through it.'

'But he'll be hopeless without Mum.'

'He's still got you.'

'Exactly. That's why I can't let him down.'

Janie knew she had walked right into it. She got up, took a towel off the radiator and tossed it at Tally. 'Come on – up you get. Have a shower and come down for breakfast – juice, tea, anything.'

Tally watched her go and felt the faintest feeling of resentment at her presence. It should be her mum chivvying her along, not Janie. Then she held her head in her hands and admonished herself for thinking such uncharitable thoughts.

Tom dragged himself up the stairs and caught sight of his face in the landing mirror – bleak, unshaven, gaunt. It reflected the inner man. He turned away and went into his study, sat down and gazed out of the window across the herb garden to Brindle Hill. He remembered the day of their picnic, Pippa trying to keep up and having to stop to catch her breath. A stab of realization. Had it really just been a stitch? Or had she known it was something worse? Pointless to wonder. He would never know.

He looked down at the folder containing the book. He picked it up and put it in a drawer. *Making Waves*. What a pathetic, hollow title. Once, he'd thought it was witty. Not any more. He looked out of the window again.

Half-way through the afternoon Janie interrupted him. 'Tom?'

He did not answer, just carried on staring into the distance.

'Tom!' She put a hand on his shoulder.

He looked up. 'Sorry?'

'I'm going to go home.'

Her remark seemed not to register. Then he came to. 'Yes. Sorry. What?'

'You look dreadful,' she said.

He half smiled. 'Yes.'

'Look. I've been thinking. It's probably better if I go home and let you two get on.'

He nodded.

'I'd stay but I really think I'm going to get in the way.'

No real reaction.

'But you must promise me you'll eat. And that you'll make Tally eat, too.'

He nodded again. 'Yes. Of course. No. You must go. Things to do.'

'That's not why I'm going.' She looked anxious that he should understand her motives. 'I think you two need to be with each other, sort each other out. I don't want to be in the way.'

Good manners overrode his preoccupation. 'You're not in the way. You've been such a help. We couldn't have managed without you.'

'You're very sweet, but I've done all I can. Look, you know where I am if you need me. Maisie says she'll keep an eye, dotty old bird, but you must ring me if you need anything. OK?'

'Yes. Of course.' And then, trying to find some inner resource, 'I'm sorry about this. About me. It just that . . . well . . . I can't take it in.' He was still sitting in the chair but had turned to face her now. And then he started to shake. She lifted him up and put her arms around his shoulders as the tears fell down his cheeks. She needed all her strength to steady him as the words tumbled from his lips. 'Oh, Janie, what am I going to do? What am I going to do?' He fought for breath. It was as if his whole body had been taken over, as though he had lost control of his movements to some palsy.

'Come on, it's all right, it's all right.' She raised her

voice to get through to him, and to give herself confidence.

'I can't live without her. I don't want to.'

'No, Tom! Come on!'

He raised his voice, trying to take command of himself but failing. 'Why did it have to be her? Why not me?'

'Don't go there.'

He was in full flood now, voice breaking, nose running. 'It's just not fair. It's – not – fucking – fair.' And then she held him as all the energy drained out of him and he cried the agonized tears of a broken man.

She did not go home that afternoon.

The following morning the two of them waved her off. She watched as they shrank in size in her rear-view mirror, and worried that she should have stayed. But Tom had promised to call if he needed her, and she had given Tally her new mobile number, insisting that she call whenever she wanted to.

They watched as the Golf, with its regulation livery of mud, wound its way down the lane and out of sight. Tally was the first to speak. 'What are you doing today?'

Tom was surprised at the question. 'Don't know.'

'Shall we go out? Just you and me?' She realized what she had said and made to cover it up. 'I mean—'

He butted in, 'Where do you want to go?'

'I don't really know.'

'Do you know what I think?'

She looked up at him. 'What?'

'I think you should give Emma a call and go and see her.'

'But she'll be at school.'

'It's Saturday.'

'Is it? I'd lost track.'

He rubbed her shoulder. 'Me too.'

'I'm not sure I can face her yet.'

'Got to do it sometime.'

'I know. But she might not be in.'

'Won't know until you try.'

She looked up at him. 'Only if you're sure you'll be OK.'

Tom smiled at her reassuringly. 'I'm sure. Just don't be late back, that's all.'

'I won't. I'll be back to tuck you in.'

'Don't set me off again.'

She stood on tiptoe and kissed him. 'You really are the best dad in the world, you know.'

He promised himself that he had cried for the last time. Apart from anything else, he was exhausted.

They sat at the kitchen table in Emma's house and Emma listened as her friend related the events of the past week. She was amazed at Tally's calm but, then,

Tally often amazed her. Occasionally she squeezed her hand, but mainly she just sat silently and listened.

'How's your dad?'

'Not very good. I don't know what to do with him, and he doesn't know what to do with himself.'

'Has he been back to work?'

'Not yet. I don't think he can face them.'

'He probably needs some time off.'

'Yes. But he needs something to do, too.'

'He's probably worrying about you.'

'I know. But I'm worrying about him.'

'You can't take it all on yourself, you know.'

'But he needs me. He's in such a terrible state.'

'And what about you? How do you feel?'

Tally looked blank. 'I don't know. I mean sad. So sad. But I can't . . . admit . . . let dad . . .' She stopped short.

Emma put her hand on Tally's shoulder. 'I don't think this is a good idea.'

Tally winced. 'I'm a bit short on good ideas,' she said.

'We could go away for a few days?'

Tally got up from the table and walked over to the kitchen window, looking out over Emma's mum's back garden, which wasn't much of a view. 'I can't leave him yet.'

'No, I suppose not.'

'I just don't want to plan ahead.'

'No.'

Emma made one last effort. 'But will you keep coming out? Just to give yourself a break?'

'Of course.'

'And what about . . . you know . . . him?'

'I can't think about that right now.'

'Are you going to see him again?'

No response.

'Do you want to see him again?'

No response.

'Only I thought you were . . .'

Tally's pale blue eyes flashed. 'No, I don't think so. And, anyway, he hasn't rung.'

Chapter 14

Rachel Jago was irritated. It had dawned on her that Pippa's death, while removing one obstacle from the route to business expansion, might have put another in the way. Tom was unlikely to be receptive to the idea while he wallowed in a sea of grief. What's more, Peter was now having second thoughts – mainly out of respect for Tom's feelings. It was typical of him to chicken out when they had come so far.

You might surmise from this that Rachel was breathtakingly selfish. You would not be wrong: when it came to selfishness, Rachel Jago was an honours graduate.

In Tom and Pippa's absence – the whole five days of it – she had not been idle. She had set her heart on the Georgian house as a home for 'her' new restaurant and had already put the wheels of acquisition in motion. The surveyor had looked over the property and already telephoned in advance of his report to say that, barring a few problems relating to the age of the building, it seemed sound.

On the strength of this, Rachel had been to the building society and cajoled the manager – an old flame – into agreeing to a mortgage, 'subject to the usual reassurances'. She wasn't quite sure what he meant by that. Still, she was sure that whatever problems arose, her old friend would find a solution. Sweet man.

And now this. How could she get round this little problem? In spite of her self-interest she knew she needed to appear kind and considerate. She'd have a dinner party, just a few close friends and Tom. She'd catch him off his guard. She could slip it into the conversation over coffee and, with other people there, Tom would find it hard to argue. There. Problem solved.

It is interesting how lack of sensitivity can lull a person into a false sense of security.

'I think you're mad to go.'

'Me, too.'

'She's an old cow and I can't think why she's invited you.'

'Thanks very much.' He was straightening his tie in the landing mirror.

'You know what I mean.'

'Yes, I do. But they've been very good over the last week, coping with the Pelican on their own.'

'She hasn't coped with it. Peter has.' The meeting in the Axbury Tea-rooms was still fresh in Tally's mind. She could recall with absolute clarity her feelings as Rachel had been sneering about their shopping. About her mother's shopping. 'And, anyway, you never socialize with them. You know you'll only get cross.'

He turned from the mirror and smiled at her. She saw the tiredness in his face. 'It'll get me out of the house.'

She brushed some dust from the sleeve of his jacket. 'You can't be that desperate.'

'Don't you believe it.'

'Thanks very much!'

He patted her head. 'You know what I mean.'

'Not sure I do.'

'I just feel that I should at least go and say thank you. I can't stand Rachel any more than you can – less, probably – but if I go tonight it means I won't have to go again for a while. A long while, I hope.'

'Well, you be careful. She eats men for breakfast.'

He narrowed his eyes. 'Not this one.'

'Just you make sure that's true. And don't be late back,' Tally said.

'Thank you.'

'What do you mean?'

'Nothing. Just thank you.'

As he drove down the lane he was aware of a glimmer of pride under the heavy blanket of sadness.

Tom had been gone only half an hour when the doorbell rang. Tally walked down the hall and saw a shadowy figure through the glass panels. She opened the door. Blip Butterly smiled nervously and held out a bunch of cottage-garden flowers. 'From home. I picked them. Just wanted to say . . . you know.'

Tally took the bunch of larkspur and marigolds from him. 'Thanks.' She hesitated, then kissed his cheek and held open the door, inviting him in.

Blip was shifting his weight from one leg to another, his hands pushed deep into the pockets of his jeans. His shirt hung outside his trousers, crisp and white. He had clearly made an effort.

He followed her into the kitchen and sat at the table while she put the flowers in water. 'Would you like a beer?'

'Thanks.'

Tally took two Budweisers from the fridge, levered off the caps and pushed one across the table towards him, before sitting down opposite.

'Cheers.'

'Cheers.'

They sat in an uneasy silence for a few moments, and

then he spoke again. 'I just wanted to say that if you need, well, you know, to talk or anything . . .'

'Thanks.'

'Only . . . I'm not very good at things like this.'

''S OK. Nobody is. I'm not.'

'Do you want to talk about it?'

'I seem to have done nothing else.'

'Does it help?'

'Not much.' She took a sip from her bottle.

Blip took his cue and did the same. Then he pushed his finger around in a drop of beer that had fallen on the table. 'Look, I kind of get the feeling you don't want to carry on with this.'

Tally looked at him. 'With what?'

'This . . . you know, relationship.'

Tally looked surprised. 'How can you say that?'

'Because you've been avoiding me.'

'I've had other things on my mind,' she reminded him.

'I know. But it was happening before that, wasn't it?'

Tally got up from the table. 'How can you bring it up now?'

'I didn't want to. I've been trying not to. But I just want to know if I'm wasting my time.'

'What do you think?'

'Well, at the moment . . . I don't want to . . .'

Tally looked angry now. 'No, you brought it up. And

the answer is yes. I think you are wasting your time.'

Blip stared at her. He had not intended to come out with it, but she had forced his hand, and now she was upset. More upset then he had ever seen her. 'I think I'd better go.'

'Yes. That's it. Walk away. Don't face up to things.'

He looked crestfallen. 'I didn't—'

'No. You didn't, and nobody else does either . . .' She tried to carry on, but failed, and spun round to look out of the window, blinking back tears.

Blip came up behind her and put his hands on her shoulders, and she turned to face him briefly then slumped against him and sobbed uncontrollably. 'I'm so sorry. It's just— I can't—'

He stroked the back of her head, trying desperately to find something to say, and failing abysmally.

Eventually the tears subsided, and Tally sniffed. 'You didn't really want that, did you?'

Blip smiled. 'Doesn't matter.'

'I'm sorry. Been bottling it all up too long. Looking after Dad, trying to sort myself out.'

'You must miss her so much.'

Tally wiped away the tears with the backs of her hands. 'The silly things most. Shopping, tea not being on the table, the house being quiet, things not moving from where I leave them. That sort of thing.'

'I know.'

Tally looked up at him. 'Oh, I'm so sorry. I forgot.'

Blip smiled understandingly. 'Football kit not being washed, running out of milk, bed not being made.'

'How long now?'

'Three years.'

'Does it get better?'

'A bit. You learn how to . . . well . . . get on.'

'I'm sorry. I didn't mean to . . .'

'No, it's all right. I know. You can't think of anything else when it happens.'

'No. But thank you – for listening, I mean. And for coming round.'

''S OK. Look, if you change your mind, or you just want . . . you know . . . a friend or to talk or anything, just let me know.'

'I will.'

Blip looked at the bottle of beer standing on the table, then back at Tally. 'I'd better be going.' He walked towards the door. 'It will get better. I mean, I'm living proof.'

She was touched at his attempt at a joke. Blip, who always seemed so serious and so earnest.

He closed the door quietly behind him.

Tally watched him walk down the path, round the corner and out of sight. A mixture of guilt and relief filled her mind: guilt at forgetting that Blip's own mother was dead, and relief that her anger had seemed to lift a little of the weight from her shoulders. She must get on. She picked up the beer bottles, emptied their contents down the sink, dropped them into the bin, then climbed the stairs and went to bed.

Tom's heart sank as Rachel answered the door.

'Tom . . . darling. How lovely to see you.' She kissed the air beside his cheeks, then wrapped her arms around him and gave him a peremptory hug. He would rather have been embraced by a boa constrictor, even though the engagement would have lasted rather longer. Rachel showed him through to the sitting room of the elegant townhouse – all oak floors and linen curtains, cushions placed on sofas with constipated precision, and oatmeal paint on the walls.

The rest of the company, all six of them, had already arrived – on instruction, he guessed – and they greeted him with muted voices, nodding their sympathy.

Peter came over and gave him a manly hug, put a glass of champagne into his hand and muttered, 'All right, mate?'

Tom made an effort to appear cheerful.

Rachel's voice rose above the soft conversation: 'Now, we're not going to dwell on sadness this evening. Tom's come out to cheer himself up and we're here to help. So here's to Pippa. We shall all miss her very much. And here's to Tom and Tally. When they need us they know where we are.' Rachel raised her glass, accompanied by polite murmurs.

Tom took in the assembled company. He knew no one well. These were Rachel's friends, ladies in expensive sweaters and trousers, men who were clearly in trading or law or something equally unfathomable. But he must be polite, see the evening through. God, he wished he hadn't come.

A couple came over to him. She was in a cream two-piece, with pearls at the neck, he in a blazer and open-necked shirt. 'Rotten luck. So sorry,' he said.

'Dreadful,' she agreed. 'Are you planning to stay where you are?'

Tom looked puzzled. 'Well, yes, I think so. Yes.'

'Only it's such a big house for the two of you.'

He felt himself become irritated. 'Not really.' He took a sip of champagne. The woman's voice became an echo. He tried to keep his eyes focused, but saw a swimming vision of the red-faced husband nodding in agreement with his wife, and the wife rattling away nineteen to the dozen. Then he was aware of silence. He looked at her face. She must have asked a question. 'I'm sorry?'

'What about the Pelican?'

He had no time to answer. Rachel's voice cut in, 'I think we'll go in and eat now.'

Tom drained his glass and put it on the mantelpiece.

He wondered if it would leave a ring mark on the polished oak. He rather hoped it would. Then he felt guilty, picked up the glass and wiped the wood and the bottom of the glass with his handkerchief.

They went into the dining room. His worst fears became reality: he was seated between Rachel and the woman with the pearls. Opposite him was a painfully thin woman with a long neck and heavy gold jewellery, her hair swept up into a walnut whip of blonde froth. Her fingernails were long and painted bright red. The men were indistinguishable from one another, all in blazers and grey trousers. He felt as though he were in a yacht club.

'Now we're not standing on ceremony,' announced Rachel. 'You know the rules: just help yourselves to everything.'

Peter had done what he often did for these dinner parties – cooked an entire henhouse full of guinea fowl, which he placed in the middle of the table, along with a dish of green beans tied into neat, faggot-like bundles with chives. Florence fennel in white sauce lay in another dish, and he dispensed a *premier-cru* Chablis into tall crystal glasses.

Tom wished he felt like eating, then breathed deeply and told himself to get a grip. He spoke to the thin, gilded woman opposite, who turned out to have a shop specializing in interior design and soft furnishings.

Typical of Rachel's friends. He tried to banish the uncharitable thought from his mind. He noticed the woman's hands – claw-like, tanned and professionally manicured. A trio of heavy gold bracelets clattered and clanged as she forked up the bony bird. Her lipstick ran into the corners of her mouth. It was all so surreal. He was here, yet somewhere else. He sipped some wine, hoping it would relax him.

Anodyne conversation followed. He was aware of talking to the woman about the state of the roof of Axbury Minster, of which he knew little, and to the man on her right about the Common Agricultural Policy, of which he knew even less. The absurdity of it all struck him like a slap in the face and he leaned back in his chair.

Rachel seized the moment. 'I've got some news to cheer you up.'

Tom raised an eyebrow but said nothing.

'Peter and I have been busy while you've been away.'

'Oh?'

At the other end of the table Peter looked up nervously. The third woman guest – an American with short dark hair – had been engaging him in earnest conversation about the merits of Loch Fyne oysters. He stood up, picked up the bottle of Chablis and carried it towards Tom. With a deftness born of experience, Tom intercepted it with a single finger laid across the top of his glass. His gaze never left Rachel and he listened attentively.

Peter accepted the futility of his intervention and retreated. The American woman interrupted her dissertation and the table fell silent.

'You know we've been talking about branching out?'

No reaction.

Rachel continued, 'Well, we've found somewhere. A Georgian townhouse in Portland Street. Perfect.'

'For what?' Tom asked calmly.

'For the new restaurant.'

'What sort of restaurant?'

Rachel looked wrong-footed. 'One that serves Peter's food.'

'I rather gathered that.'

'Aren't you pleased?'

'It's not really anything to do with me.'

'Of course it is. We're in partnership. It will be like the Albatross.'

'Exactly.'

Rachel realized her mistake. 'I mean in that we'll both own it. It will be much more successful than the Albatross, obviously.'

'How do you know?'

'Because the climate's different now. There's much more of a demand for new places to eat than there was fifteen years ago.'

'I see.'

'And it will give you both a chance to spread your wings.'

'Really.'

The atmosphere around the table became uneasy. The cold note in Tom's voice, though delivered *pianissimo*, had been audible to everyone. Except Rachel.

'And it will help to take your mind off things.'

Tom took a deep breath. 'Why should I want to take my mind off things?'

Rachel looked discomfited. 'Well. You know. It's been a ghastly time – still is, I know – but you've got to move on.' She laid her hand over his. He let it lie there. If Pippa had been here, how different things would have been. She would have nudged him under the table and tried to suppress her laughter at Rachel's interference. But now he was on his own.

'Yes. You're right. It's time to move on.'

'I'm glad you understand.' She patted his hand, then lifted her glass and took a restorative sip of her wine.

Tom nodded. 'Time for a change. You can't stand still. If you do you go backwards.' He tore a leg from his guinea fowl.

'Exactly. So you're up for it, then?'

'No. Not at all.'

The silence was icy.

'I'm sorry?'

'I'm up for a change. Not for another restaurant.'

Rachel looked bewildered. 'What then?'

'I'm selling my share in the Pelican. You can buy it if you want. Or I can sell it to somebody else.'

Rachel's mouth was wide open. Peter's face drained of colour. One of the blazers coughed nervously, another rose and went to the bathroom. With the precision of a surgeon in an operating theatre Tom removed the flesh from the breast of the naked fowl on his plate. 'Nice guinea fowl, Peter. Up to your usual standard. I shall miss it.' He turned to Rachel. 'Sorry to disappoint you. I know you've got your heart set on it – perhaps you can still do it, but not with me, I'm afraid.'

'But . . .' She was struggling for words. 'But if you don't . . . we can't . . .'

Tom shrugged. 'Sorry. Other plans.'

'What sort of plans?'

Tom laid down his fork and wiped the corners of his mouth with his napkin. 'I have absolutely no idea. No idea at all.' He got up from the table. 'Thanks so much for supper. Please excuse me. I have to go and see to my daughter. It's not been an easy time.'

Peter looked as though he was about to be sick.

'I'll be in tomorrow and we'll talk about things. I'll stick around for a few weeks till we've sorted out the financial arrangements. I'm sure everything will be all

154

right. Sally's mastered the front-of-house bit now, and you've got – what was her name? Kate Lundy. How's she been by the way?'

Peter's eyes were wide open. He replied as though he were talking to a ghost: 'Fine. Absolutely fine.'

'That's good. I thought she would be. Glad we made the right decision. You can never be sure – but you can never really be sure about anything, can you?'

Chapter 15

When he looked in on her Tally was fast asleep. He perched on the edge of her bed, and stroked a stray wisp of hair from her temple. She stirred but did not wake. Moonlight slanted in through the window, casting ghostly shadows across the room. There was no sound except her breathing.

What to tell her? She would think he'd lost it. She was his daughter but sometimes it seemed that Tally was sixteen going on forty-two. Over the past few days the role of adult and child had alternated between them. She would make a juvenile remark and he would look at her with an admonishing fatherly eye. Or he would do something she considered irrational, and she would assume the parental role. He sat on the edge of her bed now and stared at her, the only woman in his life – his daughter, his friend, his guardian. Why should she be expected to fulfil all these roles at sixteen? Where was the justice in it? And now he had burned his boats. Well, one of them. And a large one at that. What would she think?

She stirred and opened her eyes. She looked frightened for a moment, then saw him and smiled. He opened his mouth to speak, but before he could say anything she murmured, 'Good night,' and closed her eyes again. For the first time since Pippa's death the pinched look on her face had gone. He stroked her cheek with the back of his hand, then got up and walked along the landing to his bedroom. The bed now seemed absurdly large – a massive island in the middle of the oak-beamed room. An island on which he was marooned with little hope of rescue. He sat at the foot and took off his shoes, then leaned forward and held his head in his hands. He could still smell her, still feel her presence in the air. He shivered and got up to take off his clothes. The wardrobe was full of her things. What was he meant to do? Clear them out and send them to the charity shop? He didn't want to think about it. Her wardrobe was separate from his. Her clothes could stay there for as long as he wanted. It was not a problem; he would sort it when he was ready.

He slid between the sheets. The sounds and uncomfortable silences of the dinner party were still reverberating in his head. He lay back, saw the ice-white moon shining in at the window and felt as though he were frozen in time. How he wished he could turn back the clock, say the things he had never said, do the things he had never done. Why hadn't they taken those holidays together instead of working so hard and trying to fit things in? He could see, oh-so-clearly now, how happy they had been, how perfect their relationship, how lucky.

Sleep was a long time coming. It was gone three before he finally drifted off into a fitful doze, and by half past seven he was wide awake again and at the beck and call of another unwelcome day.

He was surprised to find Tally already sitting at the breakfast table. She looked up as he came in. 'You look terrible!'

'Thanks.' He ran a hand through his tousled hair. 'Not a very good night.'

'No.'

'You too?'

She nodded. 'I slept after you came in but I woke early.' She was munching a slice of toast and holding a glass of orange juice. Her body was enveloped in a massive black-and-white check bathrobe and she looked tinier than ever. 'How did it go?' she asked.

'Dreadful.'

'As expected, then.'

He lifted the kettle on to the stove.

'Rachel as friendly as ever?'

'Oh, yes. Full of bright ideas for our future.'

'What sort of ideas?'

'Expansion ideas.'

'What do you mean?'

He sat down at the table opposite her. 'She wants to open another restaurant.'

'Not that again.'

''Fraid so.'

'What did you say?'

'Too much.'

'I hope you told her where to get off.'

'Not really.'

'What, then?'

'I got off myself.'

'Sorry?'

'I told Rachel and Peter that I wanted out. That I didn't want to stay at the Pelican. That it was time for a change.'

'Good for you, Dad.'

Tom looked surprised. This was not what he had expected. 'You're not cross?'

Tally shook her head.

'You don't think I'm stupid?'

She shook it again.

'But I'm probably not thinking straight.' He looked out of the window at the brightening morning. 'What would your mum have said?'

'I don't know. But if it's what you want she'd have been glad.'

'Do you think so?'

'I know so.'

'But I'm supposed to be a responsible parent, looking after you, making sure you're cared for and that there's enough money coming in to give you an education. You've just done your O levels—'

'GCSEs', she corrected.

'Well, whatever they're called now. But there are A levels to go and then university.'

'If I choose to go.'

'Yes, but I want you to have the choice and I don't want you having a hefty student loan around your neck.'

Tally chewed her toast as her father explained the folly of his ways. 'Heaven knows what I'll do.'

The kettle whistled and he rose from the table. 'I'd better go in this morning and tell them I was too hasty.'

Now it was Tally's turn to get up. 'You will not.'

He was astonished at the anger in her voice.

'You've never been really happy there,' she said.

'But I've managed. It's given us a good living.'

160

'That doesn't mean you have to carry on doing it. And if I thought you were doing it just for me I'd hate it. If you don't want to do it then I don't want you to do it either. I want you to do something that makes you happy.' She came and put her arms around his waist while he made coffee. He could feel the side of her face nestling against his back.

'But what will people think?'

'I don't care what people think. Let them think what they want. If they think you've gone barmy, who cares? I know you haven't. You've always wanted to write. Why don't you do that?'

Tom turned to face her. 'Because I'm probably no good at it.'

'You don't know until you try. And, anyway, you've got your novel.'

'I doubt that anyone will want to publish it. And I haven't really got stuck in for ages. I think it's all a bit tired, really.'

'Well, start another.'

'I don't think I can . . . just yet.'

Her voice lowered. 'No.' She paused. 'But that doesn't mean you won't be able to . . . sometime. When . . . you know . . .'

'I know.'

She brightened again. 'Why don't you write short pieces for newspapers? You could write about . . .'

'What?'

'I don't know. Life. Things.'

'I think I've had enough of life and things for a while.'

'Oh, Dad! What am I going to do with you?'

He looked up from his coffee to the scrap of a girl he was meant to be bringing up. 'I don't know, Tally. I really don't know.'

He was not looking forward to the meeting with Peter. They had not really spoken the night before and he felt guilty at having made a spur-of-the-moment decision that would affect Peter's life as much as his own. He peered anxiously around the kitchen door at the Pelican. There was no sign of Peter, just a fair-haired figure pulling pans and dishes out of a cupboard.

'Hello,' he said.

Kate Lundy spun round and a smile flashed across her face, to be replaced in an instant with a look of sympathy. 'I'm so sorry.'

'Thanks.'

There was an awkward silence. Then he asked, 'How are you getting on?'

'Fine. Well, you know, learning fast.'

'Yes.'

'Look . . . would you like a coffee? I'm just making some.'

'Yes, please.'

She poured coffee from a jug into two mugs. 'Milk and sugar?'

'Just milk.'

'Look, I must thank you for getting me this job.'

'It wasn't me.'

She handed him a mug. 'Oh, I know you had to convince Peter. He's told me so – and that he thought I was a waste of space.'

'He didn't waste much time.'

'No. But, then, neither have I. I hope I've convinced him.'

'I think you have, from what he said last night.' Tom recalled the brevity of their farewell, and realized that he had assumed rather a lot from Peter's brief affirmation of Kate's worth.

'How are you?'

'Oh, you know . . .'

'I don't think I do, but I can imagine. Look, if there's anything I can do, you only have to ask and . . .'

'Thanks.'

'It's funny, really.'

'What?' He was unsure of her meaning.

'When we met my life was at rock bottom. Then you took me in. A couple of weeks later and things have changed, for both of us, in different ways.'

Tom picked up his mug. 'Why were you in such a state?'

'My divorce papers had just come through.'

'Oh, God! I'm so sorry.'

'Don't be. I wasn't. Just at a crossroads, that's all. One part of your life ends . . . Well, that's probably a bad choice of phrase.'

'No.'

'It had been going on so long. Then when the papers arrive you suddenly realize the finality of it all. No going back. But at least mine was out of choice.'

'Yes,' he agreed sadly.

'This is terrible. Talking about me and my problems when—'

'No. It makes a change. Takes my mind off . . . For a while.' Tom drank some coffee. 'You should have said when you came for the interview.'

'What – and sounded like an over-emotional wronged woman? Not a good start, especially when you're being interviewed by two men.'

'At least Peter might have been more understanding.'

She looked at him disbelievingly. 'Do you think so?'

He smiled. 'No.'

'I knew that if I sailed in with my personal problems on day one you'd think you had a real moaner on your hands. Then I got caught in traffic and it all went pear-shaped. Well, I thought it had, until you gave me the job.'

'What now, then?'

'Oh, I don't know. Just happy to have something to

get on with – stop me brooding on the past.' She spoke more softly. 'I expect you're the same.'

'Well, yes. But—'

They were interrupted by the sound of the kitchen door opening and Peter's hurricane-like entrance. 'Will somebody hold this bloody door open? I can't get these bloody crates in on my own.'

'Coming, Chef.' Kate walked to the door and took its weight as three crates of fresh vegetables rounded the corner, with only a pair of legs visible beneath them.

'Christ knows what we're going to do for herbs now.'

The remark was as wounding to Tom as any knife.

Before Peter could dig himself a deeper hole, Kate cut in, 'Not a problem. I know someone in West Chortle who grows them.'

She took the top tray from him and then he saw Tom.

'Ah. Hello.'

'Hi.'

'Take these from me, will you?' he said to Kate. 'Tom and I need to talk.'

Kate relieved him of the vegetables and put them on the large table at the centre of the kitchen. Tom held open the door of the restaurant and the two men walked through.

For half an hour she could hear them in earnest conversation, Peter's voice occasionally rising in volume.

When they returned to the kitchen she sensed the atmosphere between them.

Peter said nothing, but grabbed a jacket from the back of the kitchen door and stormed out. 'Going to find some herbs.'

She shouted after him, 'I told you, West Chortle. There's a man who—'

'Not listening, I'm afraid,' said Tom. 'My fault. Bit of a bombshell.'

Kate looked at him enquiringly.

'I'm opting out.'

'Sorry?'

'I'm leaving the restaurant.'

'Oh, God!'

'It's good of you to be concerned but there's no need. Peter will be fine when he's calmed down. He just needs to have a stomp around and get it out of his system. I expect you've worked that out by now.'

She stared at him. 'Is it because of what's happened?'

'Yes. Just need a change. Rachel – Peter's wife – wants to open another restaurant and I couldn't face it. Been there before.'

'The Albatross?'

'You've heard?'

'Peter's talked about it, and about expanding. I didn't realize you weren't keen.'

'I just don't think it's the right time. And not just

166

that. I want to move on. They'll get over it. They might even go ahead. I'm not sure. But I know it will be OK here – Sally can do my job even better than I can, and now that you're here, well, Peter knows he's got a good second-in-command – he said as much just now.'

'But what will you do?'

'I don't know. It's stupid, really, but I just know I can't go on doing this. Not really cut out for it.'

'But people ask for you.'

'Only because I'm here. Because I'm the one who can get them a table. They'll soon learn to ask for Sally.'

'You undersell yourself, you know.'

'I'm sorry?'

'Look, I know we don't know each other very well, but I pick things up. One of the reasons this place is so successful is that people like the atmosphere here – not in the kitchen, out there.' She pointed at the door to the restaurant. 'That's down to you.'

Tom shrugged. Kate came over to him and leaned against the table beside him.

'Tally thinks I ought to write. I've always dabbled, but never done anything about it.'

'How is she?'

'She's a great help. I just keep telling myself that I should be helping her.'

'Same here.'

'What do you mean?'

167

'I have a son. He's at university. I tell myself that I'm supposed to be the one supporting him – well, I do, financially – but he seems to look after me most of the time.'

'Role reversal?'

Kate nodded. 'I think that's what happens when you're a single parent. The usual rules don't apply. It's almost like a marriage, in a funny sort of way.' She looked reflective, then changed her tone. 'When you feel like it, come over for supper. I'll ring you if you don't.'

Tom was surprised at the offer. 'Thanks.'

'Only it strikes me that you might be a bottler, too.'

Tom smiled at her. 'Last week you were an unemployed divorcee and now you're a full-time counsellor.'

'That's what mums are for.' She could have bitten off her tongue the moment she had said it.

Chapter 16

During the weeks after her mother's death Tally had watched her father carefully. He had been to the solicitor, muttered about insurance polices and probate and she had wished that he could be allowed to get through without being tied up by legalities. What had they to do with real life?

Neither of them had wanted to do much, go anywhere. It seemed enough to stay at home and try to take things in – not to be morose, although that happened as a matter of course, but to get to grips with their changed lives, to help each other through.

At night, when he went to bed alone she grieved for him. She thought, too, of Alex, and that he would not know what had happened. She wondered when she

169

would see him again – *if* she would see him again. Then one day he called out of the blue and asked if he could take her out for the evening. She had hesitated, but in the end agreed. She said nothing about her mother on the phone, preferring to tell him face to face. He said he would pick her up at six, if that was all right.

'Would you mind if I went out?'

Tom was washing up the tea things and looking out of the kitchen window reminding himself that he must weed the herb garden. 'What?'

'Only Alex has asked me out and I'd like to go.'

'Is he the one with the car?'

'Yes.'

'The fast one?'

'Yes. But I make him go slow.'

'As long as you do. Where will you go?'

'Dad!'

He looked contrite. 'Sorry. Just . . . well . . .'

'I'll take care.'

'I hope he does.'

'And in answer to your question I think we're going to Nutley Marina.'

'Does he sail?'

'A bit.'

'Not going out on a boat, are you?'

'No, just for a bite at the Spinnaker – the bar there.'

170

'Fine. Sorry. I sound like an old woman.'

'Glad you care.' She came up and kissed him. 'I'll go and change.'

'Does he know?'

'Not yet,' she murmured. 'Thought I'd tell him face to face, not on the phone.'

'You OK?' He was drying his hands now.

'Yes. Better get ready. He'll be here in half an hour.'

She did not have to tell Alex to slow down once on the way to Nutley. He had the roof down, and the evening was warm, although lumpy clouds were gathering in the west. He watched her get into the car – elegantly in spite of her short skirt. Her slender legs were golden brown, clearly due to the Italian sun, he thought. Her hair was held back in a single, short plait. She looked stunning, but thinner than he remembered.

They swapped pleasantries on the twenty-minute journey, and finally drew up in the marina car park with the bonnet of the car pointing at the water.

'You hungry?' he asked.

'A bit.'

'I'm starving.' He got out and came round to open the door.

She looked at him, leaning over her side of the car in his pale blue shirt and cream chinos. He wore old brown deck shoes with no socks, and his fair hair had recently been cut. He looked scrubbed, clean and well turned-out. She caught a whiff of aftershave – nothing too strong, just enough to remind her that last time he had smelt of soap. She was glad he'd ditched the shades.

'Could we walk for a minute?' she asked.

''Course.' He opened the car door and let her out, then locked it.

They walked along the edge of the marina, where sailboats and cruisers bobbed gently alongside the pontoons. When they came to a wooden jetty Tally stopped. She leaned on a handrail and looked out over the water. 'I've lost my mum.'

For a moment he was silent. Then the reality of the statement struck him. 'Oh, God! Oh, I'm so sorry. I didn't know.'

Tally kept staring out over the rippling water. 'No reason why you should. You've been away.'

'But . . . when . . . what happened?'

Tally spoke quite calmly. 'She died when we were on holiday – in her sleep. Heart failure – we had to come back early.'

He put his arm around her. 'I don't know what to say.'

'I just wanted you to know.'

They stood quietly for a few minutes, then he asked, 'How's your dad?'

'A bit lost. Doesn't seem to know what to do with himself.'

'The funeral and everything . . . when?'

'All done. The week after we came back.'

'Why didn't you ring me?'

'I haven't got your number.'

Alex slipped his hand into hers, then turned her round to face him. He looked down at her, then bent and kissed her lips. His were soft and warm, and Tally felt herself melt into him.

When he raised his head her eyes were full of tears. She did not speak, but managed a shy smile, then turned and brushed them away.

Tally could not remember feeling like this before. She had little appetite, but managed a plate of smoked salmon and scrambled egg and a glass of mineral water. Alex's appetite, too, had diminished, and he was struggling to get through the plaice and French fries, helped down with a bottle of Beck's.

They talked easily now – he about his weekend in Salcombe with the family, his dad barking orders from the helm like some latter-day Captain Bligh. He made her laugh with a tale of picking up a buoy – he leaning over the bows of the tiny sailing-boat and trying to secure the painter, while his father fought to stop the boat in the right position and finally tipped his son into the water.

She watched his face as he talked and ate. His eyes and cheeks seemed to glow. She could see where the sun had tanned his skin before his haircut, and the faint pale border at the edges.

He listened attentively as she spoke about her mother, explaining that there had been times when they were more like sisters, especially when it came to shopping and coping with her dad. There was concern and love in her voice when she talked about him.

Over coffee Alex asked a waitress if he could borrow her pen. Tally watched as he wrote on a paper napkin, which he passed to her. 'My phone number – if you still want it. The top one's home, the bottom one's my mobile.'

Tally smiled and slipped it into her bag. 'Thanks.' Then, hesitantly, 'Would you like mine?'

'I've already got it.' He grinned. 'How did I ask you out?'

She took another napkin and wrote down a number. 'My mobile,' she said. He folded it carefully and pushed it into his back pocket.

Tally looked at her watch. 'Better be getting back. I don't want Dad to worry.'

'No.' Alex got up and went round to where she sat, easing away her chair as she stood up.

Tally grinned.

'What is it?'

'Nothing.'

'Come on!'

'It's just that you're the only person I know who does that, apart from my dad.'

Alex stopped the car a few yards down the road from Wilding's Barn, as Tally had suggested. He switched off the engine and she turned to face him. 'Thank you for tonight.'

'No. Thank you. I'm just so sorry . . .'

She lifted a finger and laid it lightly across his lips. 'Thank you for being there. You know, when I first met you I thought you were so cool, with your fast car and your shades and all that.'

He looked disappointed. 'But I am cool . . . aren't I?'

'In the nicest possible way.' She leaned over and kissed him. After a few minutes she eased away, then laid her head on his chest.

'Can I see you again?' he asked.

'Just give me a couple of days.'

Alex touched her face. 'How did you get so brown?'

'Sitting in the back garden, thinking.'

'Don't think too much. Mmm? At least, not about sad things.'

She opened the car door and stepped out into the night before he could get out to help her. He started the engine and the Mazda growled off down the bumpy lane. As he rounded the corner and disappeared from view Tally waved.

That night she lay awake again, but not all her thoughts were sad, and when she finally drifted off to sleep, she could still smell the fragrance of his aftershave on her shirt. It was lying next to her on the pillow.

'Damn!' Tom was looking out of the window at the soft but steady rain.

'What's the problem?' asked Tally.

'I wanted to weed the herb garden and it's peeing down.'

'Good.'

'What do you mean by that?'

'You can't go out so you'll have to stay in and that means you can start writing.'

'Look, sweetheart, I'm not sure about this writing thing. I haven't an idea in my head and I've no confidence either. The two things don't make for a winning combination.'

'You won't know until you try.'

Tom came and sat beside her. 'What is it?'

'What's what?'

'You look different. Have you done something to your hair?'

'Don't be ridiculous, Dad! I haven't touched it yet.'

'Well, something's different.' Then a dawning

realization crept over him. 'Ah. Last night. How did it go?'

'Fine, thanks.'

'Only fine?'

'Yes. Isn't that enough?'

'I suppose so. Is he . . . nice?'

'No, he's horrible. Of course he's nice.'

Tom shrugged. 'Just curious, that's all.'

Tally sighed. 'His name's Alex Blane-Pfitzer, he's eighteen, he's just finished school at Sherborne and he goes to uni in autumn – if he gets a place.'

'Blane what?'

'Pfitzer. It's a bit of a mouthful, isn't it?'

'Is he foreign?'

'No. English.'

'Aristocratic?'

'You're fishing again. No. He's not. Quite well off but just . . . lovely.'

Tom saw the glow in her eyes. 'Well, that's all right, then. Only . . .'

'What?'

'Be careful. Don't get hurt.'

'I'll try not to.'

Tom watched as Tally got up from the table and walked towards the stairs. There was a dreamy faraway look in her eyes. He tried to be glad that she had something to take her mind off Pippa's death – he *was* glad. He just hoped she wouldn't shut him out. He felt a sudden stab of deep loneliness, isolation. Then he told himself he was being overly dramatic and feeling sorry for himself. He followed her upstairs, went into his own bedroom and stared out of the window at the miserable day.

The shower hummed in the bathroom, and above the splashing sound of the water he heard another hum: his daughter's voice and a Westlife song. A few days ago such a display of happiness would have been unimaginable. Now, he was glad it had come. He knew it would help her get through. He just wished he could hum, too, but right now he couldn't even bear to hear music on the radio.

Chapter 17

The call came sooner than Tom had expected. Kate Lundy had said she would phone but he had assumed it was just a kind gesture.

'Would you like to come round on Saturday night?' she had asked. 'Peter's given me the night off.' He could not think of any good reason to decline so he accepted.

Getting ready that evening he was irritable and nervous. It was the first time he had been out on his own since Rachel and Peter's dinner party. He told himself that that was why he was apprehensive.

Tally watched, curled up on the bed, as he changed into navy blue trousers, suede loafers and a blue polo shirt. 'You look handsome,' she said lightly, with the intention of boosting his confidence. She was startled by his reaction.

'I'm not trying to look handsome, just clean.' Then he regretted his churlishness. 'Sorry. It's just that it seems all wrong, getting dressed up, and not for your mum.'

'You're only going out to be friendly.'

'Yes. I know. Stupid, really. It just feels odd.'

'I suppose it will.'

Tom sat down on the bed beside her. 'How do you think we're doing?'

'As well as we can . . . considering.'

'It's a bugger, isn't it?'

'Yep. A bugger. I remember when you'd have told me off for saying that.'

Tom sighed. 'It doesn't seem to matter now.'

'No.'

'More important things to worry about.'

She pushed him in the middle of his back. 'Like getting you out of here. Come on. You look great, so just go and have a nice time.'

He looked into the mirror and ran his fingers through his hair. 'I think that's the best I can do.' Then he turned and bent to kiss her goodbye. 'Are you in tonight?' he asked.

'Yes. I thought I'd watch a video.'

'No Alex whatsisname?'

'Not tonight.'

'Well, I shouldn't be back too late, but don't wait up.'

'Oh, I think I might. I've had too many early nights lately. I'll see you later.'

Tom grabbed a bottle of something red from the wine rack in the kitchen. When the door slammed behind him, Tally switched on the TV in the corner of the kitchen. Then she switched it off again. She had never liked *Blind Date*.

Kate Lundy's directions had been precise and were easy to follow. She lived on the outskirts of Portsmouth, a good forty-five minutes from Axbury Minster. Tom admired her willingness to travel but pitied her the return journey from the Pelican in the early hours of the morning. He found the modest block of flats in a wide street and pressed the button on the entryphone. A whirring buzz, followed by a click, opened the steel and plate glass door, and he climbed three flights of lino-covered stairs to flat six. As he did so, the music became louder, not the country music he had heard when he called to give her the job, but the softer notes of piano, drums, double bass and saxophone.

He rounded the corner and saw her standing in the doorway. She looked smaller somehow, and softer-featured. Her face was relaxed, her smile welcoming. 'You found it?'

'I guess so. Good directions.' He offered her the bottle. 'Nothing terribly exciting, but not bad for summer evenings.'

The flat was small but pleasantly furnished. It lacked the opulence of Rachel and Peter's Georgian villa, yet had a warmth and friendliness that Rachel's impeccable furnishings could not match.

Kate motioned him to a fat sofa decorated with a bright red throw. She held up the bottle. 'Some of this or what I've already opened?'

'Oh, what you've opened will be fine.'

Tom looked about him as she poured. Kate's flat had clearly been furnished on a shoestring, but the wall sported bright prints of John Miller seascapes, and the worn carpet was cheered up with Indian rugs. The furniture was a mixture of periods, from early Habitat to late Ikea. He felt comfortable, welcome, and he took the glass from her gratefully.

'It's all a bit simple, I'm afraid.'

'It's lovely.' He raised his glass. 'Cheers! Thanks for having me.'

'Cheers!' Kate took a sip, then leaped up and put down her glass. 'God! I've forgotten the vegetables.'

As she ran into the kitchen, Tom shouted after her, 'But you're a chef!'

'Day off today. Doesn't count.'

He got up, walked over to the kitchen door and stood

there as she cut up broccoli, then topped and tailed mangetouts on a thick wooden block. She wore a baggy white cotton shirt and black trousers, her feet were bare and her face free of makeup apart from eye-liner and mascara. Her skin was clear, and her cheeks were flushed from the heat of the kitchen. She was prettier than he had remembered.

Above the worktop he noticed the photograph of a young man, dark-haired and smiling. 'Yours?' he asked.

'Yes. All nineteen years of him. Harry. At Bangor doing marine biology.'

'That's funny.'

'Why?'

'Marine biology is what Tally wants to do. I don't think she's thought where to do it yet, though.'

'It was there or Edinburgh. Both of them seem to be a million miles away, but you've got to let them go, haven't you?'

'Yes.' He looked reflective. 'I think mine is on her way already.'

'What do you mean?'

'Just found her first real boyfriend.'

'Oh. Bit tricky for Dad?'

'Mmm.'

'I shouldn't worry. She'll still need you, you know.'

'I hope so.' He was unsure whether to continue. Kate said nothing, but carried on chopping vegetables.

'Before I left tonight she kissed me.'

Kate raised an eyebrow.

'On the cheek. She's always kissed me on the lips before.'

'Oh.' She grinned.

'I think it must be love.' He looked thoughtful, then brightened. 'I didn't think you were old enough to have a son of nineteen.' As soon as he had said it he realized how like a chat-up line it must have sounded.

Kate laughed. 'I'll take that as a compliment. I'm thirty-nine. I married young.'

He felt ill at ease, and at that moment he wished he hadn't come. It seemed there were reminders everywhere just waiting to trip him up. Kate read his discomfort. 'Come on. Let's go and sit down for a bit. These can cook on their own.' She lit the gas under the two saucepans and ushered him back into the sitting room.

Tom sat on the sofa, Kate in an armchair opposite with her legs curled underneath her. As they sipped the wine they swapped notes on children, restaurants and the relative merits of Portsmouth and Axbury Minster. Eventually Kate said, 'Time to eat.' Tom sat quietly while she returned to the kitchen, and listened to the soft music playing in the background. For the first time since Pippa's death, he didn't want to switch it off.

Kate returned with two dishes of vegetables and two plates of Dover sole. 'Fish OK?'

'Perfect.'

'Bit stupid to ask now.'

'It looks great. Sorry about the red wine.'

'You weren't to know. Anyway, I'm not one of those "red with beef, white with fish" types.'

'Glad to hear it.'

Tom helped himself to vegetables.

'Have you decided what to do yet?' she asked gently.

'Not really. I'm finding it a bit difficult to concentrate.'

'It's hardly surprising, is it?'

'No, but I can't go on like this. Rudderless. I need to sort myself out.'

Kate looked agitated. 'Look, I hope you don't think my timing's all wrong.'

Tom looked up from his fish. 'Sorry?'

'Well. It's the restaurant. The Pelican. Are you set on pulling out, selling your half of the business?'

'Yes.'

She took a sip of wine to bolster her courage. 'Would you sell it to me?'

He was taken aback. 'But you . . .'

'I know. I've only just arrived and I hardly know either of you. But I think I know enough.'

'But what about . . . ?'

'The money?'

'Well, yes.'

'At the moment I haven't a bean. You can tell from this place.' She looked around her. 'Clean but not exactly classy.'

Tom demurred.

'It's just that now my divorce has come through I should be able to get my half of the proceeds.'

'I see.'

'It may take a few months, though. Oh, I know it all sounds very hasty, and I've no reason to expect you to agree. After all, I'm probably not a very good bet.'

'Have you asked Peter what he thinks?'

'No. I wanted to talk to you first.'

'Right.'

'You must think I'm an insensitive cow.'

'No. Not at all.' Tom stared straight ahead. He had settled on selling, but it had not crossed his mind that Kate would be a potential buyer.

'I thought very carefully about it and decided that I should just keep my head down and get on with life. But the more I thought about it the more I knew it was what I wanted. I don't want a flashy apartment or a fast car. I've no need for either, but I would like to get stuck into a restaurant.'

'And you've seen enough to want to get stuck in at the Pelican?'

'Yes. Oh, I know Peter can be a shit, but he's a good chef and I can cope with the fireworks.'

'It's a hell of a risk.'

'After what I've been through over the past few years it seems like security. I'm prepared to take a chance.'

Tom could not think what to say next.

'Don't say anything now. Just promise me you'll give me first refusal,' Kate said.

Tom nodded slowly.

'And I'm sorry to bring it up now. It's not a good time, I know, but I didn't know when would be a good time. I thought at least if I asked you quietly, in private, you could tell me where to get off.'

'No. Not at all.'

'I'm saying all this without having a clue what you would want for your share, but Rory – that's my ex – reckons I'll have the best part of half a million once the sale of the house goes through.'

Tom was dazed. It was so unexpected. He didn't know whether to be pleased or sad – pleased that someone wanted to buy his share in the Pelican, or sad that he really was leaving the place.

When he left Kate's flat at a quarter to midnight he felt strangely detached from it all. He stopped in the doorway to thank her for the evening. She kissed his cheek. Without thinking he kissed her back and she smiled. 'Let me know. And thank you for coming. It was fun.'

'Yes, it was. Thanks for getting me out of the house.'

'You're welcome.'

He drove home, hardly noticing the journey, and pulled into the drive of Wilding's Barn at half past twelve. The light was on in the kitchen, but there was no sign of Tally. He switched it off and climbed the stairs, noticing the faint glow from her bedroom. He stuck his head around the door and found her propped up in bed reading *Cosmopolitan*.

'You'll get the wrong idea from reading that,' he said.

'How do you know?'

'Experience.'

'Ha! How did it go?' She put down the magazine and folded her arms.

'Fine.'

'Only fine?'

'Where have I heard that before?'

'Well? What's she like?'

'She's very nice.'

'Oh. How disappointing.'

'Don't be rude.'

'Just teasing.'

'But she did drop a bit of a bombshell.'

'What's that?'

'She wants to buy my share in the Pelican.'

'Wow!'

'Precisely.'

'Do you mind?'

'I don't know. I did at first. Felt a bit annoyed that all she'd got me round for was to ask if she could buy me out.'

'So what did you hope she'd got you round there for?'

'Just for a chat.'

'Sympathy?'

'I guess so.'

'Serve you right!'

'Mmm. But, then, you can't blame her. I'd said I wanted out so she offered me the chance. What do you think?'

Tally frowned and folded her arms. 'If you think she's got the money – and you did like her right from the start, didn't you? – then, why not? As long as you're sure it's what you want . . . What does Uncle Peter think?'

'He doesn't know yet.'

'That could be tricky.'

'Well, he hasn't said anything since I told him. Hasn't made me an offer or expressed any interest in buying me out.'

'So how did you leave it?'

'I said I'd give her first refusal.'

'Well, there you are, then. Sorted.'

'Yes, but . . . I can't believe it's that easy.'

'Seems to be.'

'I know.' He got up from the bed and stretched. 'But

one thing I've learned during the years that I've been your dad, all sixteen of them . . .'

'And two months.'

'And two months . . . is that life is seldom as straightforward as it seems.'

'Pessimist.'

'Realist.' Tom bent down and kissed her, then tapped at the magazine. 'Not too long.'

'Half an hour?'

'If you must. Though as you're sixteen years and two months old I don't suppose I can stop you doing whatever you want now, can I?'

She grinned.

He was deeply asleep when she woke him. First he was dimly aware of a figure at the foot of his bed. Then, as his eyes focused, he saw Tally standing with her hands by her sides. She was shaking.

'Mmm? What?' He surfaced slowly, but came to rapidly when he saw the state she was in. Her nose was running and she was trying to speak. He sat up, got out of bed and went to her. 'What on earth's the matter?'

Tally tried to hold back the tears. 'I couldn't see her – Mummy. I tried to see her face and I couldn't see her.'

The words sliced into him. He pulled her into his arms and held her close. 'Oh, sweetheart.' He rocked her gently for a little while, then disengaged one hand

and switched on the lamp. 'There you are, there she is.' He pointed to the photo on his bedside table.

Tally looked at it, then closed her eyes and leaned into him once more. 'Tell me it doesn't mean I've forgotten.'

'No. Of course it doesn't. It just happens. It's your mind playing tricks.'

'Only I thought it might be because of Alex and things.'

'No. You mustn't think that.'

She sobbed now, and he was grateful for the release of her emotion, letting his own tears splash into his daughter's hair. 'Oh dear. Just when you think it's getting better, eh?' Tally nodded, her face buried in his pyjama jacket.

'I'm sorry', she murmured.

'No need. We'll get there, poppet, but it might take a bit of time.'

Chapter 18

Tom had not seen Maisie for the best part of a fortnight and felt guilty. She had probably been trying to stay out of the way but he wanted her to know that he and Tally were mending, slowly, and that he was grateful for her restraint.

She met him at the door of Woodbine Cottage, dressed in her customary eccentric fashion, and threw her arms around him. 'Oh, Tom! Wonderful to see you! Missed you both so much. Didn't want to interfere.'

He returned her hug.

'Come in for a coffee?'

He nodded. 'Thanks. But I can't stay long, I have to go into town – sort things out.'

Maisie busied herself with cups and saucers, kettles

and jugs. She could turn even coffee-making into a complex hybrid of art and chemistry. 'What sort of things?'

'The Pelican. I'm selling up.'

Maisie stopped what she was doing and turned to face him. Her turban today was orange and puce, her trousers and cardigan black. 'Goodness. Are you sure?'

Tom nodded. 'Time to move on.'

'Where to?' There was a note of alarm in her voice.

'Oh, not geographically, just mentally.'

'Thank goodness for that.'

Tom was flattered by the look of relief on her face.

'I thought for a minute you might be leaving . . .'

'Don't want to do that.'

'But what will you do?'

'Tally wants me to write. I'm not sure.'

'The arts, yes. That's where you belong.'

'How do you know?'

Maisie's eyes glowed. 'I can tell a fellow artist a mile off. Body language. Aptitude. Impossible to disguise. What you need is a shed.'

'Sorry?'

'All the best writers have a shed. Bernard Shaw had one that revolved. So it could always face the sun.'

'How could he write with the sun in his eyes?'

Maisie eyed him suspiciously. 'I don't know,' she said deliberately. Then she warmed to her subject. 'Robert

Graves lived in a house in Mallorca, with the most wonderful view. He built a brick wall outside his window so that he could concentrate.'

'Really?'

The coffee was decanted from an earthenware jug into two lopsided pottery beakers. Maisie's artistic efforts had become part of her everyday life.

'Ian Fleming had a house called Goldeneye. In Jamaica.'

'I wasn't thinking of going that far,' Tom said.

'No. Quite. Good. But we need to set you up with some kind of sanctuary.'

Tom was anxious that she should not get too carried away. 'I have a room in the house, Maisie, I think that'll do to start with. Anyway, I don't know what I'm going to write.'

'Good God! Yes. Just the thing. Here somewhere.' She leapt up from the kitchen table, dived into a drawer and pulled out a fistful of letters. 'Correspondence. A bit behind.'

There were envelopes of all sizes, some buff, some white, a few of lurid shades, and one in rich blue, which Maisie plucked from the pile and opened. 'Here we are. Perfect. Dear Maisie . . . Oh, it's from an old school chum. Works for that glossy magazine . . . What's it called?' She turned the typewritten letter over and screwed up her eyes. 'Can't really see.'

Tom pointed at the half-moon spectacles, fastened to a chain and resting on her bosom.

'Oh, yes.' She put them on. 'That's better. Stupid. Forgot. Yes, here we are . . .' She broke off again. 'This came just before you went on holiday. I was going to tell you when you came back. Well, you are back but . . .' She began to sound emotional.

'Go on,' Tom prompted.

Maisie sniffed, cleared her throat and regained her composure. 'Yes. Right. The *Metropolitan* – that's it. Very prestigious.' She nodded gravely. 'They need . . . now, how did she put it? Yes, "someone who can write about country life without sounding twee or sentimental". Preferably someone who understands about farming and wildlife but who can talk about them in such a way that town dwellers would understand.'

'Oh, Maisie, that's not me. I don't know anything about Brussels.'

'But you grow them.'

'No. I mean Brussels, Belgium.'

Maisie shot him a withering glance. She spoke slowly in order to make herself understood. 'They do not want a political pundit who can drone on about the Common Agricultural Policy. They want someone who can write "readable and provocative articles on life out of town", she says. Real country life, not the imagined life of the nostalgic townie.'

'But what sort of subjects?'

Maisie peered down through her lenses and scrutinized the letter. 'Anything you like, as far as I can see.' She took off her glasses and looked up. 'She thought I might be interested. But words . . . not my thing. I'm more into the physical arts . . . if you see what I mean. I should have replied and said sorry, but I haven't yet. So, shall I introduce you?'

'Well, it isn't really what I intended. I'd thought of fiction but I haven't an idea in my head at the moment.'

'It would start you off. Worth a try. I mean, you may not like them and they may not like you but at least you could talk to them.'

'I suppose so.'

'Good.' She brightened. 'What fun. So glad we're . . . I've been able to help. A little rung on the ladder.'

'Mmm. *Scoop.*'

'Sorry, dear?'

'Evelyn Waugh. Boot. The plashy fen . . .'

Maisie shook her head. Pippa's death had clearly left him a little unhinged.

Peter was sitting outside the back door of the Pelican drinking coffee when Tom arrived. 'What are you doing here?' he asked. Then he felt guilty at his abruptness. 'I mean, I thought you'd be busy writing or whatever.'

'Not yet. I just wanted a chat about this place. Fancy a walk?'

'If you like.' Peter put down his mug, then shouted behind him into the kitchen, 'Back in a few minutes.'

The two men made their way down the back alley behind the Pelican and out into the street, eventually crossing to the expanse of grass that flanked the Minster. It was a warm, sunny morning, but not late enough to be seething with humanity. Both men had their hands pushed deep into their pockets. They looked at the ground a lot.

'I just wanted to sound you out,' said Tom.

'Oh, yes?'

'About my share.'

'What about it?'

Tom came straight to the point. 'Kate's interested.'

Peter stopped walking. 'Bloody hell! She didn't waste any time.'

'No. But what do you think?'

'Do you care?'

Tom sighed. 'Of course I care.'

Peter looked apologetic. 'Sorry, mate. It's just a lot to take in, you know?'

'I know.'

'Oh, shit! This is so fucking awful. Look at what's happened to you, and here I am feeling sorry for myself.' Peter struggled for words. 'It was all a bit of a shock,

197

that's all. After all this time. Look, you do what you need to do. I don't mind. She's a good worker. Decent enough, too. You were right, you know. If it had been down to me we'd still be looking. And Kate's really the business.' He met Tom's gaze. 'Yes. OK. Sell to her. If that's what she wants. And what you want.'

Tom nodded. 'Yes. I think so.'

The two sat down on a bench. 'You OK?' asked Peter.

'I'm not sure what to say when people ask that. "Yes, fine," or "No, I'm bloody not." I mean, how long are you supposed to feel miserable? Right now I just want to go away and hide, or else go out at night and scream at the stars. I worry that people will start avoiding me because I'm a sad old sod who ought to be moving on. But every time I feel like climbing out of it I start to feel guilty.'

'It'll take time.'

'The way I feel now it will take for ever.' He looked up at the Minster spire, silhouetted against a pale blue sky, the rays of sunlight spearing through its crenellations and dazzling him. 'I miss her so bloody much, Pete, so bloody much. I can't think why I should bother carrying on – except for Tally.'

Peter put his arm around Tom's shoulder. 'You can't think like that.'

'No. But I do.'

'How is Tally?'

'OK. Better than I am, I think. Except that last night

198

she had nightmares. Couldn't see her mum's face.'

'That happened to me when my dad died.'

'And my mum. Tally was really scared, though. Looked terrified.'

'She OK this morning?'

'I think so. She came and said sorry. Sorry! I ask you! What for? Loving her mum?' He stopped abruptly. 'Oh, Christ, Pete, I didn't know it was possible to cry so much.'

'You need to take your mind off it.'

Tom shook his head.

'I know what you're going to say, but you do. Just give yourself something else to think about.'

'But all I want to think about is Pippa. And Tally.'

'And how healthy is that? You've got to start living for yourself. Then you'll be of more use to Tally.'

'I suppose so.'

'I know so. Look, sunshine, sell your share in the restaurant by all means, but get yourself a project, a direction. I know it sounds callous and selfish but it's not. It's a way of making sure you survive. It doesn't make Pippa any less important, it just means that you'll be able to find a way out of all this. Right?'

'Yeah, I guess.'

'Anyway, pity me.'

Tom turned to face him. 'Why?'

'Because I'll have to tell Rachel that our new

partner is female.' He slapped Tom on the back. 'Go on, bugger off to your writing. I've got a hundred lunches to cook.'

When Peter returned home that afternoon Rachel was in high spirits. After two days in London she was clearing out her wardrobe to make way for the new season's acquisitions. But there was something about her mood that made him nervous.

After kissing him on both cheeks she told him the news. 'Darling, you'll never guess what.'

'Try me.'

'Sarah and her husband.'

'Richard with the red face?'

'Don't be unkind.'

'Well, he has. Too much port and cheese and not enough exercise.'

'Listen, you silly boy. You know how he loves his food?'

'I had noticed.'

'Well, they've come up trumps.'

'What do you mean?' Even as he asked it, warning bells began to ring.

'They've agreed to come in with us on the restaurant. Not only will they take Tom's share of the Pelican, they'll also put up some money for the new place. Isn't that wonderful?'

Peter paled, and sat down suddenly on the edge of the bed.

'Well, you might look pleased. After all, it's got you out of a spot, hasn't it?'

Peter had never been good at lying to Rachel, but that night he drew on hidden resources. 'I don't think we should be too hasty. I saw Tom today and I'm not at all convinced he's going to sell. I think we should give him time to consider. If we rush him into things it might undermine him. We need to be patient.'

'But what about Richard and Sarah?'

'Oh, I think they'll be prepared to wait, don't you?'

Patience was not one of Rachel's natural attributes, and she took a great deal of convincing that the best course of action would be no action. Peter was late getting to sleep that night. He kept breaking out into a cold sweat.

Chapter 19

'Well? How did it go?' Tally threw her arms around him and gave him the now customary peck on the cheek.

Tom flopped down on a kitchen chair.

'Tell me! *Tell me!*'

He looked dazed. 'I got the job.'

'*Yes!* Well done! Gosh! That means you're a writer. Wow!'

'Not yet it doesn't. Not until I write something.'

'But what did they say? Did you show them what you could do? What did they think of it?'

'They chatted about what I did, asked why I wanted the job, looked at what I'd written – briefly – then said they'd give me three months' trial.'

'Wow! And what about the money?'

Tom frowned. 'None of your business.'

'Oh, Dad! Is it OK? Can we live on it?'

He was touched by her concern. 'Sweetheart, I don't think it will keep you in the manner to which you've become accustomed, but by the time the sale of the restaurant goes through and what with insurance policies and stuff . . .' he swallowed hard '. . . we'll be OK. And it won't take up too much time so I think I'll be able to start writing something a bit bigger.'

'The novel?'

'Maybe.'

'Great! Come on, then.' She got up and walked across the kitchen.

'What?'

'Time for a celebration.'

'Oh, Tal, I don't think—'

'No buts. We need things to celebrate, you and me, and this is our first step.' She smiled ruefully.

He took the hint. 'Go on, then.'

She opened the fridge and took out a bottle of Laurent Perrier.

'Where did that come from?'

'Never you mind.'

'What would I do without you?'

'You'd have more money for a start.'

'Ah. Did I pay for that?'

Tally nodded.

'I see what you mean. Come on.' He opened the bottle with a well-practised twist and poured the fizz into the two flutes Tally passed him. He handed one to her, took one for himself and looked her in the eye. 'Here's to us, my love.'

'Here's to us.' She chinked her glass against his. 'And the future.'

As the bubbles hit the back of his throat he felt a sense of relief at the day's events. He could think of no other person with whom he would rather celebrate. Except one.

Tally wrinkled her nose and spluttered as the champagne went down the wrong way. He patted her on the back. 'You're not used to it.'

'No, but if you do well with your writing I could get used to it.'

'Cheeky monkey! Develop a taste for this and you'll need a richer man than I am to look after you.'

He wondered why her face had taken on a glazed expression. She did not tell him that two hours earlier she had rung Alex Blane-Pfitzer. She had worried over it for days, but finally something inside her snapped. She could not go on like this – longing to travel in one emotional direction with Alex but being pulled in quite another by her concern for her father. It was better that she end it . . . wasn't it? For a while anyway. Then at least she could get her head round things. She tried to sound as casual as possible and told Alex quite lightly that she needed time to herself for a while. When he asked her how much time, she was unable to say.

Tally's GCSE results had arrived in the middle of August. Tom could not remember seeing her so apprehensive. He hoped with all his heart that they would be good enough to encourage her rather than setting her back. He need not have worried. Three As, five Bs and two Cs saw her jumping up in the air and throwing her arms around him. 'Not bad for a dyslexic!' she'd yelled.

'I'm so proud of you,' he said, hugging her tightly and fighting back the tears. They drank champagne, and Tom allowed himself to say how proud Pippa would have been.

Tally thought wistfully of Alex and longed to call and tell him, but she did not; instead she set about cooking a celebratory meal for herself and her father.

Tom waited for the OK from Kate to proceed with the sale of the Pelican, but things moved slower than she'd expected. Rory was being 'a bit of a bastard' at getting things moving. Tom wondered if he had made a mistake, but Kate's openness and honesty persuaded him to trust her. He hoped he would not be proved wrong. Whenever he bumped into Peter in town, he prevaricated, hoping that matters would not come to a head, but Peter always changed the subject anyway, saying that he'd go along with whatever Tom wanted.

As summer turned to autumn, father and daughter began to notice changes in one another, nothing too marked at first, just an easing of tension and the slenderest lightening of sorrow. Anniversaries were celebrated – as Pippa would have wanted – but in a muted fashion.

The most difficult time was Christmas, when the jollity of the rest of the world seemed to be at odds with their own sense of loss. Tom even suggested a holiday abroad, but Tally insisted that they had to get through the festivities as best they could. And they did, with Maisie coming round for lunch in an outfit that made Santa Claus look dowdy, and Janie dropping in on Boxing Day on the way to her mother's.

Blip had arrived on their doorstep on Christmas Eve, a small, neatly wrapped present in his hand. 'I brought you this,' he said, reminding Tally of a shepherd boy approaching the infant Jesus.

'Shall I put it under the tree or open it now?' she had asked.

'Open it now,' he'd said, and folded his arms while she tore away the wrapper to reveal a small leatherette box. She felt anxious in case it was something too significant, too meaningful: she did not want to disappoint him again. She opened the box, gasped, then laughed and asked, 'What's it for?'

'For when you need me. Just blow it.'

She lifted the shiny football referee's whistle and cradled it in her hand. 'You're very kind.'

Blip looked at the floor. 'I just wanted you to know that I'm here when you need me.'

Tally bit her lip, then said, 'Thank you,' softly. She gave him a hug. 'I'll keep it with me all the time.'

On Christmas night she gazed out of the window and across the fields, holding a white and gold Christmas card inscribed 'Love from Alex'. She looked at the shiny whistle in her palm and wondered why things never turned out quite the way you expected them to.

Winter turned to spring and spring to early summer. Tally had set aside thoughts of marine biology, and plumped, instead, for A levels in English and Italian, with thoughts of working in travel. Tom was surprised, having worried that the tragic Italian holiday would have far-reaching consequences, but proud that Tally had grasped the nettle. He'd done it himself to a degree, by battling on with his novel and bursting through a dreary period of writer's block.

When a year's worth of anniversaries had passed, and just when they were both wondering what would happen next, Janie telephoned out of the blue at the start of the summer holidays and invited herself over. 'Are you sure you don't mind?'

'Positive. We could do with some company. I think Tally's finding me a bit tiresome.'

Janie Giorgioni was her usual forthright self. 'Bollocks. She adores you. Anyway, I'll only come for the weekend on condition that you let me cook.'

'Are you expecting me to refuse?' There was a note of irony in Tom's voice.

'You'd be the first man who did.'

'So I've heard.'

'Cheeky bastard – you're certainly back on form.'

'Almost.'

She spoke more softly. 'I know. Look, I'll be with you late afternoon on Friday, if that's all right.'

'Fine.'

'I'll bring all the stuff – don't worry about that – just get some decent wine in, OK?'

'The best of my cellars will be at your disposal, madam.'

'I should bloody well think so.'

Tom shook his head. She was all bluster, as usual. It rather cheered him up.

'Oh, and I'm bringing you a present.'

'What sort of present?'

'Something to give you inspiration in your writing. A sort of leitmotif for your bits for that magazine.'

'A sort of *what?*'

'Wait and see.'

'Janie, don't do anything rash.'

'When do I ever do anything else?'

'Exactly.'

He put down the phone, smiling to himself, then turned to see Tally standing in the doorway looking dazed, her hair tousled and her face pale.

'What on earth's the matter?'

'It's Alex.'

'Alex?'

'The boy I went out with . . . for a bit.'

'What's happened.'

'He's just rung.'

'Well?'

'He wondered if we could meet up again.'

'Do you want to?'

'I think so.'

'You don't sound very sure.'

She hesitated. 'It's just that I'm surprised he's rung. After all this time.'

'Shows he's got stamina.'

Tally stood quite still. She'd convinced herself, over the months, that she had blown it – sent Alex away just when their relationship was about to develop. How could any male ego recover from such humiliation? And yet he had called back. It must mean something. He was desperate, clearly. Unable to find anybody else and so happy to settle for her. For the time being. Either that or . . . She stopped herself from going any further. She did not need to go any further. Life had moved on. She would move on, too. It had taken the best part of a year.

Tom was surprised by the faraway look in her eyes, and the apparent dawning of a certain realization.

'How stupid. What a waste,' she said softly.

'Why a waste?'

'Because we've lost a whole year.'

Tom looked at her sympathetically. 'Yes,' he said softly. 'So what are you going to do about it?'

'I don't know.'

It was Friday afternoon and Tally had been closeted in her bedroom with her mobile for the best part of an hour. Tom had stuck his head round the door twice now, and she had waved him away. Eventually she came downstairs and exercised her best wheedling voice: 'Da-a-ad?'

'What do you want?' He was at the sink, washing up.

'How do you know I want something?'

'Years of experience.'

'Oh.'

'Go on, then,' he said, without turning round.

'Well, it's just that – you know Alex?'

'I've heard of him but we've never been introduced.'

'Very funny.'

'Well?'

'It's just that Mr and Mrs Blane-Pfitzer . . .'

'Is that really their name?'

'Be serious, Dad. They've asked me if I'd like to go on holiday with them to Devon.'

Tom turned from the stubborn remains of a lasagne he was trying to scrape off a Pyrex dish.

'When?'

'The first two weeks in August. They'll be there for the whole month but they've asked if I could go for a fortnight.'

'Oh.'

'Can I?'

Tom was temporarily lost for words. 'Can I think about it? When do they need an answer?'

'Well, now, really.'

He was rattled. 'Well, I'm not sure. I mean, we hadn't planned on a holiday.'

'I know. I said you might not be sure so Mrs Blane-Pfitzer said if you'd like to give her a ring she'd be happy to talk about it with you.'

'Oh, did she?'

His loss of cool surprised her. 'I just thought . . .'

'I don't think you did think. That's the trouble. How can I let you go off with someone who's had nothing to do with you for a year then suddenly decides out of the blue he'd like to take up with you again?'

'It was my decision to end it – not his.'

'Well, you can't have thought that much about him if you could happily do without him for a year. Why did you pack up with him if he was so special?'

'Because of . . . things.' She wanted to say, 'Because of you,' but she could not. Why did he have to make such an issue of it? She had stopped going out with Alex because she could not split herself into two emotional halves. She had put him to one side to help her dad through, and now that she felt able at least to contemplate an outside relationship he was being unreasonable.

Tom was well into his stride now. 'And he's someone I don't even know from a family I've never met. You're only seventeen, you know.'

Tally was hurt. 'But it's only for a couple of weeks, and they sounded very nice on the phone. Even his dad—'

'Oh, if his dad's all right that will be fine.'

'Dad, don't be ridiculous. I just thought I'd ask, that's all, but you're clearly not keen so I'll say no.'

'Thank you.'

Tally's lip trembled and she fought to control herself. 'I didn't think you'd mind.'

'Well, I do mind. You're all I've got and I don't want

you swanning off with any Tom, Dick or Harry.'

'He's not a Tom, Dick or Harry. His name's Alex and he's very nice.' Tally stormed out of the room.

Her father shouted after her, 'There's no need to get a strop on. How can you expect me to agree when I don't even know them?'

He heard the slam of her bedroom door. He threw the tea-towel into the sink, where it landed with a splash. 'Bugger!' He sat down at the table. 'Bugger, bugger, bugger!' He glanced at the kitchen clock. Half past three. Janie would be arriving within the hour and they were in the middle of a family row. 'Oh, shit!' He pulled the soggy tea-towel out of the greasy water and wrung it out, then tossed it into the washing-machine to join a waiting heap of coloureds.

Why had nothing prepared him for all this? He'd worked in the catering trade, was used to dishes, pots, pans, glasses, organizing meals. But organizing a household was a different matter. His meals, her meals. His washing, her washing, shopping, cleaning, and making sure she had what she needed in the way of clothes. Underwear. She seemed to be buying that – he hoped. Why should he think about her underwear now?

Sometimes it seemed that there was hardly enough time to write, what with organizing Tally's timetable and keeping the garden going. He'd been determined that the herb garden should be just as good as it was when Pippa looked after it. At the outset he knew little about herbs, but Pippa's books had helped, and he'd learned as he'd gone along. He'd even managed to sell a few in town, though not to Peter. That didn't seem right somehow. Tally had offered to help, as had Maisie, but he wanted to do it himself. It mattered.

Perhaps now it was all coming to a head. Since Pippa's death he and Tally had had hardly a cross word. There had been tensions, certainly, even a few sulks, but never a full-blown row. He wasn't being over-protective, just cautious, so why was she being so unreasonable?

He walked from the kitchen to the bottom of the stairs. 'Janie will be here soon.'

No answer. He was clearly *persona non grata*. Well, tough. If she wanted to be childish that was her problem. Anyway, what else could you expect from a seventeen-year-old? She was far too young to be allowed to go on holiday with people he didn't know. She could bloody well stew in her own juice. And, anyway, if she went there for a fortnight what would he do?

It stung him like a bee. Was he being selfish? No. He was genuinely concerned for her, didn't want to let her out into a world he didn't trust. Who were the Blane-Pfitzers anyway? In a moment of irritation he stomped up to his study and pulled the copy of Debrett's *People of Today* from the shelf. He found the entry: 'Blane-

Pfitzer, David. Chairman and chief executive of Unicorn Holdings.' Married with two sons. He scanned the potted biography, his eyes glazing. Blane-Pfitzer was clearly a high flyer. Sherborne and Cambridge, patron of a couple of charities. Not that that made him automatically fit to take care of Tom's daughter: there was still people who thought that Jack the Ripper had been the Duke of Clarence. He cursed his childishness and stuffed the heavy volume back on to the shelf.

Why couldn't she go on holiday with this Blip guy? He seemed harmless enough. No flash car there, gentle and quiet, clearly cared for her. Then he remembered talking to Pippa about him and calling him wet. Perhaps he couldn't have it both ways.

He heard Janie's car pull into the drive, and went downstairs to welcome her. She was already untangling herself from the paraphernalia of her automotive lifestyle when he came out of the house.

'Christ! What a journey!' she said.

'Traffic?'

'And the rest. Look at that – some bastard carved me up at a junction near Chichester. Scraped right down my wing.'

Tom studied the bodywork of the battered Golf and did his best to spot the blemish to which Janie was alluding. She got the message. 'Oh, all right, so it's in a bit of a state already but why should the bastard make it worse?'

Tom kissed her cheek. 'No. Give me a hug, I'm in need of TLC.'

'You and me both.' He put his arms round her and squeezed.

'What's up, then?'

Tom drew away from her. 'Oh, we've just had our first row. Well, our first row since . . .'

'It had to happen. Real life and all that.'

'I'm just sorry it happened now – spoiled your entrance.'

'Bollocks. Doesn't matter.' She pushed the spilling residue of her lifestyle back into the car and slammed the door before it could effect another getaway. 'What was it all about?'

'Holidays.'

Janie raised an eyebrow.

'Tally wants to go to Devon with her new boyfriend. Well, new old boyfriend.'

'Oh, I see. And Dad's not too keen?'

'Would you be?'

'I'm not her dad.'

'Exactly.'

Janie opened the back door of the car and proceeded to drag out crates of food. 'Can you grab these?'

'Good God! How many are you expecting to feed?'

'Just us – unless you want to invite anybody else, boyfriends, for instance.'

'Don't push it.'

Their conversation was interrupted by the appearance of Tally at her bedroom window.

Janie looked up. 'Hello, lovely! I gather he's being a bit of a bastard.'

Tally smiled and shrugged.

'Are you coming down to help?'

She disappeared from the window.

'Do you mind not taking sides?' said Tom irritably.

'I'm not taking sides, just helping to clear the air.'

'Yes, well, I'd rather it cleared in its own time.'

She dug him in the ribs with her elbow. 'SOHB.'

'What?'

'Sense of Humour Breakdown.'

'Janie, it's serious.'

'Of course it is. Very serious. Otherwise she wouldn't be asking to go on holiday with him.'

'That's not what I meant.'

'I know.' Janie winked at him. 'Come on, there's stuff that needs to go in the fridge before it goes off. Leave the car windows open, will you? Bit of a pong. Hello, sweetheart!' She greeted Tally on the doorstep and handed her a crate piled high with packets of pasta, fresh strawberries, double cream and peaches. 'I gather I've arrived at just the right time.'

*

They ate in the garden at an old oak table covered with a gingham cloth. Candles flickered in tin lanterns that Janie had found in the lean-to at the side of the barn. It was a warm evening, and Tom steered the conversation away from holidays. As he cleared the table and went indoors to make coffee, Janie turned to Tally. 'Tricky time?'

'You can say that again,' Tally said, with feeling.

'Don't worry. He'll come round. He's just being protective, that's all.'

'Well, why can't he ring them up and talk to them? Then he'd see it's all right.'

'Because he's your dad, that's why.'

'But it's so annoying.'

'Look, leave it to me. I'll have a chat with him.'

'No. I don't want him to think I've gone behind his back.'

'How very nice.'

'What do you mean?'

'I think it's lovely that you care.'

'Loyalty. I do care, even if he thinks I don't.' She looked at Janie with wide, pale blue eyes. 'It's just that I really would like to get to know Alex better – *and* have a bit of fun. Dad and I have been looking after each other for a year now.'

'And you want your own life back?'

218

'Well, yes, I suppose so. But that sounds dreadful. I just think we should both start to live our own lives again.'

'Have you told him this?'

'No. Half of me thinks it's wrong but the other half . . .'

'I know. Just be patient.'

'But I have to let them know by the end of the weekend, otherwise Alex's brother is taking a friend.'

Janie looked sympathetic. 'I'm sure he'll come round.'

'Yes, but by then it might be too late.'

Tom emerged from the kitchen with a tray of coffee.

'Anyway, I've got a present for you both,' Janie said.

'What sort of present?' asked Tally.

'Something to cheer you up. Inspiration for your father and company for you.'

Tom looked concerned.

Janie walked over to the car and lifted the tailgate. In the gathering darkness Tally and Tom could not make out what she was doing, but she returned through the gloom carrying a cardboard box tied with string.

'What is it?' Tally asked excited.

Janie put it on Tally's knee. 'Open it and see.'

'Janie!' Tom's voice held a warning note.

Tally pulled off the rough string and eased open the top of the box. 'Oh! Oh – how wonderful! He's lovely!'

'He's a she.'

Tally lifted out a tiny white and buff kitten.

'What the . . .' Tom was horrified.

'Now, before you start, I thought it was time you both had something to think about.'

'But it will need looking after.'

'Animals usually do, but most people manage without much trouble.'

'But—'

'Oh, stop butting, Tom.'

'Well, why?'

'I've been looking at all these writers who do columns in newspapers and magazines and they all have an animal to write about. Several guys have made a passable living writing about their dogs and I thought it was time that a cat got a bit of attention.'

'That's ridiculous.'

'Well, I think she's gorgeous.' Tally was cradling the kitten in her hands. 'Have you left her in the car all this time? It's a wonder she didn't cook.'

'Rubbish, it's cool enough. And anyway she was asleep when I arrived.'

'Probably knew it was the only way to survive your driving,' muttered Tom.

'I'll ignore that.'

Tally lifted up the kitten and looked into her eyes. She mewed. 'What's her name?'

'That's up to you,' said Janie.

Tally deposited the kitten in Tom's lap thoughtfully, and watched as her father stroked the little animal. 'Wendy,' she said. 'I won't be long. I have to make a phone call.'

Tom watched her go. 'Wendy! What a name.' He turned to Janie. 'Why Wendy?' he asked.

'Don't you remember *Peter Pan?*'

'Of course.'

'Well, who was Wendy?'

'She looked after the Lost Boys.'

Janie smiled. 'So she did.'

Chapter 20

Mrs Blane-Pfitzer – 'Call me Helen' – had seemed very pleasant. 'You must be worried but please don't be. We can keep a close eye on them and there are plenty of rooms in the house.'

Tom assumed she had said this to reassure him, but he felt like saying, 'Yes, and who's going to make sure they don't tiptoe into each other's at dead of night?' But he checked himself. It wasn't that he didn't trust Tally: he trusted her implicitly, and her common sense. But how could he trust the boy? He had been one and he knew.

'Why don't you come down yourself for the middle weekend? There's plenty of room.'

'Oh, no, that's all right.'

'You must. We'd be really happy to see you.'

'Well, if you're sure . . .'

'Absolutely. Look, we'll pick Tally up on the Saturday morning around eleven and you can meet us all then. Does that sound OK?'

'Fine. Yes.'

What else could he say? How could he object? The Blane-Pfitzers were being so reasonable and considerate. Tally would be going to Devon on holiday and he would have to get used to the idea. Though he did feel a bit put upon. Janie had started it all – asked him how he could refuse, especially as he had done the same sort of thing when he was fifteen, never mind seventeen. It wasn't long before he realized that he didn't have a leg to stand on, and he had rung up Mrs Blane-Pfitzer to see if they still had room. 'Plenty,' she had said. So why had Tally told him she would have to let them know soon or a friend of Alex's brother would take her place? Or had Alex himself used that as a ploy to ensnare her? He admonished himself for his distrust.

A couple of days later he had told Tally over breakfast, having deliberately let her stew. He felt bad when she flung her arms around him and kissed him. 'I'm sorry I was so foul,' she said, and he felt worse.

'Oh, don't worry. Just promise me you'll be careful.'

'I will.'

'There is one thing.'

'Mmm?'

'I won't do it if you'd rather I stayed away, but the Blane-Whatsits have invited me down for the middle weekend.'

'Great!'

'You don't mind?'

'Of course I don't mind – as long as you don't cramp my style!'

'I'll try not to.'

'Oh, cool!'

He watched her running upstairs, doubtless to phone her beau and tell him the good news. August was just a fortnight away. He had two weeks of worry to look forward to, and then what? A gap. The prospect of being in the house alone did not appeal one bit. He went out into the garden to pull weeds from among the herbs and try to think of something else. It didn't work.

'So, what made you ring me when you did?' she asked.

'I couldn't wait any longer. I had to find out if you really didn't want to see me again or if you did just need a break.'

'After all that time?'

'I thought you'd need a year to get through all the anniversaries and stuff.'

'Yes.' She was surprised by this thoughtfulness. 'And what about Edinburgh?'

'I didn't go.'

'What?'

'Took a gap year instead.'

'But where? Why?'

'To Europe. I thought I needed to sort myself out. Glad I did. I had a lot to think about.'

By the end of the call her head was reeling. Had she had anything to do with his decision to postpone going to Edinburgh? She felt the strangest sensation – a mixture of pleasure and guilt that perhaps she could have affected him as much as he had affected her. And now she would be with him for a fortnight. The prospect was exciting, but scary. What if they didn't get on? They *would* get on. What if his family were difficult? She'd take the chance. And, anyway, if her dad was coming down half-way through the holiday she could always go back with him if things had got a bit sticky. She had not admitted that this was one of the reasons why she was pleased he would be joining them. But it would be good to see him, too, to check that he was all right.

She leaned on her window-sill and watched her father in the herb garden. He worked at it daily now. He would weed for a bit, then sit on the grass and gaze into the distance, then work again.

Sometimes she felt so sad that she ached, while on other days she seemed to find strength and optimism from somewhere deep inside herself. She could never predict which of the two states of mind would prevail on a given day. Life seemed like a roller-coaster. She tried to keep a sense of balance, even if she did not quite understand how to achieve it.

The kitten lay in a basket at the foot of her bed. Tom had insisted that it slept downstairs, until one day he found it climbing the curtains. Tally had said that it would be more easily looked after in her bedroom. He lacked the will to argue, so the litter tray, bowls and an igloo-like basket had been arranged in Tally's room.

She would often sit in the easy chair by her window, the kitten in her lap, looking out over the rolling Sussex Downs. Slowly her ability to concentrate had returned. In the first few months after her mother's death she'd been able to settle to nothing, but the doctor had suggested she take things easy and not push herself too hard. Tally had objected to seeing him, but a few weeks after the funeral Tom had insisted. She was glad she had given in: she felt a failure, and the doctor had reassured her that this was natural and only to be expected. She tried to believe him, and slowly she began to pick up the threads. But some things still hurt. Most of all she missed her mum's physical presence. Sometimes she wished that she had been buried, rather than cremated. Then at least she would have had something on which to focus. But that was silly, Tally told herself. Her mum was still with her in spirit – what did it matter that her ashes were scattered on the grass in some distant part of

Sussex? She tried not to think about it. It was still too frightening.

The letter from Kate Lundy came with the morning post. Tom would have expected a phone call and was surprised at the formality until it occurred to him that Kate would want to do things properly. The offer was couched in legal terms and it was a good one. He would not haggle. He rang her at home.

'Hello?'

'Kate? It's Tom Drummond.'

'Hi!'

'I've just got your letter.'

'Is it all right? I'm sorry it's taken so long. I hope you haven't given up on me?'

'No. Not at all. And, er, I think that'll be fine. I'll contact my solicitor and get something drawn up.'

'Oh, that's fantastic.'

'I'm glad you're pleased. Has Peter said anything?'

'Not a word.'

Odd, he thought. 'And have you said anything to him?'

'No, I didn't want to count my chickens. And I wasn't sure how he would take it.'

'OK. I'll give him a call and tell him we're going ahead.'

'Right. I'll get things moving at my end, then.'

There were a few more pleasantries, and then she said goodbye. He had done it. Tom's relief was tinged with sadness, although he had not set foot inside the Pelican for more than a year. He'd been surprised that neither Peter nor Rachel had made a fuss, but he'd suspected that they were lying low and that Rachel was being un-characteristically understanding about his state of mind.

What pleased him was that he had managed to make headway with the novel. There were days when it seemed as though he was trying to spoon treacle with a feather, but the manuscript was growing thicker. Writing allowed him to escape into another world, and gave him a brief respite from his loneliness. He was moving into a new phase of his life, with no one beside him. Tally was with him, yes, but that was different: she was there to be steered, watched over and guarded, not dumped on. He was conscious that he had nobody with whom he could share those things that required intimacy on a different level from that of father and daughter. Tally had her own row to hoe. Funny phrase. He looked out at the garden. The grass was long and drenched with the crystals of early-morning dew. He would cut it later, tidy things up a bit. That seemed to be all he was capable of today – tidying things up.

He phoned Peter before the dew had disappeared from the grass. The response was brief, accepting but not joyous. Half an hour later Peter called back. 'Look, mate, I think we might have a bit of a problem.'

'What sort of problem?'

'The restaurant. You see, Rachel's got a couple of friends interested. You met them at our place last year, Sarah and Richard – you know, the guy with the red face and the woman with the jewellery.'

'They all had jewellery.'

'Sarah had more than most. Anyway, they want to buy your share of the Pelican and come in with us on the new place. Great, eh?'

'Well, it would have been if it had come earlier.'

'But it's not too late, is it? I haven't mentioned it so far because . . . well because I thought you had enough on your plate, and things seemed to be ticking over OK. No new developments. I mean you can tell Kate you've had a better offer, can't you?'

'I've already accepted.'

The silence at the other end of the phone was epic. Finally Peter responded: 'Tell her you can't.'

'Why?'

'Because . . . Well, we've been together for years. You owe it to me.'

'But you didn't say anything when we talked last year. I told you about Kate and you admitted it was a good idea.'

'That was then. This is now.'

229

Tom felt a germ of irritation. 'Just because you've changed your mind, Pete, I can't go and change mine.'

'But I've only waited because . . . the thing is Rachel desperately wants Sarah and Richard on board.'

'Ah. I see.'

'You bloody well don't.'

'No, I think I do. Sorry, Pete, your problem. I've given Kate my word and I can't go back on it now.'

'But you haven't signed a contract.'

'I've said yes to Kate and that's all there is to it. It's taken her ages to sort herself out, and I'm not going to let her down. She's been let down enough.'

'Oh, bollocks, bollocks, bollocks.'

'Probably. But there we are. I'm sorry, but that's that.'

'I wish it were. I bloody well wish it were.' Peter put the phone down without saying goodbye.

Tom replaced his handset with great care and exhaled deeply. 'Oh dear, oh dear, oh dear.'

He suspected he had not heard the last of this.

'Now have you got plenty of underwear?'

'I bet you say that to all the girls!'

'Don't be facetious.' Tom looked at his daughter meaningfully. 'I can get some more washed quickly if you want. If I put the machine on now it'll be ready by morning.'

'Dad, I've got underwear coming out of my ears.'

'What you call underwear and what I call underwear are two different things.'

'I should hope so. I wouldn't want to see you in lace.'

'Oh, very funny.'

'Lighten up, Dad! I'll be fine. I won't talk to any strange men – only the one I know.'

'And his dad. And his brother.'

Tally walked over to him. He was standing by the airing cupboard on the landing, his arms full of towels, his hair tousled, his face careworn and weary. 'Are you sure you're going to be all right without me?' she asked.

He shrugged. 'Probably not.' He pushed the towels into the cupboard and closed the door. 'What about your time of the month?'

'Just had it.' Tally put her arms round him and gave him a hug. 'You are funny.'

'What do you mean?'

She sighed. 'Oh, nothing.' She looked up into his eyes. 'Thanks for being there.'

Tom ruffled her hair. 'Oh, I'll always be there.'

'Hope so.'

He patted her shoulder. 'Come on, glass of something before bed. I don't know about you but I'm knackered.'

'You know, Dad, your language has really gone off lately.'

'Yes, well, I've been under a lot of stress, most of it brought on by an errant daughter.'

'Errant? I rather like the sound of that. Sort of knights in shining armour.'

'Yes, well, just remember that shining armour can tarnish.'

'And that knights can turn into knaves?'

He looked at her thoughtfully. 'Sometimes I worry that *your* vocabulary isn't up to much, and at others you take the wind out of my sails.'

'Like with my Italian.'

'Yes. It was lovely. I was very proud of you. So was your mum.'

It seemed right to let her know, before she left him for the first time, that her mother and father had both been proud of her. Tom swallowed hard and battled to survive the moment. He only just won.

'Come on, little girl, a glass of wine and then I'll tuck you up in bed. Though why, at your age, you should still need fussing over is beyond me.'

Tally stood open-mouthed. Tom winked at her. 'Last one to the wine rack's a cissy.' He pushed past her and raced down the stairs. She overtook him at the kitchen door, grabbed a bottle of red wine from the rack and held it triumphantly over her head. 'I win.'

'Now, there's a change.'

Chapter 21

There were butterflies in Tom's stomach. He'd have happily lain in bed watching the sun rise higher in the sky, but for the sickening feeling that churned inside him. After turning over a few times he got up and went to the window, opening it wide and breathing in the fresh air. The trees on the brow of the distant hill rose like fountains through the morning mist. He shivered and went downstairs to make coffee.

By the time he had showered and shaved it was eight thirty, and Tally had still not risen. He tapped gently on her door, to be answered by the low murmuring he knew so well. He eased open the door and regarded the mound huddled under the Winnie-

233

the-Pooh duvet. She might be leaving to go on holiday with a man, but she still clung to some childhood comforts. 'You awake?'

A grunt.

'They'll be here in an hour and a half.'

A groan. Still no sign of an arm, a leg or a head.

'Do you want some coffee?'

Another groan, and a hand flapped out from beneath the printed honey jar. Then her face blinked into view. 'What time is it?'

'Half past eight.'

Her head dropped back on to the pillow. 'Oh, no.'

''Fraid so.'

'I don't want to go.'

'What?'

'Scared.' She hid her face under the duvet.

'Don't be silly.'

'Supposing they're awful?'

'They won't be awful.'

'They might be.'

'Who's trying to convince who? I thought you wanted to go.' Tom went across the room and pushed the hair out of Tally's eyes. 'Come on, silly girl, into the shower. You'll feel better when you're clean.'

'Bet I don't.'

'Well, you needn't go. You can stay here and cook for me.'

'All right, I'm going.' She sat up and swung her legs out of bed.

'I thought that might work.'

Tally rubbed her eyes and staggered across the bedroom towards the bathroom.

Tom looked at her open suitcase, piled high with the things a girl might need on holiday. He walked over to where it sat on her desk and wondered how she would get it shut. In one corner he saw a tiny teddy bear, almost hidden by a towel, and in another, a neatly folded triangle of black silk.

He sat down heavily on the bed. It took a supreme effort of willpower to leave the case exactly as she had packed it.

The Blane-Pfitzers were punctual, arriving at ten on the dot. The Mercedes estate, filled with cases and bags, crunched up the lane and cut a graceful arc in the gravel outside the barn. Father and daughter heard its approach from Tally's bedroom.

'Well, here we are, then,' said Tom.

'Yes.'

He put his arm around her. 'Have a great time.'

'I'll try.'

'Just—'

'Yes, I'll be careful. And don't worry.' She stood on tiptoe and kissed him. 'I'll be fine.'

'Maybe that's what worries me.'

She gazed up at him. 'I still need you, you know. You're still my dad.'

'Only your dad.'

'No. Not only my dad. Lots more than that.' She took his hand, and without looking at him said softly, 'I love you.'

With his forefinger he turned her head to face him. He wanted to say, 'And you.' In the event, all he could do was nod. He sniffed and took a deep breath, then looked at the suitcase – bulging but closed. 'I'll carry it down for you.'

'I can manage.'

He raised his eyebrows.

Tally smiled. 'Thanks.'

They stepped out of the front door to be greeted by the Blane-Pfitzers, who were spilling out of the silver car. As the parents exchanged pleasantries, Tally went and stood by Alex. Mrs Blane-Pfitzer lifted up the tailgate of the car and came over for Tally's suitcase. She took one look at it and summoned her husband. 'David, I think you'd better lift this one.'

The two men turned. 'Oh, don't worry.' Tom hurried over and carried it towards the car. 'In here?'

Then they all climbed into the car, Tally sandwiched between Alex and his younger brother on the back seat.

Tom lip-read his daughter's valediction as the car

eased out of the yard and down the lane. 'Be careful,' she said, and gave him a little wave. It would have been funny, if it had not hurt so much.

After they had gone, Tom tried hard to settle to something. He cut the grass, even though the dew had not yet burned off. The mower left little bits of chewed green cud everywhere, and he spent half an hour picking them up. He pulled flower-heads off the rhubarb, and fought with the apple mint, forcing it to retreat back into the border where it belonged.

Then sat down at the laptop, but he could think of nothing except Tally. Where were they now? Poole? Exeter? Surely she would ring to let him know when they arrived. Maybe she'd forget, caught up in the excitement.

The phone rang at two o'clock. They had made it. The traffic had been a bit grim but they were there now, and the house was wonderful, looking out over the harbour. There were palm trees and boats and the sun was shining and . . . She seemed happy.

Half relieved and half heartbroken he put down the phone. She was on her own now – till next weekend. He told himself he was being over-protective, neurotic even. For God's sake, the girl was seventeen. She had to have a bit of independence. The trouble was, he missed her.

He turned on the laptop once more, and the words flowed.

The journey to Salcombe had been tense. The traffic had irritated Alex's father, resulting in an uncomfortable tension between him and his wife, and Alex's brother, Henry, had been glued to his Gameboy, his elbow digging into Tally's side as he punched away at the buttons. She'd tried to talk to him but had received only a scowl in return.

Alex had once squeezed her hand tentatively and smiled at her, but their conversation was constrained by the company and the atmosphere. When they pulled into the drive of the long, low cottage at the top of the hill she had feared the worst, but as the journey ended the tension evaporated. Even Henry flung his Gameboy on to the car seat and charged out of the car cheering.

'Welcome to Salcombe,' whispered Alex in her ear. 'It'll get better now.'

And it did.

Alex's father, so grumpy in the car, stretched his arms and legs and said, 'Thank God for that!' then smiled at her and said, 'Sorry. A bit tense. Better now. Alex, you go and show Tally the view.'

Alex took her by the hand and walked her round the back of the cottage to a stone-flagged terrace, fringed by orange-flowered montbretia and dumpling-shaped hebes. A low stone wall ran round it, and beyond, the land fell away to reveal a view of the harbour, glittering like dark blue velvet sprinkled with sapphires. It shimmered beneath her in the afternoon sun, and above it rose the soft green domes of Devon hills. Boats bobbed on their buoys, pleasurecraft ploughed across the water, and the green swords of the montbretia rustled in the sea breeze.

'Oh, wow! It's beautiful!'

'Thought you'd like it. Do you want to see your room?'

Without waiting for an answer he pulled her through the French windows into the sitting room, with its chintz-covered armchairs and sofa, and up a lopsided staircase to the first floor. The ceilings were low, with dark oak beams, the doors were of simple planks painted glossy white. At the end of the landing he lifted the iron latch on a particularly low doorway and guided her in. The small room contained a single bed covered in a rose-patterned quilt, a small white-painted wardrobe, a dressing-table stencilled with flowers, and a washbasin. But the most striking thing of all was the view: through the tiny dormer window, whose thin white curtains seemed to float in the warm breeze, she could see the harbour laid out before her. A bench seat with a rose pink cushion was arranged in front of it, and she leaned out to get a better look. 'It's stunning. Thank you so much for asking me.'

'Thank you for coming.' He bent down and kissed her. There was the slightest moment of awkwardness, and then he said, 'I'd better get your case. I hope the wardrobe's big enough.'

She watched him go, in his white polo shirt, dark green shorts and ancient deck shoes, then turned back to the view. It was just heavenly. A stab of sadness seared into her. She was on holiday for the first time without her mother and father. She rested her head on the window-frame and breathed deeply to steady herself. Then she looked once more at the glittering bay below, her emotions a tangled web of sorrow and delight. How she wished her dad could see it. And then she rang him to say she had arrived safely.

Tom was staring out of the window when the phone rang again. It was five o'clock. The day had flown by, and although it had once looked as though he would have nothing much to show for it except a chewed-up lawn, a half-tidied border and a washed Winnie-the-Pooh duvet cover, he now had a healthy pile of manuscript pages at one side of his desk.

'Tom? It's Janie.'

He was surprised. 'Hello, you. How are you?'

'More to the point, how are you?'

'Bloody.'

'Thought so. Fancy some company?'

'If you'd asked me this morning I'd have said no. I was drowning in self-pity. Right now I'd love some.'

'I'll be there in an hour.'

'I thought you were with your mum.'

'I can take just so much Scottish common sense before I need to run kicking and screaming. I'm in a service station near Andover. I'm desperate to get drunk and swear.'

'Well, for God's sake, come here then, and I'll drink and swear with you.'

Tom was laughing as he put down the phone. Thank God for Janie. The belligerent voice of reason in a confusing, worrying world.

He greeted her on the doorstep with a hug and a kiss. 'You look nice.'

'Steady. Don't flatter a girl too much. Mind you, you clean up pretty well yourself.'

Tom was wearing a white linen shirt and navy chinos, and his face and arms were tanned from weeks of therapeutic weeding in the herb garden.

'Mind you, your hair needs cutting.'

He was opening a bottle of chilled white wine. 'I haven't thought about it – I don't have to look smart for anyone now. The restaurant, I mean, not . . .'

'I know. Well, you look pretty good to me.'

'Chicken all right? A bit boring I know, but I wasn't expecting you.'

'Fine. Sorry to ring so late.'

'No need to apologize. Glad of the company.'

Janie sat at the kitchen table, watching him prepare the meal. 'Was it hard seeing her off?'

Tom nodded. 'Stupid, really. I know she's growing up and I can admit that to myself, but I don't want her to get taken advantage of.'

'All part of it, I'm afraid.'

'I guess so.'

'I know so. I've made an art form of it, sweetheart.'

Tom grinned. 'And survived?'

'By the skin of my teeth.'

Tom could never understand why Janie of all people had not managed to hold on to a man. She was strikingly attractive – her glossy dark brown hair was swept up into a French plait tonight, and she wore a pale blue linen shirt that did not quite meet the waistband of her white jeans, and flat Italian shoes. Her eyes were dark brown – black when she was angry or excited – her skin a soft shade of olive, and her teeth white and even. She ate like a horse, and had exasperated Pippa by never seeming to put on weight, but pacified her with the assurance that, as with all Italian women, it would come when she reached her forties, which were now only moments away.

While the chicken cooked they moved outside, and sat under the branches of an old apple tree at the gingham-covered table where they had dined before. Janie felt something soft and warm brushing past her leg. She looked down. 'Hello, you, where've you been?'

'Where she shouldn't have. In Tally's bedroom.'

'Oh dear! Making the boss cross, are you?' Janie looked from the cat to Tom. 'How's she getting on?'

'Too well. I'd like to complain but I hardly see her. Well, until now. I expect I'll have to take over now that her mistress is away.'

The kitten curled itself round a table leg and proceeded to do battle with it until suddenly it closed its eyes and fell asleep.

'She's supposed to be your cat as much as Tally's. You're to take care of her and she'll take care of you.'

'Oh, I think I'm past being taken care of.'

'Hey, you miserable sod, I didn't come here to listen to you complain.'

'Sorry. But I've made decent headway with my novel. Funny, really, I didn't expect to. It started to flow and I couldn't hold it back.'

They sat under the apple tree for supper, one on each side of the table, the candles flickering in the lanterns. A second bottle of wine relaxed them both, and Janie spoke rudely about her mother's Scottish canniness, which, over the last few days, had driven her to distraction. Finally Tom dissolved into laughter and begged her to stop.

'Oh, I'm just grateful if hasn't rubbed off on me. Thank God I'm more Milano than Morningside. Christ! Can you imagine! *The Prime of Miss Janie Brodie?* What a thought!'

'You're mad.'

'God, I hope so. I'd hate to think I'd ended up like this if I was normal.'

Tom leaned back on the bench. 'So, what are you looking for, Janie? A career or a man?'

'Oh, fuck the career. I'd rather have a man any day. Though you'd think now that I'd have been put off it, wouldn't you? I've tried hard enough.' She narrowed her eyes. 'But I'm not giving up just yet. Poor misguided old cow.'

'Don't be stupid.'

'Oh, that's more difficult. Stupidity is my stock-in-trade. Heigh-ho, maybe one day.' She paused and took a large gulp of wine. 'What about you?'

'What about me?'

'What of the future?'

'Can't really think that far.'

'No. I suppose not.'

'So much to try to understand.'

Janie nodded.

'Some days I don't seem to have one. Most days, really. Other days I don't want one. Then, very occasionally, I have this yearning to get up and get on. Like today. But it doesn't last long. I feel I can't let it last long.'

'But you must.'

'Must I?'

'You have to. Otherwise you'll just waste your life.'

'It seems as though that's happened already.'

Janie got up, walked round the table and sat down next to him on the bench. 'You mustn't believe that. If you do, you're finished.'

Tom lowered his head.

Janie lifted his chin with her finger. 'You're a lovely man and you mustn't let it happen.'

'You're very kind. It's just that I get so bloody low. Life seems to stand still. There's only Tally to think and worry about. And it won't be long before she goes, university or whatever. She's slipping away now, really. I know I have to let her, but it's hard.'

Janie put her arm round his shoulder, and pulled him towards her so that he lay across her lap. 'You'll cope. You're tough.'

'I don't really want to be tough, Janie. I just want to let go.' He was looking up at the stars now, his eyes distant.

'I know, I've been there – but only ever through my own fault. I can't begin to imagine what it must be like when things are taken away from you.'

He sighed a long, deep sigh. 'It sounds so selfish, and I feel so guilty to admit it . . . but I do so miss having someone to love.'

Janie said nothing, but ruffled his tousled hair. For several minutes they were silent, Tom with his head in her lap, she stroking his hair. Then she spoke, slowly and softly. 'Oh, Tom,' she said, gazing upwards to avoid his eye, 'this is so bloody hard, and you can tell me to shut up and go away if you like . . . but I do love you so very much.'

He said nothing. Her heart pounded in her chest and she knew that she had blown it. Then she looked down at him and discovered that he was fast asleep.

Tears welled up in her eyes. She continued to stroke his hair until the last of the candles guttered and went out.

Chapter 22

'I'm sorry if I got a bit maudlin last night.'

'No need.'

They were sitting at the kitchen table, Tom, unshaven, in an old shirt and a pair of shorts, Janie in a long, baggy white T-shirt, her hair scraped back into a clip.

'That's not why I said yes to your coming round. Just so I could moan at you.'

'I know that. And that's not why I came round – just to listen to you moaning.' Janie sipped her orange juice.

'So why did you come?' he asked lightly, hardly expecting a serious answer.

'You really want to know?'

'Yes.' He bit off a mouthful of toast.

She put down the glass and looked across the table at him. 'I came because I wanted to make sure you were OK.'

'What?' He chewed. 'Me and Tally?'

'No. Just you.'

He swallowed, then grinned. 'Steady. I might take that the wrong way.'

Janie shrugged.

Tom looked puzzled. 'If I didn't know you better . . .'

'But you do know me better. Better than most.'

'What are you saying?'

'Nothing. Nothing at all.' She smiled, ruefully. 'Don't worry, Tom. I'm not going to do anything stupid. Last night I nearly did. I so desperately wanted to take you to bed. To hold you and tell you that everything would be all right.'

'Oh, Janie.' He shook his head. 'It's very kind of you but there's no need . . .'

'Come off it, Tom. I'm not kind, I'm selfish.' She took another sip of juice and looked out of the window. 'I'd just love to spend some time with you, that's all.'

'What?'

'I'm sorry. I shouldn't have said anything.'

Tom took a deep breath. 'You're not serious!'

'Oh, I am.'

'But you've never said . . . I didn't know . . .'

'Why should you? Pippa was my best friend. You were her husband.'

'But you were always so . . .'

'Rude?'

'Well, yes.'

Janie smiled. 'Just a front. Fancied you like mad.'

Tom rubbed his chin.

'Oh, Tom! There really is no reason to worry. I won't make a nuisance of myself. It's just that while you've been struggling to get your head round this so have I. I've never felt so guilty in my life. And I don't do guilt. But it feels as if I must have wished her ill. I didn't for one moment. I loved her so much. You know how they say that the worst thing that can happen to you is that your dreams come true?'

Tom said nothing.

'Well. That's me.' She drained her juice. 'I'd better go.' She got up from the table.

'No. Look. Don't go.' He reached up and held her by the wrist. 'Sit down for a bit.'

Janie turned her head away and he saw that she was fighting back tears. 'Christ, look at me. Miss Tough Cookie. I should write a book: *How to Fuck Up Your Life in Five Easy Stages*.'

'As many as that?'

She turned and saw that he was smiling.

'Sorry, you old bastard.'

'No. Don't apologize. I'm very flattered. And . . .'

'Offended?'

'No. Not offended.' He looked thoughtful. 'Stunned. And confused. It's only been a year and a bit.'

'But how long can you go on mourning?'

Tom drew a deep breath.

'No. Don't. I'm sorry. That was a dreadful thing to say.'

'No. It's just that . . .'

'What will the neighbours say? What will other people say? How long is long enough? Two years? Three? It's such a waste.'

He was standing up now, leaning against the sink. 'Janie, I think you should stop now before you say something you'll regret.'

'It's the things I don't say that I regret.'

'But what about Tally?'

'I don't know. I'm not asking you to do anything dramatic. Just think about it, that's all. I just want you to know that if you fancy a bit of company then I'd rather it were me than anyone else.'

He looked around, as if searching for reinforcements. 'I can't believe this.'

'Oh, Tom, stop being so hard on yourself. You said last night that you were desperate for someone to love.'

'I'd been drinking.'

'And that's all it was? What about *in vino veritas?*'

'That's not very fair.'

'It's perfectly fair. You haven't just lost your wife, you've lost yourself, too. Your way of life. Did you know that married men live longer than single men? Women can hack being on their own, but men can't.'

Tom raised his eyebrows. 'So, you're trying to tell me that I should start another relationship for scientific reasons?'

Janie shook her head. 'No. Perhaps you're right. I'm just a stupid woman who's got into a conversation she should never have begun.'

Tom walked over to the table and sat down opposite her. 'I'm sorry. It's just that I'm having trouble letting myself go. I'm moving on slowly, but it's not that easy. Pippa's gone but she's still here, everywhere I look. Still in every cupboard and drawer. In the garden.' He turned to the window. 'I see her out there sometimes, clear as day, kneeling among the herbs. Then the garden's empty again, she's gone, and I'm on my own again.'

'And you're happy to be like that?'

'No, I'm not. But I need to be sure I know what I'm doing.'

'Are we ever sure?'

He shrugged.

Janie got up. 'I think I'd better go before the neighbours start to talk.'

Tom frowned. 'That's not like you – to care what anyone says about you.'

'No, but I care what they say about you. And Tally.'

'I don't think Maisie will even notice.'

'Don't you believe it. Maisie is sharper than you'd think.'

'What do you mean?'

'Oh, I'll tell you some day. Nothing for you to worry about.'

Tom got up and put his arms around her. 'You are funny. All these years you give me hell and now this.'

'I'm sorry.'

He held her at arm's length. 'Will you stop saying you're sorry? It's just a bit of a shock, that's all. And, you know, I'm really not your type.'

'Isn't that for me to decide?'

'I think I have a say in it, too, don't I?'

She lowered her eyes. 'Yes. Stupid of me not to have realized.'

Standing in the doorway of the house in something of a hypnotic trance, he watched her drive away, and wondered if it had all been a dream. Distractedly he picked up the post: two bills, one circular and a letter in a crisp cream envelope. The writing looked vaguely familiar. He opened it and sat down at the breakfast table:

Dear Tom,

I am sorry to have to write this letter, but it seems that it is the only course open to us. Peter and I have worked with you at the Pelican for some years now and were, obviously, really saddened by recent events, not least your decision to pull out of the restaurant.

However, we really do feel that we must be given the chance to buy your share, rather than let it go to an outside party or someone who is new to the business. Peter has explained your unwillingness to sell to us and so we therefore have no alternative but to seek legal advice.

If you have second thoughts and think that this would be unnecessary we will be only too pleased to negotiate with you and sort this out amicably.

Please do let me know at your earliest convenience.

Yours sincerely,
Rachel

Tom folded the letter and placed it back in the envelope. Then he went to the telephone and called his solicitor.

'You've done what?'
'Written to him.'

'Saying what?'

'That if he didn't sell his share of the Pelican to us we'd resort to legal action.' Rachel was sitting at the chrome and limed oak breakfast bar at No. 1 The Cloisters, picking at a slice of dry toast like a dyspeptic sparrow and thinking of her waistline. Or trying to.

Peter's voice grew in volume. 'You stupid woman!'

'Don't talk to me like that. Tom had no right to go behind our backs.'

'He didn't go behind our backs. He told me exactly what he was going to do. Asked me, even.' Peter was standing at the other side of the kitchen, sipping strong black coffee from a large mug.

'And you let him sell his share to Kate Monday.'

'Lundy!'

'Tuesday, Wednesday, who cares? It's our restaurant and we should be able to do with it what we want.'

'Wrong. It's *my* restaurant and I should be able to do with it what *I* want.'

Rachel spun round to face him. 'You don't mean that.'

'I bloody well do.'

'There's no need to get angry.'

'Oh, there is. There's every reason to get angry.'

'Well, if that's how you feel, I'll have to find some other way of sorting things out.'

'I don't think so.'

'What do you mean?'

Peter's voice was quiet and steady. 'This is my business, mine and Tom's. Not yours. You want a restaurant, you go and buy one.'

Rachel's voice was disbelieving. 'What are you saying?'

'You heard. Use your own money. Or your friends'. Not mine.'

'There's no need to throw one of your tantrums.'

Peter held her gaze. 'I'm not. I'm just telling you. You follow this through and you're on your own.'

A hundred and fifty-three miles away, outside a cottage above Salcombe harbour, Tally was watching Alex and his father pull out a small sailing boat from the garage. It was the first morning of her holiday. She had slept well the night before, and woken up to the sound of seagulls squawking among the chimney pots.

At dinner the night before the conversation had been friendly and easy, although she had detected a slight tension between Alex and his father, even though she could not put her finger on the reason for it. She half wanted to ask him, but thought better of it.

They had gone to bed at eleven, and there had been that tricky moment outside her bedroom door when she was sure that Alex had wanted to kiss her goodnight, but instead just smiled as his parents and younger brother went in and out of the bathroom in a seemingly endless choreographic routine.

In the morning she got out of bed and leaned on the window-sill, having flung the window wide to let in the fresh air. There was little activity on the bright, ice-blue water, but she could hear the distant *ting* of halyards on masts, and feel the sun on her face. The cries of squabbling gulls echoed around her. She felt a sudden pang of emptiness, in spite of the brightness of the morning and the beauty of the view, and tiptoed along the landing to the bathroom, locking the door carefully while she showered and readied herself for the day ahead. A hopeful day. A scary day.

She put on a pair of shorts and a T-shirt, and fastened her hair back from her face with a band. She pulled out from the wardrobe a pair of deck shoes she had bought specially, and looked at herself in the dressing-table mirror, craning her neck to see how her legs looked in shorts and shoes. She hoped she would do.

Alex had not seemed to notice her much over breakfast. Apart from the occasional nod he seemed intent only on locating the Shreddies and the milk. But after a while he came to and smiled at her. Maybe he was not a morning person. What a time to find out.

Then the boat was discussed. Alex's father had said that they would get it on to the water together and Alex and Tally could take it out on their own, if they were careful and wore life-jackets. Tally would have been happy to go for a walk and discover the town, but she did not want to disappoint either father or son so she smiled and said, 'Lovely.'

Getting the boat on to the water had resulted in a few sharp words from father to son. 'No! Watch the centreboard! Alex, grab that painter! Quickly!'

Alex said little, but did as he was asked, and glanced sheepishly at Tally a couple of times as if to apologize for his father's behaviour. Tally did her best not to get in the way.

Then they were out on the water and alone, with the voice of David Blane-Pfitzer ringing in their ears from the slipway.

Alex sighed a deep sigh. 'Thank God!'

Tally remained smiling, hoping that Alex's father was far enough away not to have heard.

'Sorry,' offered Alex. 'He's always a bit of pain with his boat. I'm surprised he's let us out on it so soon.'

'Lovely day.'

Alex looked up at the sky. 'Yes. I'm sorry it's been a bit tricky.'

''S all right.'

'It'll be better when we've all relaxed – and Henry's got over not being able to bring his friend.'

'I thought you said there was no room, but there seems to be plenty.'

'Yes. Only Mum doesn't much like Eddie, so she says that to Eddie's parents.'

'But you told me I had to make up my mind quickly or Henry's friend would come instead.'

Alex blushed and looked guilty. 'I said that to hurry you up. I just wanted you to come.'

Tally grinned. 'You wicked boy.'

Alex grinned back. 'I know. Do you mind?'

Tally shook her head, and for the first time in two days she knew exactly why she was there.

Chapter 23

The printer hummed as the twelve pages of copy slithered out on to the tray. Tom picked them up and scanned them to make sure the machine had done its job properly – it had been temperamental of late – then leaned back in the chair and looked out of his study window at the full-blown summer garden and the distant pale grey Downs.

How long had he looked at this view? Sixteen years? Seventeen? He never tired of it, but there was something irksome about it now, about the fact that his chair had always faced in this direction. The fat manuscript of *Making Waves* sat in its red folder on a small chest of drawers. He gazed at the words 'The End', then added the final twelve pages, picked up the folder and slid it into the desk drawer. It was finished. Put away. Done. Now he could start on a new one. The thought surprised him. He had concentrated on *Making Waves* for so long that he had never imagined writing another. But the title was already in his head. It meant a fresh start.

He got up from the chair and heaved at the corner of the desk, sliding it round so that it faced the wall and he had to look sideways out of the window. No good at all. He would end up with a crick in his neck. He swivelled in the chair and faced the view once more. Tally had been gone two days and he had heard nothing since that first call. But she would have rung if things were not going well . . . wouldn't she? He must stop worrying about her. And about Janie.

He walked to the window, leaned out and breathed deeply. He had hardly dared ask himself how he felt about her. Too frightened. He was still raw from the shock of Pippa's death, and yet . . . for the first time since he had lost her he felt a deep warmth inside him. It was comforting to know that he was wanted, maybe even loved.

How *could* he be thinking like this after just a year? But, as Janie had said, how long does a man have to mourn? How long would he have to wait before he inhaled the scent of someone's perfume, found bags of shopping dumped on the worktop, felt a soft, warm body beside him in bed and heard laughter in the house?

A shed, that's what he needed. Maisie was right. Bernard Shaw was right. He looked out across the herb garden. In the far corner was a space where he had parked the Land Rover while he was doing it up. It was a clear patch of grass now – perfect for a shed. Over there he would still be a part of things but sufficiently detached to think. He could run electricity to it from the house and it would be a new place. It would not burden him with memories. He would be able to move on. A little.

A phone call to a local firm was all it took. Yes, they had a variety of sheds. Yes, he could come and look. Yes, they could supply and deliver it within the week. He was on his way.

Tally had deliberately avoided ringing her father on the second day of her holiday. She had come close to it on several occasions but was determined to stand on her own two feet. If she rang too often he would probably expect a daily phone call, and she wanted to be independent. Sort of.

By the second day Alex had taken care to make sure that he and Tally could operate independently of the rest of the household by asking his parents if they could have breakfast in the summerhouse that overlooked the harbour. Could they have barbecues there in the evening? To Tally's surprise they did not object, but she had still been nervous when Alex had suggested they meet at the summerhouse at half past eight the following morning – worried that his parents might think they were being rude or, worse, up to something.

But Alex had been persuasive, the parents seemingly unconcerned, so she had given in. Early that morning she had got dressed and tiptoed downstairs, out into the garden and the sunny morning. She walked silently along the uneven flagstones of the terrace at the back of the house, and down across the small, sloping lawn where the dewy grass pricked at the soles of her bare feet. When she reached the bleached wooden summerhouse it was empty. She was about to turn round and go back to the house, when a low voice at her shoulder said, 'Hello!' She spun round, and found Alex beside her with a packet of cornflakes in one hand and a pint of milk in the other. His fair hair was tousled, and glinted where the early-morning sun caught it, like golden thread. He wore a faded red-and-white-striped rugby shirt with the collar up, and a pair of shorts.

Tally blushed. 'Hi!'

'Hi!' He nodded at the door of the summerhouse. 'Can you . . .?'

'Oh. Yes. Of course.' She turned the handle and opened the door. Alex walked past her and placed the packet and the bottle on an old plywood table flanked by two even older Lloyd Loom chairs, their weaving in a late stage of disentanglement.

She watched as he moved across to a small cupboard in one corner, opened the door and took out two bowls and two spoons.

'How did you know . . .?'

He smiled. 'Put them there last night.' He pulled out a carton of orange juice and two glasses.

Tally grinned. 'I didn't know you were a Boy Scout.'

'Seagull patrol. Only a seconder, though, not patrol leader.'

'That figures.'

'Cheeky!' He put down the glasses and the carton and walked up to her. 'You look lovely.'

'You look as though you've just woken up.'

'I have.' He put his arms around her. 'Been dreaming about you, though.'

She felt herself blushing. 'Nice dreams, I hope.'

He nodded, then bent down and kissed her. Tally felt the fluttering sensation in her stomach again. She put her arms around him and felt his tongue slide into her mouth. She did nothing to stop him. Slowly his hands slipped up from her waist until they almost reached her breasts. She lifted her own hands to intercept them, and held them firmly.

Alex eased away and spoke softly. 'Sorry.'

Tally smiled and lowered her eyes. 'No need.' Then she looked up at him and said brightly, 'Breakfast?'

All day she felt as though she were walking on air. That morning they messed about in the boat, taking it up the estuary and pulling it up on small patches of beach, before devouring shop-bought sandwiches and cans of Coke. She had brought her camera with her for the first time since the fateful Italian holiday, and took photographs of the harbour and of the boat with Alex at the helm. They sat back to back on the sand, watching other boats butting through the gentle waves, and talked about everything and nothing. He leapt up at one point, and asked a startled holidaymaker to take their photo – he with his arms around her, she looking faintly awkward. Occasionally he would kiss her, and she him, but his hands explored nothing more than her arms and shoulders.

In the heat of the afternoon she slipped off her T-shirt to reveal a Lycra bikini top and Alex exclaimed, 'Wow!'

'Too much?' she asked, concern in her voice.

'No. Just right.' And then, seeing her raised eyebrows, 'It's all right. I'll try to control myself.'

'I don't want you to think . . .'

'Ssssh! It's hot.' He took off his own T-shirt, to reveal his broad but trim torso, the honeyed skin dusted with freckles. She turned away, embarrassed, and watched the boats as they tacked across the channel.

He sat down and put his arm round her. 'What are you thinking?'

'Just how lucky I am.'

'Not sad?'

'A bit, but not too much.'

'I'm glad.'

She turned to face him. 'Thank you for asking me.'

'Thank you for coming.'

There was a moment of silence between them, but it was not uneasy. Tally leaned across and kissed him lightly on the cheek. 'What shall we do tonight?'

'Ah, now I was going to ask you . . .'

'Ask me what?'

'I've a few friends down here. They came last week. I wondered if you'd like to meet them.'

'Oh.' At first Tally was disappointed at the prospect of having to share him, but if he wanted her to meet his friends it would be unkind to refuse. Perhaps she should take it as a compliment. 'Fine. OK.'

'Not if you don't want to.'

'Oh, I was just being selfish.'

'That's nice.'

'No, it's not. Yes. I'd love to meet your friends.' She was lying. Inside she felt nervous and taut, where moments ago she had felt relaxed for the first time in weeks. She admonished herself for being so unsociable, for not being happy to meet his friends. For the rest of the afternoon she tried to enjoy herself, but the prospect of an evening with strangers hung over her like a dark cloud. Alex appeared not to notice – either that or he was too polite to mention it.

When the phone rang Tom was convinced that it must be Tally, but it was Peter, asking if could come round for a drink.

'Look, I'm sorry,' Tom said, 'only I really don't want—'

'I just want to clear things up.'

'What about Rachel's letter?' Tom's solicitor had said to hold fire on the matter of Rachel's threatened lawsuit, and await developments.

'Oh, fuck the letter. And fuck Rachel.'

Tom had been surprised at the last remark – he was used to Peter swearing, but he had never heard him apply it to Rachel. He told Peter to come round, then laid down the handset and went to the fridge for a beer. The phone rang again. That would be Tally. At last.

'Tom?'

'Janie.'

'I thought I'd better ring.'

'Oh?' He was pretty sure of what was coming. The apology. Things said in the heat of the moment.

'It's just that I didn't want you to think . . .'

'That you really meant it?'

'No. That I didn't mean it.'

Tom stood perfectly still, his powers of speech temporarily suspended.

Janie continued, 'I did mean it, but I shouldn't have said it. I'm so sorry. I had no right to. You've enough on your plate without me adding to life's complications. I think it's probably a good idea if I stay away for a while.'

'Janie!'

'No. Really I do. I feel embarrassed. Me! It seems as though I'm letting Pippa down. And Tally. And you. There are some things one should keep to oneself and that was probably one of them.'

'I don't know what to say.'

'Don't say anything. Look, I'll call you in a while. I just think it would be best if I weren't around for a bit.'

'What about Tally?'

'Tell her I had to go away unexpectedly, that I'll be back in a month or so.'

'But she'll want to speak to you.'

'She wouldn't want to speak to me at all if she knew what I'd said to you.'

Tom searched for the right words, but failed to find anything suitable. 'If you're sure.'

'Positive.'

He sighed. 'OK. Only . . .'

'No. Don't say any more. I'll be thinking of you, you know that. Take great care, you old sod.'

Before he had time to reply she was gone, to be replaced by the sound of car tyres crunching over the gravel drive outside the Barn. He put down the phone and saw Peter storming up to the front door with a face like thunder.

'Give me a beer.'

'What?'

'Give me a fucking beer – quick.'

'Right.' Tom went to the fridge and took out a bottle of Beck's, flipped off the cap and handed it to his soon-to-be-former partner. Then he leaned back against the kitchen worktop as he watched Peter drink from the neck. 'Now, look . . .' he said, as the bottle was lowered. Then he saw Peter's face properly. He looked almost frightened, and the hand holding the beer was shaking. 'What the hell's the matter?'

'I've left her.'

'What?'

'Rachel. I've had enough.'

Tom stared at him, unsure for the umpteenth time that day what to say.

'It's just impossible. I've tried reason, I've tried agreeing with her, I've even tried arguing, which comes very easily.' He took another gulp from the bottle. 'I just can't hack it any more. Why the fuck did you let me marry her? Don't answer that. Oh, Christ, Tom, I'm just worn down. I'm not myself any more. I mean, look at me, flying off the handle all the time. I never used to be like this.'

Tom looked doubtful.

'Well, not as bad, anyway.'

Finally Tom managed to speak. 'When did this happen?'

Peter looked at his watch. 'Seventeen minutes ago.'

'I see. Any particular reason?'

'That letter to you.'

'Oh.'

'That was the last straw. I had a go at her about it. I mean, what the fuck did she think she was doing writing to you like that? It was as if we didn't know each other.'

Tom looked at him enquiringly.

'I know. Point taken. I suppose we do hardly know each other now. Not like it once was. But why? No reason other than Rachel.'

'Peter, I don't think—'

'Don't say anything. I've not come round to blame you for the break-up of my marriage, I've come round to say I'm sorry for what's happened and that it won't happen again.' He looked out of the window. 'Christ, Tom, when I think what you and Pippa had and what

269

you've lost, and when I think of what I'm stuck with
. . . *was* stuck with.'

'I'm not sure comparisons are a good idea.'

'No. But they make you think.'

'Aren't you being a bit hasty?'

Peter turned to face him again. 'You call two years
hasty?'

'But you were besotted with her.'

'Until I found out what she was really like. And that
took about a fortnight. No wonder she'd been through
two husbands. They think the second did away with
himself – and after two years of living with Rachel I can
quite understand why.'

'I'm not sure you should be telling me this,' Tom said
quietly.

For the first time there was a crack in Peter's voice.
'Well, who the fuck else do I tell?'

Tom walked up and put his hand on his friend's
shoulder. 'Sorry.' He had never expected to see him in
such a state. Peter, the confident, arrogant but good-
hearted chef, he of the bolshy temperament, the
colourful, high-volume kitchen vocabulary, looked
crumpled and desolate.

Peter rubbed the back of his fist across his eyes then
drained the bottle. 'Look, mate, I'm sorry,' he said softly,
almost respectfully. 'Christ knows, you've got enough
on your plate right now without me.'

'No. It's not a problem. I mean—'

'Anyway. I should be glad. Glad I'm out of there. And you shouldn't think you've had anything to do with it. Other than being a role model.'

'What?'

Peter stood the empty bottle carefully on the draining board. 'When I saw you and Pippa it used to make me so jealous. You were so good together. Not in a lovey-dovey way but just so . . . right. You fitted together. You *liked* one another. I so wanted to like Rachel. And I couldn't. She was great in bed – couldn't get enough of it. But you need more than that to build a marriage on. When she wasn't on her back she was buying clothes to put on it. Or making grandiose plans for another restaurant.'

Tom felt faintly guilty.

'D'you know, she never once talked about us? Her and me. Not in a loving way. You know – things we might do together, places we might go. Everywhere she went, she went with her friends, those braying stuck-up bitches and their red-faced wankers of husbands. The only time she ever made plans for us was with that other bloody restaurant. I never wanted it, but she didn't seem to care about that.'

He fell silent, and stared into the middle distance.

'So, what now?'

'Mmm?' His eyes were unfocused.

271

'What will you do now?'

'Fuck knows. Stick a bed in the attic at the Pelican for a bit. Then see what turns up.'

'You're sure about leaving?'

'Oh, yes. Burned my boats. Told her to fuck off. Except that the house is in her name so she won't.'

'What?'

'Oh, don't worry. I kept the restaurant in my name, but I expect it'll be ages before I can get any money off her – if ever. What a state, eh? What a fucking state. You and me both on our own again, but for different reasons.'

'Yes.'

Peter opened the door to leave. 'Look, I'm sorry if this has all come out wrong. Bad time and all that. Anyway, you know where I am. And the company will be better now – just me and my canine friend Delia.'

'Yes.'

Peter walked across the yard to his car. 'Be seeing you.'

'Yes.'

He disappeared into the night and Tom stood at the doorway enveloped in an uneasy kind of emptiness. He had never liked Rachel, yet he felt sad for both her and Peter. It had been a sudden decision on Peter's part but, he knew, a final one. Peter had never before gone back on anything, and it was unlikely that he would now.

Chapter 24

Tally took longer than usual to get herself ready for the evening out. She bathed, washed her hair, took ages over her makeup and even longer deciding what to wear – not that her holiday wardrobe was extensive. When she emerged on the landing, in a pale blue and white striped cotton dress with pencil straps, Alex greeted her with 'Wow!'

'What are you doing here?' she asked.

'Just waiting.' He looked about him to make sure the coast was clear, then kissed her lightly. 'Can't wait to show you off.'

'Is that what this is all about?'

'Of course.' He ushered her towards the narrow

staircase. 'Can you walk in those?' he asked, as they left by the front door.

'It depends how far.' Tally looked down at her strappy sandals, then at the steep hill down into Salcombe. 'You don't bring the car down here, then?'

'No point, really. The lanes are narrow, and someone might trash it when it's parked. Better to leave it at home.'

'We haven't seen much of your parents.'

'Never do. Mum's off visiting friends, and Dad's looking at boats. He wants something bigger. A yawl, I think.'

'Is that why we've been allowed to use the little one?'

'Guess so.'

Tally hesitated. 'I haven't talked to him much yet.'

'He doesn't say much.'

'I've noticed. Why is that, do you think?'

Alex struggled. 'He doesn't know how to, I guess.'

'What do you mean?'

'His dad died when he was tiny. Maybe he didn't see how it's done.'

'Neither did my dad, but at least he talks to me.'

'Mine talks to me. Sometimes. It's just . . . tricky, that's all.'

'Do you think that being brought up by a single parent makes you a different person?'

Alex looked at her. 'That's a big question.'

'I suppose it is. Only I seem to have come across a lot of people lately who've lost a mum or dad.'

'And how do you think they differ from people with two parents?'

'They stay more inside themselves. Usually.'

She left it there. It seemed that Alex was unwilling, or unable, to take the subject further, and she was reluctant to spoil their evening, even if, in prospect, it was already daunting.

'So where to?'

'I said we'd meet them at the Jolly Sailor and then we can see what we feel like doing.'

'Who are they?'

'Right, well, there's two school chums. Mark is the one with ginger hair and he's a great winger – rugby. And Raife – he's dark-haired, and a dark horse, too, bit of a wheeler-dealer. Then there's Anna, you'll like her – she's Mark's sister, but she doesn't look anything like him. She's tiny with short dark hair. Clee, short for Cleone, is a long-haired blonde who's had an on-off relationship with Raife for about three years.'

'What's she like?'

'Flighty is the word my mum uses. Can be a bit of a whinger, too.'

'Oh.'

'You'll like them, I promise. They're good fun.'

'Where do they stay?'

'In Mark's parents' house in East Portlemouth – just the other side of the harbour. They have to get home by boat at eleven thirty otherwise they're stuck over here.'

'Do you come here every year?'

'Yes. Every August. And a few other weekends.'

'Spoiled.'

'Yes, I know, but I try not to let it go to my head.' He was beginning to get used to her mock disapproval, Tally thought. Where once he had looked puzzled, or even hurt, now he returned her gentle jibes with top spin. She rather liked that.

The Jolly Sailor was seething with bodies. Loud conversation drifted out of the open windows on to the narrow, thronged street, along with the smell of beer and cigarette smoke. They did not have to go in: Alex called out to the two young men coming down the front steps with a tray of glasses and crisps. 'Hi, you guys!'

His greeting was returned by a fresh-faced, towering figure with a mop of ginger hair, and a slightly shorter one with dark, spiky hair and sunglasses pushed on to the top of his head.

'We're round the back. On the quay. Walk this way,' instructed the taller of the two, affecting a limp as he balanced the tray on one hand and grinned maniacally.

'Don't mind him,' Alex said. 'He's a bit touched. At midnight he turns into a pumpkin.'

'Or a werewolf.'

'You wish!'

They followed as instructed and sat down at a combined bench and table of the sort regularly found in pub gardens – fiendishly difficult for a woman to sit at gracefully, and amazingly efficient at laddering tights. Tally perched at the end.

Alex went through the introductions: 'This is Tally. Tally, this is Mark, and Raife and Clee and Anna.'

Mark said, 'Hi,' with a warm grin.

Raife said, 'Hi,' coolly, trying to impress and not look impressed. Clee waved and managed a brief smile, and Anna said, 'Hello, lovely to see you. We've heard all about you.'

'Oh,' said Tally, smiling nervously.

'All good,' said Mark, 'and there's no need to be shy. We're a perfectly acceptable bunch, if you don't count the fact that these two had a row this afternoon and aren't speaking to one another – or, rather, they weren't until you came along but now they will be extremely well-mannered and their conversation will sparkle.'

Raife said, 'Shut up, bastard,' and Clee raised her eyes heavenward.

Anna attempted to make Tally feel more at home. 'Give them a few minutes and half a glass of lager and they'll be fine.' And then, noticing that Tally and Alex lacked glasses, 'Guys, you haven't bought Alex and Tally a drink.'

Mark cut in, 'Yes, we have. Here you are, squire, a pint of Mr Foster's best, and for the lady a Smirnoff Ice. OK?'

'Thanks.' Tally was a little unsettled. She wondered if they knew her age. Clearly they were all a couple of years older than she was, more sophisticated, worldly.

'So, Alex,' said Raife softly, 'where did you find this babe?'

Alex brushed off the implied sarcasm. 'We met in Axbury.'

'Ah, the country retreat.'

'That's right.'

Raife turned to Tally. 'And you fell for the fast car and the smooth talk.'

Alex attempted to cut in, but Tally beat him to it. She said sweetly, 'No. I thought he was a jumped-up little shit, actually, when I met him but then I discovered otherwise.'

The table fell silent. Clee's jaw dropped. Raife's sunglasses fell off his head and on to his nose like a closing visor. Mark's eyebrows disappeared into his hair, and Anna threw back her head and laughed. 'Good for you, Tally.'

Tally felt ashamed and, at the same time, empowered. She had guessed that unless she stood her ground at the outset there would be little chance of her holding her own. But she wished that she had not been quite so crude. Still, it was over now, and it seemed to have broken the ice.

Raife pushed his glasses back on to the top of his head. 'First hit to Tally, then.'

'How nice to see you put in your place, Raife,' Clee retorted. 'First time today.'

Mark, sensing it was time to move on, opened up the conversation: 'So, what have you two done today?'

Alex, with occasional contributions from Tally, told them about the boat, about how they seemed to have it to themselves now that Alex's father had gone in search of a larger vessel, and about their plans for the next few days.

While the boys were in conversation Anna leaned over and whispered in Tally's ear, 'Well done. They take a bit of mastering, these guys, but I think you've sorted them.'

'Thanks. I'm a bit nervous.'

'I'm not surprised.'

Tally studied the elfin-featured Anna in her little black dress, with her brown shoulders and legs. 'How long have you been here?' she asked.

'Oh, a month or so. It's the end of my gap year. Need to unwind. Knackered.'

'What have you been doing?'

'Classroom assistant in a nursery school. More little shits. They were sweet, actually. How about you?'

At this point Clee joined in, having clearly found boys' talk not to her liking.

Tally continued, 'Just finished my first year of As.'

Clee raised her eyebrows. 'Wow!' she said, with irony.

Tally had had her moment of glory and could think of no suitable rejoinder.

'Hardly a criminal offence,' said Anna.

'Oh, I don't know,' said Clee, sipping her own Smirnoff Ice defiantly and nodding at Tally's glass.

'Oh, come off it, Clee. Stop being so stuck up. Just because Raife's had a downer on you today.'

Clee got the message. She put down the bottle. 'Sorry, I'm just a bit pissed off that's all. Need a few more of these.'

'Well, if we could get those guys off the subject of boats and babes, maybe we'd get served. Mark! Are we getting another drink or what?'

Mark got up, made placatory noises at Anna and Clee, then went off again to the bar.

They ate – eventually – at a fish bar, by which time Mark was pleasantly sloshed, Raife silent and brooding, and Anna glassy-eyed. Clee could not stop talking, about boys, shoes and handbags. Tally began to find her rather funny, if a little wearing, but the drinks had helped her to relax a little. She had moved on to orange juice after the third Smirnoff Ice, much to the amusement of Clee and the barely veiled disgust of Raife.

Alex was still upright, but she noticed that he lurched from side to side a little and that his S's were over-enunciated. Her reverie was cut short by Anna shrieking, 'God, look at the time! We'll miss the boat.'

'I think I've already missed it,' mumbled Raife. 'Same time tomorrow night?'

There was muttered agreement from the rest of the group.

Clee disappeared under the table in search of the shoe she had taken off to illustrate her point about straps and buckles, and Raife hurried towards the door, saying, 'I'll go and ask it to wait. Just get a move on.' Then he was clearly struck by another thought. He lumbered over to Tally, beamed and said, 'See you again, Princess,' then kissed her hand and bowed his way out of the door backwards.

Clee scowled at him, then turned to Tally. 'He's mine,' she whispered, before picking her way through the tables in Raife's alcoholic slipstream.

Quite suddenly they had all disappeared, leaving Tally and Alex among the remains of a fish supper.

'I think we'd better go,' she said.

Alex nodded. 'Suppose so. Up the wooden hill to Bedfordshire.'

She helped him up the road to the house, his arm draped around her as he tried to walk in a straight line.

They climbed the stairs together, with difficulty, she pushing him ahead of her, and at his bedroom door they stopped. She expected to have difficulty in persuading him to go into his own room, but he smiled beatifically, said, 'Goodnight, Tally-Wally,' and almost fell through the door.

She closed it quietly behind him and murmured, 'Goodnight, Alex,' before walking to the end of the landing and letting herself into her own room.

As she lay in bed, watching the clouds pass over the moon like grey gauze, she wondered what her mum would have said if she could have seen her now.

Chapter 25

'How much?'

'Four hundred and ninety-five, sir. That's including the VAT.'

'I should think that's including the staff, isn't it?'

The man at the timber yard looked implacable. ''Fraid that's the going rate, sir.'

'But I could buy a house for that, in a remote part of Lancashire.'

'That may be true, sir. I've never been further than Chichester.'

Tom scratched his head. 'But it's only shiplap, with a bit of felt on the roof. Supposing I made it myself?'

'That's up to you, sir. Plenty of timber.' The man

gestured over his shoulder with his thumb, to the tall stacks of wood in the yard.

Tom took the bull by the horns. 'Right. You any good at quantity-surveying? I want a shed eight foot by ten with windows down one side and a door at one end. Nothing fancy, but it needs to be well lit.'

'You got half an hour, sir?'

'Yes.'

'Right, then, we'll sort you out.'

And they did. Tom came back to Wilding's Barn with timber sticking out of the back of the Land Rover and his red-and-white-spotted hanky tied to the overhang. ''Tain't strictly legal, sir, that hanky. You needs a luminous triangle, really.'

'I'll risk it,' he'd said, and arrived home without incident.

He unloaded the planking, the timber supports, the glass, two rolls of roofing felt and stacked them in the barn, then went to survey the potential building site – the square of turf in the corner of the herb garden.

The familiar 'Oooh-ooh!' greeted him from across the lane.

He turned round. 'Hello, Maisie.'

She was pushing a wheelbarrow containing an easel and a chair. 'Hello, Tom. How goes it? Everything tickety-boo?'

'Not too bad, Maisie. How's the garden coming along?'

Maisie shook her head, and the tassels on her bright pink turban executed a neat somersault. 'Not terribly well, I'm afraid. I think I underestimated the power of the manure last year. Now I can't see anything for nettles and buttercups. Perhaps there's more to it than I thought. I'll have another go next year.' Her kohl-rimmed eyes took on the expression of a bloodhound that had lost its quarry.

Maisie's summer clothing was even more bizarre than her spring outfits. The pink turban topped off a loose-fitting tie-dyed yellow blouse, a pair of baggy Indian-style trousers in turquoise, and an orange silk sash. On her feet she wore odd flip-flops, one green and one blue, with fake chrysanthemums hovering above her toes. She looked rather like a well-loved doll that had been dressed by a small child.

She spotted the timber and felt stacked against the wall of the barn. 'Something new?'

'I'm taking your advice, Maisie. Building myself a shed.'

Maisie clapped her hands. 'Oh, I'm so glad. You'll find it a real plus, I know. And perhaps . . .' she hesitated '. . . perhaps it will help to give you a fresh start.'

'That's what I thought. So, if you'll excuse me, Maisie, I'd better get cracking.'

'Yes, yes, of course. Glad it's all starting to work out.

285

My friend – the one who wrote me the letter about the magazine job – says they're all thrilled to have you. Love your stuff.'

Suddenly he felt guilty at having tried to extricate himself from the conversation, when it had been Maisie, after all, who had thrown him the lifeline.

'Oh. That's nice.' Then, with feeling, 'Thanks, Maisie, I'm really enjoying it. Gets me thinking about . . . well, other things, you know, anything from butterflies to bicycles. Helps take me out of myself – I couldn't have done it without you.'

She looked embarrassed now, like a blushing schoolgirl. 'Happy to help out.' She backed away in the direction of Woodbine Cottage. 'Must get on. I've a painting to finish. Easel to set up. Tackling the buttercups. As they're there. Shame to waste them. Speak soon. 'Bye!' And she was gone, with only the rustling of her clothing against the hawthorn hedge to give any indication of her whereabouts.

Tom went to look for his tools. A bit of sawing and hammering was just what he needed to get a whole heap of things out of his system.

At the end of the day he was surprised by what he had achieved. The floor was down, much of the superstructure was in place, and he had cut the timber to length for two of the sides.

He ran a bath, poured himself a glass of white wine and lowered his weary body into the soothing water. His mind wandered over all-too-familiar terrain: he could see Pippa, and hear her, but her voice seemed more distant, almost like the memory of an old film. He saw Janie, too, and found himself smiling. He sipped his wine, and tried to clear his mind of a jumble of thoughts, but as he lay back and let the fragrant suds rise to his ears, he felt an unusual warmth inside him. Then he wondered, as he wondered at almost every minute of the day, what his daughter was doing now. He could always ring her on her mobile and find out, but he guessed that that would not go down well. She would ring him when she was ready. He would just have to come to terms with that.

If anything, Tally's day had been even better than the previous one. The sun had shone all morning. They had left the boat on its swinging mooring in the harbour and climbed the steep path to Bolt Head, where they had sat among the scrubland and grasses and looked out to sea.

'What did you make of last night?' Alex asked.

'I liked Mark and Anna.'

'But not the other two?'

'They'll take a bit of getting used to.'

'But you don't mind going out again tonight?'

'As long as we get some evenings on our own.'

'We will. I don't want to share you all the time, you know. I just thought you might be a bit bored if it's always you and me.'

She cocked her head on one side. 'And I used to think you were so confident and cool.'

'All a front, I'm afraid. I'm as unsure as the next man.'

'But a bit of a smoothie when it comes to cars.'

'Only because my dad bought me one.'

She looked thoughtful. 'Why does he buy you an expensive sports car, which most dads wouldn't do, yet not spend much time with you, which most dads would do?'

'I told you, he finds it difficult. I suppose the car is his way of showing me he loves me.'

'Funny sort of way.'

'I guess. Anyway, can we stop talking about my relationship with my dad, and get on with our own?'

'Sorry. Just curious. I've never really known anybody else's dad except my own. I suppose they're all different.'

'I suppose.'

By noon the sun had lodged itself behind thick cloud. They walked down towards the harbour, had a snack lunch at a quayside café, then made their way back up to the cottage, where Henry was fussing that the batteries on his Gameboy were flat. Alex nodded towards the garden. He and Tally pulled a pair of ancient sun-loungers from the summerhouse in time for the sun's re-emergence, then lay by the low stone wall, looking at the view and reading books – she lost herself in Freya North, and he in John Grisham. Once, she caught him looking at her over the top of his book. 'I can see you,' she said.

'Well, you shouldn't look so gorgeous.'

For once she did not blush. 'Do you think so?'

'Mmm.' He nodded.

The sun had caught her arms and legs, but thanks to the good sense instilled by her mother she had been generous with the sun cream and had turned a gentle shade of golden brown rather than pink. He had been less cautious, and although he was quite brown already she noticed the reddening on his shoulders. 'You're beginning to burn. You should put some more cream on.'

'Do it for me?'

She smiled. 'Only on your shoulders.'

'Spoilsport.' He threw her the bottle of Ambre Solaire. She caught it, got up, poured some into her hands then rubbed it into his neck and shoulders. She was surprised at how taut he felt, and how smooth his skin was. She felt slightly guilty at enjoying the sensation, and perhaps took rather longer than necessary to make sure that all the cream was rubbed in. He leaned forward as she massaged him. 'That's nice.'

'Just don't get too used to it. There you are.' She dropped the bottle into his lap from a height of about three feet.

'Ow!'

'Sorry!'

'No, you're not.' He took off his Storm shades. 'Do you want me to do yours?'

'No, thanks, I've done it.'

'Double spoilsport.'

She felt almost sorry for him, sitting there with his tousled fair hair and perfect body, trying his best to behave. She wondered if he would be put off by her reluctance to be too intimate, wondered how long she could resist his advances, then wondered if there would be any more. She picked up her book and tried not to think about it. She did not notice, for a few moments, that it was upside down.

That night they all met up again at the Jolly Sailor. Mark and Anna were as friendly as the previous evening, Clee seemed to have got over her fit of pique, and even Raife was less surly, giving Tally a sly wink in greeting.

'Look, guys, how about a beach party,' suggested Mark. 'I've blagged the keys of the putt-putt from Dad so we can get up the river a bit then be back in time for the ferry.'

'Are you sure you'll be in a fit state to bring the boat back?' asked Alex.

'Sober as a judge. You lot can get plastered and I'll drive home.'

Anna looked at him disbelievingly.

'Well, I might have a couple but I'll be careful.'

'We're hardly dressed for it,' said Anna, pointing at the girls' clothing – she was in another little black number, Clee was in a long linen dress, and Tally had on a short white skirt and strappy top that showed off her tan.

'And what are we going to do for food?' asked Clee, with a trace of the previous night's whinging tone.

'Crisps and stuff. Nuts.'

'Yeah, nuts!' offered Raife, more than usually articulate.

'The deli is still open,' said Anna. 'We can get something there. You guys sort out the booze, we'll get the food and we'll meet you at the boat in . . .' she looked at her watch '. . . fifteen, twenty minutes. OK?'

Alex looked at Tally. 'OK?'

'Fine.'

So they went their separate ways, Tally with Clee and Anna in search of something more substantial than crisps and nuts, and Alex with the guys in search of assorted six-packs, Smirnoff Ice and orange juice.

Without the men around, Clee seemed more outgoing, if a touch preoccupied with her appearance. Her topic of the day was shampoo – finding the right kind to cope with the bleaching effects of the sun and leave her hair sleek and shiny. It was a problem to which she had given a lot of thought and considerable experiment.

'Clee, why don't you just use Vosene?' asked Anna, winking mischievously at Tally.

'What? That gloop? Catch me using that on *my* hair! It stinks like a gents' loo.'

'I didn't know you'd ever been in one.'

Anna caught Tally's eye, and they did their best to suppress their laughter.

They found the deli, and bought ready-boiled quails' eggs, smoked-salmon sandwiches, shortbread and peaches, then walked down the street to the harbour. The boys had beaten them to it and were waving from a small blue and white dory named *Miss Isle*, in the bottom of which lay several carrier-bags filled with assorted bottles and cans.

The dory tilted a little as Tally put one foot on the side to step aboard. Alex took her hand and helped her in, then did the same for Clee, who took off her strappy sandals first. This did not stop her stumbling, and Alex had to grab her arm to prevent her falling out of the other side of the boat. While he was helping her upright, Tally, too, slipped off her shoes and took Raife's outstretched arm to steady her. She felt his hand brush lightly across her bottom. At first she thought she must have imagined it, but she glanced at him and saw him smile, the shades pushed back on his head, his dark brown eyes glistening in the early-evening sun. She half smiled, unsure whether he was flirting or teasing. She walked to the front of the dory and sat down next to Alex, who took her hand and held it.

Mark started up the engine. 'OK, cast off, Raife. Up the river for a bit of fun, boys.'

They moved off slowly between assorted boats moored at bobbing white and orange buoys, then out into the centre of the river, where Mark opened up the engine. Tally looked backwards at the foaming crescent of brilliant white water spinning out behind them.

All conversation stopped under the roar of the outboard, until fifteen minutes later when Mark slowed the engine and pointed the dory towards a small apron of deserted beach perhaps a mile upriver from the harbour. 'This should do.' He turned off the engine as the boat nosed in towards the sand and shingle, and pressed a button to lift the outboard clear of the bottom. With a sliding crunch the bows of *Miss Isle* came to rest on the beach.

Hands were offered – Tally careful to take Alex's this time – and when everyone was safely on the beach the three men manhandled the dory out of reach of the tide.

'So, where are the cans?' asked Raife. 'Let's get stuck in.'

Mark handed him a Foster's, then tossed one to Alex. 'Can you sort the girls out, Raife? I want to make sure the boat doesn't go anywhere.'

'No problem.'

Raife busied himself with the drinks while Anna, Tally and Clee pulled out the contents of the two carrier-bags from the deli. Mark threw them a couple of car rugs, and they spread the food in a corner before slipping off their shoes and sitting back on the rug to admire the view across the harbour.

'Do you do this sort of thing every year?' asked Tally.

'Most years,' said Anna.

'When I'm invited,' muttered Clee.

Raife came over with a tin tray, clearly 'borrowed' from the Jolly Sailor, loaded with three Smirnoff Ices poured into plastic glasses. 'Your drinks, ladies.' He handed them out with mock servility. 'Will there be any more?'

'Quite a few more, if last night is anything to go by,' said Anna.

'It took me all morning to get rid of the hangover,' muttered Clee. 'Not so much for me tonight, I think.'

Tally smiled and took a sip of her drink. After a hot

day in the sun it tasted wonderful, and the more she sipped at it, the more relaxed she became.

They sat in a circle, swapping holiday stories, eating and drinking. Alex cracked open quails' eggs for Tally and dipped them into celery salt before feeding them to her, taking a bite himself every now and then. He put his arm around her, and once or twice his hand lightly brushed against her breast. She felt a strange sensation of being all-powerful.

As dusk fell, the conversation became more riotous, and Tally was aware that she was talking rather a lot. But they were all laughing, so it must be all right. She was developing a taste for Smirnoff Ice. When Mark suggested they play hide and seek she volunteered to hide before anyone else had a chance. She had never imagined she could enjoy herself so much.

She slipped off her shoes while they closed their eyes and counted, then sneaked away from the beach up through gorse bushes and long grass, between waving willowherb and faded foxgloves, finally pulling herself behind a gnarled hawthorn and leaning into the trunk. She felt dizzy, but pleased with her hiding place. In the fading light she was convinced that she would be invisible. She had forgotten that she was wearing white.

'A hundred! Coming, ready or not.' Laughter followed, then the sound of rustling foliage and snapping twigs, one to the left, and two more to the right, way down below her. She breathed deeply, pulling the fragrant sea air into her lungs. It was a rich mixture and her head spun. She clung to the hawthorn trunk for support. Her head cleared a little and she scanned the path below her for moving figures. Nothing. They must have missed her. She leaned back against the trunk of the tree. 'Found you!' She nearly leaped out of her skin. The whispered voice was right beside her ear, and she turned to see Raife, one arm round the trunk of the tree, beaming at her.

Her heart was thumping in her chest, and she laughed nervously. 'You made me jump.'

'Sorry.'

'That's OK. Now we'd better go and find the others.'

'What about my reward?'

'What do you mean?'

'For finding you?' His eyes were glazed, his smile lopsided.

'What sort of reward?'

'A kiss for finding a princess.'

She had no time to say anything, or even to move. He had her backed up against the hawthorn tree. She felt him press against her, and as she drew breath to cry out, his lips were on hers and his tongue forced its way into her mouth. She brought up her arms to push him off, but he was stronger and pinned them to her sides by putting one arm around her. She felt his other hand on her waist, kneading her skin, his tongue still in her mouth. She thought she would choke, and then he moved his hand up inside her top until it reached her left breast. He cupped it and squeezed it as she fought for breath. She began to feel a hardness at the front of his body, had difficulty breathing. She felt powerless to move and found, suddenly, that she was crying, in halting, breathless sobs.

Suddenly he jumped back from her, and she saw Alex with his hand on Raife's collar, then on top of Raife on the ground hitting him. She could do nothing but sob, and cling to the hawthorn tree.

'Hey, man! Hey!' Raife cried, between punches. 'It was just a bit of fun.' And then the final punch landed on his jaw, cut his lip, and the fun ended.

The boat journey back was undertaken in silence, Raife looking outboard and holding his jaw, Mark driving with an ashen face and a grim expression, Clee sitting with her head in her hands. Tally shivered and did her best to stifle the sobs as Alex cradled her in his arms. No one said anything as she and Alex stepped from the boat and on to the pontoon in the harbour, but she saw the look of distress on Anna's face as she turned to leave, and felt sorry that their brief friendship had ended so abruptly and in such stupid circumstances.

When they arrived the house was dark and quiet. Tally wrapped her arms around her body, as though she were trying to preserve it as well as keep herself warm. Alex opened the front door, led her up the stairs, along the landing and into her room, where she sat on the edge of the bed, shaking.

'I'm so sorry, so bloody sorry,' he said. Tally began to cry. 'I really don't think he meant to harm you, just got a bit carried away.'

She nodded between sobs.

'God! I could kill him. Just tell me what I can do, what I can say to make it all right.'

Tally sniffed back the tears. 'Not your fault.'

'Yes, it is. I should have bloody well noticed what he was doing.'

'But you couldn't see.'

'Not when you went to hide, no. But I should have seen what he was doing to your drinks. I should have realized when you started getting tipsy. I just thought you were enjoying yourself.'

'What do you mean?'

'He was lacing your glass with more vodka. I found it when we were clearing up.'

She fell back on the bed. 'Oh, God! I'm so stupid. Why am I so stupid?'

He put his arm underneath her and scooped her up. 'You're not stupid. You're the cleverest girl I know. You just happened to fall for the oldest trick in the book. I'm the stupid one for not grasping what was going on.'

'But I'm seventeen. I've been allowed away on holiday on my own because I persuaded my dad that I could be trusted and look what happens – I get groped by some guy in the bushes, and if you hadn't been there, God knows what would have happened.'

'No, it wouldn't. Raife's a stupid sod but he's not . . . Well, anyway, it didn't.'

She was disconsolate now, and a mixture of tears and saliva was taking its toll on her face.

'Here.' He tore a bunch of tissues from a box on the bedside table and handed them to her.

'Thanks.' She blew her nose and wiped her eyes. 'I must look a sight.'

'You do a bit. But you're still gorgeous.'

They sat quietly for a few minutes until she had stopped shaking, then he put his arm around her. 'I suppose you'll want to go home now.'

She looked up at him. 'I'm not sure. I really want to ring my dad, but I don't want to give in. Don't want to be a failure.'

'You don't have to ring your dad. You could let me look after you.'

'Like tonight?'

'I know. Not a very good advert for my services. What about if I promise to try harder?'

'Not sure.'

He squeezed her hand. 'I promise I'll try. You'd better get some sleep, and so had I. I'll see you in the morning and we can decide what to do. You sure you're OK?'

She nodded amid the fistful of tissues.

He kissed her forehead lightly and got up. He walked towards the door, then turned to face her. 'You won't say anything to Mum and Dad about what happened, will you? Only I'd rather we sorted this out ourselves if that's OK?'

She nodded again, and he left the room, closing the door quietly behind him.

It was too late for a shower. She might wake the rest of the household. Instead, she took off her clothes and washed herself from head to toe with the flannel at the washbasin, cleaned her teeth, put on a clean T-shirt and slipped between the sheets.

What would her dad say if he could see her now? Suddenly she wished she were at home, with him sitting at the bottom of her bed, then ruffling her hair in that infuriating way he had when she'd just brushed it, and telling her everything would be all right. She fell asleep, eventually, a thousand drums beating in her head.

Chapter 26

Someone had cleanly sliced off the top of her head. That was the only thing that could account for the pain. She put up her hand and ran it gently over her skull. Then she lifted her head from the pillow, tilted her face forward, rested it in her hands and said, very softly, but with great feeling, 'Owwwww!'

It took her a few moments to discover that if she moved very slowly she could just about retain her equilibrium, so she slid off the bed and crept to the other side of the room, where she steadied herself on the towel rail next to the washbasin, trying not to breathe too fast and send the blood pulsating through the veins in her head in a rhythm like something from *The Very Best of Meat Loaf*.

It was half an hour before she emerged in baggy shorts and T-shirt from the French windows into the garden, squinting, even though her eyes were protected by the peak of a baseball cap and sunglasses. It did not take her long to discover that the garden was empty of people so she made her way to the kitchen in search of something to stop the pounding in her head.

'Hello? You're late up.'

She pulled the sunglasses down to the end of her nose, peered above them, and found herself face to face with Alex's father.

'Oh dear! Hard night?' he asked.

She nodded, then regretted it as the percussion section of the orchestra played overtime. She winced and closed one eye.

David Blane-Pfitzer smiled understandingly. 'And you only seventeen!'

Tally felt guilty. He had invited his son's girlfriend into this house and she was clearly an alcoholic.

'I didn't – I mean – I wasn't . . .'

'There's no need to explain.' He tilted his head on one side and looked at her. 'Does it hurt?'

She nodded, and the drums started again.

'Right. Sit over there, under the tree, in the shade, and I'll make you something that will sort you out.'

'I really don't think . . .'

'No arguments. Just walk slowly, no sudden movements, and lie back on that lounger.'

She did as she was told. The pounding seemed to ease
when she sat still.

Within a few minutes Alex's dad was back with a
glass in his hand, which he held out to her. 'Here you
are. It looks revolting, it tastes even worse, but it always
does the trick.'

Tally opened one eye, looked at the yellow and
brown mixture in the glass and then up at her host
pleadingly.

'Drink!' he instructed. 'All down in one. If you pause
you'll be sick.'

Her eyes widened, but she took the glass and drained
it, grimacing as she handed it back, then clamped her
lips together to keep whatever it was down. She had
tasted raw eggs and Worcester sauce, but the other
ingredients of the vile brew remained a mystery.

Alex's dad sat on the lounger next to hers, and leaned
forward so that his arms rested on his knees. 'We
haven't seen much of each other since you arrived. Are
you having a good time – or shouldn't I ask?'

'Yes, thank you. Very nice.' It hurt less when she
didn't nod.

'I've been out looking at boats.'

'Alex said.'

'I thought it was time he had the little one to himself.

I rather like it but he gets fed up with me shouting at him when we sail. Funny, really. I'm not a shouter – except on the water.' He grinned. 'Oh, yes, I asked Alex to help his mum with the shopping. He was reluctant to go but I told him I'd keep an eye on you. He should be back any time now. He seemed very concerned that you were all right, not keen to leave you at all.'

She had not imagined him to be like this. From Alex's explanation she had expected a dour, humourless man, grumpy, with little time for his son. He was tall and dark with a tanned, creased face, attractive rather than handsome, and wearing a polo shirt with shorts and deck shoes of a similar vintage to his son's. She wanted to ask him how he got on with Alex, why he had bought him the car, and why, when they were together, the atmosphere seemed so tense. But now was not the moment.

'Is this your first time away on your own?' He spoke slightly louder than was necessary.

'Yes.'

'And are you OK? It must be a tricky time.'

'Yes, thanks.'

'Well, it's only a couple of days till your dad comes down. Will you go back with him or stay on?'

She was surprised at his question. 'I don't know. I'm not sure. I mean, I'm having a lovely time . . . It's just that . . .'

'Too much too soon?'

'Yes. In a way.'

'And missing your dad, I expect?'

'Yes.'

'More than you thought?'

'Yes.' She looked at him quizzically.

He spoke more quietly now. 'I think daughters do.'

'Not sons?'

'Oh, in a different sort of way.'

'How different?'

He shrugged. 'Sons aren't really allowed to miss their fathers. They have to get on. Conditioned to do their own thing.'

'That sounds a bit hard.'

'Oh, it is.' He looked wistful, then brightened. 'I never knew my father. Died when I was a few months old.' He became more reflective. 'It's funny being a dad – especially with a son. You're never quite sure how much they need you, and they never let on. It's handed down from generation to generation, that fierce independence.'

It was as if he was talking to himself. Tally listened attentively. She had not expected such a conversation and felt slightly uncomfortable, but at the same time flattered that he should confide in her, as he never had in Alex.

'Different with daughters, I expect, not that I've any

experience of it. I suppose you can be more obviously protective of a daughter – rather like with a wife.'

'But daughters have to stand on their own two feet as well.'

'Yes, but you can be forgiven for trying to stop them. And you can allow them longer to grow up. It's seen as being a good father. More difficult with a lad, somehow. You're always conscious of letting them be their own person. Of trying to give them all the advantages you never had and at the same time making sure you don't smother them. Tricky, really, getting the balance right. I'm not sure that Alex and I have cracked it. I try to stay out of his way as much as I can, let him get on. But I do enjoy his company.'

He slapped his knees and stood up. 'Listen to me going on. And you with a hangover. Now just you stay there until that brew takes effect. As soon as you feel the slightest bit hungry, go inside and have two slices of dry toast. You'll be right as rain then. OK? I have to nip up to the City, I'm afraid. Back in a day or two. See you then . . . I hope.'

And he was gone, leaving Tally to look out over a silvery harbour and a few days of uncertainty.

Within half an hour of his father's departure Alex had returned with his mother and Henry. He came straight out into the garden. 'You OK?' he asked.

'Just about. Your dad sorted me out.'

The colour drained from his face. 'Did you tell him about last night?'

'I'm afraid it was pretty obvious from the state I was in.'

'I mean . . . about . . . you know?'

Tally shook her head. It was the first time she had been able to do so without it hurting.

Alex sat down beside her as his mother and brother set about transferring the bagfuls of shopping to the kitchen cupboards and the fridge. Henry had come home with a new piece of software for his Gameboy.

'So how are you feeling. I mean, about staying on.'

'Not sure.'

'You might go back on Saturday?'

'Don't know yet . . . Only . . .'

'Yes?'

'Can we have some time together now? Just you and me?'

''Course. I could do with a de-coke anyhow.'

'Me, too. Though I think after what your dad gave me I've probably had a ten-thousand-mile service.'

'Oh, no, not one of his "morning after" jobs?'

''Fraid so.'

'And you kept it down?'

'So far.'

'That's more than I can do.' Tally got up and walked

to the low wall surrounding the garden. A warm breeze rustled through the montbretia. Alex came and stood by her.

'Your dad talked to me today.'

'Mmm?'

'About sons and daughters.'

'But he hasn't got a daughter.'

'I know. I think he probably wishes he had.'

As the second roof panel slid on to the shed, Tom felt pleased with himself. He screwed it into place, then set about fitting the felt. Little pieces of grit worked their way under his clothing, his hands felt rough, and the sun on the felt generated a nose-tingling aroma of tar. Soon his shed would be weatherproof. Soon it would have a door and windows, but there was enough of it now, after two days of working from dawn till dusk, to show that it would serve its purpose nicely.

He felt something brush past his legs. He looked down to see Wendy. Her whiskers twitched at the tarry tang, and she took a tentative step up on to the floor and padded slowly forward, as if admiring his work. Tom stood, hands on hips, watching the cat explore. 'What do you think, then?'

Wendy looked back at him, then turned away and climbed into the cardboard box filled with timber offcuts in one corner of the shed.

'That's not very comfortable, is it? Come here.' He picked up the old sweater he had been wearing until he had got too hot, and slid it underneath her. She kneaded it with her claws, then sank into it, closing her eyes and purring loudly.

'Well, I guess that's you sorted. Room for two, I suppose. With any luck we'll have the door and windows on tomorrow and you'll feel properly at home.'

He looked at his watch. A quarter to seven. Time for a bath. He half looked forward to it, for the soothing effects of the water, and half dreaded it, for the thinking time it provided. It had become a daily ritual, a sort of cleansing operation, not only of body but of mind. He would lie back in the water and think of Pippa. Go over things. Remember things said, and her last words to him, 'I'm so glad I met you.' And then would come the emptiness – the aching blackness – and the realization that she had slipped away from him. 'Slipped' – such a sly, surreptitious word. She had not slipped, she had gone. But he could keep her close in his soul, couldn't he? She was still with him deep inside. Yet something seemed to be getting in the way, an invisible barrier that numbed his senses and prevented him feeling the rawness of their previous intimacy.

He found himself talking out loud.

'What's happening to me? Why can't I *feel* you? I mean, I *can* feel you, but not like I could. I can remember what it was like – exactly – walking across the yard, hearing the music playing through the open door, going into the kitchen, seeing you standing there, turning round, smiling at me. I can still smell you, touch you. I can remember putting my arms around you and kissing you. Making love to you. I can remember exactly how it felt but . . . I can't feel it. *Properly*. I don't want to let it go, don't want it to slip away. I still want you so much . . .'

Chapter 27

That evening after supper Tally rang her dad.

'How is it? What have you done? Are you OK? Is he behaving?'

Tally laughed. 'Which do you want me to answer first?'

'All of them!'

'It's fine. We've boated, and eaten out. They're very nice – except for Henry who hasn't spoken two words to me since we arrived – and Alex has been the perfect gentleman.' Her mind returned to the evening on the beach and she did her best to change the subject. 'But how are you? What are you doing?'

'Oh, I've been very busy.' She noticed that his voice

had a forced jollity about it. 'I've finished *Making Waves*.'

'Oh, wow! Well done! Are you pleased?'

'Oh, I think so. But I've put it away. I'm starting on another.'

'That's great.'

'And I've decided that I need somewhere else to write, so I've been building a shed.'

'A what?'

'A writing shed. On that patch of grass next to the herb garden. Give myself a fresh start – fresh surroundings.'

'Is it working?'

'I don't know, I haven't moved in yet. Almost finished it, though.'

'Wow!'

'Yes, wow!'

'And how's Wendy? Is she behaving?'

'I have to admit grudgingly that she is. She moved into the shed before I'd even got the door on. She spends most of the day sleeping in a cardboard box on top of my old sweater.'

'How funny.'

'Not for me. I like that sweater.'

'No, I mean can't you see what you've built?'

'A shed. That's what I've built.'

'No, you haven't. You've built a Wendy house.'

Tom laughed. 'Trust you.'

'I'll have to call you Peter Pan.'

'I'll settle for Dad.'

There was a pause. 'I miss you.'

'I miss you, too, sweetheart.'

'When are you coming down?'

'I'm leaving here first thing on Saturday morning, and I should be with you around lunchtime. Do you think that will suit the Blane-Whatsits?'

'Yes, I'm sure. It's all very relaxed here.' She looked back at the house from her perch on the garden wall, just to check that she was not being overheard. 'I've hardly seen Alex's mum – she seems to visit friends the whole time, with Henry, which is a plus – but I spoke with his dad today.'

'Nice?'

'Very nice, strangely enough.'

'Why strangely enough?'

'Oh, nothing. I'll tell you later. How's Maisie?'

Tom explained about the garden of gigantic nettles and buttercups and Tally laughed at his description of Maisie's outlandish costume.

'And any news of the restaurant?'

'Well, a bit.'

'Go on.'

'Peter's left Rachel.'

'Shit!'

'Tally!'

'Sorry. I mean, wow!'

'That's better.' He gave her a rough account of the last few days.

'Well, where's he living? What's he going to do? Is there anybody else, do you think?'

'Now who's asking a lot of questions? The answers in order are: above the shop, I don't know, and I don't think so.'

'Have you spoken to Janie?'

'Not recently. She's gone away for a while. Working. Not sure where she is.'

'But you can ring her on her mobile.'

'Oh, I've been a bit busy and I don't like to bother her.'

Tally was puzzled. There was something odd in his tone, but she could not put her finger on it. Granted, her father was not the world's greatest gossip, but she'd have thought he would confide in Janie. Maybe he was just a bit busy, with his shed and everything. She let it go. 'Well, anyway, I'm looking forward to seeing you.'

'And I you, my love. It's been lovely to hear your voice.'

'I'll see you Saturday, then.'

'You will, God willing.'

'Don't say that.'

'Sorry. I'll see you Saturday. I can't wait.'

'Love you.'

'Love you, too, Tal. And tell that Alex Blane-Whatsit to take care of you or I'll have his guts for garters.'

'Glad you care.'

'See you soon.'

''Bye.'

She pressed the red button on her mobile and put it into the pocket of her shorts, then drew her knees up under her chin and looked out over the water. She hadn't told her father that her intention was to go home with him on Saturday. Maybe she was just keeping her options open. Large grey clouds were rolling in from the south-west. It would be raining before bedtime.

Tom was staring at Janie. She was leaning on the farm gate, smiling at him, her shiny dark hair brushing her brown shoulders. He stretched out to touch her and awoke, breathless and covered in perspiration. He leaned over the side of the bed, gasping for air, and looked at the clock on the bedside table. Three a.m. He flopped back on to the pillow. The dream had been so real. He felt annoyed with himself for his reluctance to admit that he had feelings for her. But he felt guilty, too, that he had been so cold and undemonstrative when she had said that she loved him.

What a God-awful mess. He was mourning the

woman he had loved for seventeen years, missing her and trying to get over her, yet turning away another woman for whom he felt a growing love. But how could he ever love her as much or as well as Pippa? Not yet, surely. Not fourteen months after Pippa's death. It was too soon. It couldn't be love. Maybe it was just need.

He remembered his mother talking about men and their needs. 'Men are hopeless without women. They can't cope. Useless on their own. Like children. They need to be looked after and loved.' Wasn't that what Janie had said, too?

Yes. But not yet. He would pour himself into work. He would try to forget it all. He could not keep going round in emotional circles, he had to strike out in a different direction. Get stuck into the new novel. Put some kind of space between himself and the past.

He got up, dressed and went down to the shed. Maisie's ability to sleep long and deep came in handy that night. She did not hear the sounds of hammering that rang out from behind Wilding's Barn, and by morning the writing shed was finished.

By Friday evening the grey weather had settled over Salcombe like a shroud. Earlier in the week the family had been sweltering in shorts and T-shirts, but now they were in long trousers and fleeces. The forecast in the long term was not too gloomy, but it would be a day or two before another halo of high pressure hovered above them.

Heavy showers sent them scuttling for cover in the house, where Tally and Alex pulled out the Scrabble board, or Monopoly, and argued over who should have Mayfair and who Park Lane. Even Henry put down his Gameboy for half an hour at the prospect of a good argument. But it was good-natured, and they ended up rolling on the floor trying to wrest the dark blue cards from each other.

At around eight thirty a gap appeared between the clouds, and a blackbird began its twilight chorus. Alex looked up. Henry was now glued to the television, his mother was preparing food in the kitchen and his father had still not returned from London. He got up, walked to the French windows that looked out across the garden and called to Tally, 'Look at the sun on the water.'

She came and stood beside him. 'Wow!'

He turned to her. 'I love your wows!'

'Sorry. My dad always says it's a sign of a poor vocabulary.'

'Mine, too. But your wows are more expressive than most.' He opened the windows. 'Fancy a walk?'

Tally looked up at the approaching clouds. 'We might have to make it a quick one.'

'Come on, then.'

He took her hand and walked with her to the far corner of the garden. They sat side by side on the low wall and looked out across the water, streaked with fiery copper in the dying evening light. 'Doesn't it look wonderful? Like it's on fire,' she said. Then she shivered, and Alex put his arms round her. The clouds moved over the sun, and the fiery water turned an inky black. Tally looked up as the first spots of rain began to fall. 'Oh dear.' It began to rain harder.

'Quick, in here. We'll run up to the house when it slackens off.' He pulled her inside the summerhouse and closed the door.

She looked at him and her face creased into a grin. 'This was just a ploy to get me in here, wasn't it?'

He looked at her innocently. 'Do you think I'd do something like that?'

'I hope so.' She put her arms around him, tilted her head upwards and kissed his lips. He responded, running his fingers through her fine fair hair.

She eased away from him for a moment, then laid her head on his chest.

'Are you really going home tomorrow?' he asked.

She nodded.

'Why?'

'Because it's so lovely.'

'But if it's so lovely, why not stay?'

She looked up at him. 'Because I'm frightened it might be too much, too soon.'

He looked hurt. 'But if it's so good, how can you go away?'

'Because that way it stays good and it can't go wrong.'

'You mean you don't want to see me any more?'

'No, silly, I want to see you lots. I just want to make sure it lasts. You're my first proper boyfriend and I want it to go on and on. I don't want you to be bored with me.'

'Or you with me?'

'That's not my worry.'

He looked serious. 'Am I really your first?'

'The first real one. There was another for a while.'

'Blip?'

She looked up. 'How did you know?'

'Girls talk.'

'Yes, I know.' She sighed.

'What was he like?'

'He's very nice.'

'But?'

'Sometimes being nice isn't enough.'

'No. Can I tell you something?'

'Depends what it is.'

'I've never felt like this before.'

Tally slid her hand up to his lips and sealed them with a finger. 'Ssh! Please.'

He stepped away from her, sat down on one of the fraying chairs and rested his chin in his hands. 'Sorry.'

Tally leaned against the glass doors of the summer-house and watched the rain fall on to the parched grass. 'Neither have I.'

She turned to look at him, then, without speaking, walked towards him and offered him her hands. He took them and stood up. She moved towards him and looked up into his face, then gently moved his hands upwards and laid them on her breasts.

He bent down to kiss her, and she felt his tongue exploring her mouth, gently, sensuously, so different from Raife's clumsy attempts. She whimpered slightly as his hands stroked her breasts, her skin tingled and she felt the strength of his body pressed against hers. Slowly he lowered one hand to her bottom, and caressed it through the smooth fabric of her jeans.

They were both breathing heavily now. He moved away from her slightly, saw the expectant look in her eyes and heard her breath coming in short gasps. He pulled the fleece and T-shirt over her head in one, let them fall to the floor then held her to him, running his hand down her smooth back and feeling her breath on his neck.

Her hands began to unbutton his thick shirt, until she could press herself against his naked chest. The heat of his flesh took her breath away, and he began to kiss her more passionately, on her neck, and her firm, rounded breasts, his hands running over her back then down to her bottom and, finally, between her legs. She gasped and let out a cry. 'Sorry,' he murmured.

She shook her head gently and kissed him lightly on the shoulder.

'You don't . . .?' he asked.

She smiled and shook her head. 'Not yet.'

They held each other close until their breathing became slow and even, and the chill of the evening air made Tally shiver. Then he helped her back into her clothing.

'Do you mind?' she whispered.

Now it was Alex's turn to shake his head.

'But boys are supposed to be impatient.'

'I *am* impatient.'

'You might have to wait a while.'

'Don't care.'

'It might not be worth waiting for.'

'I'll take the risk.'

'It might all go horribly wrong and we might never do it.'

'I'll still take the risk.'

Tally looked searchingly into his eyes.

'What is it?' he asked.

'I don't know whether to say it.'

'What?' He looked down at her, half hoping, half scared.

'You see, the only other man I've ever said it to was my dad.'

He saw the tears spring into her eyes, and carefully tilted her face towards him. Several moments passed before he whispered slowly, and very softly, 'I do love you.'

She lowered her eyes and nodded, then whispered, 'And you.'

Chapter 28

Tally got through to Tom on his mobile while he was *en route* to Salcombe.

'Dad?'

'Tal? Yes?'

'Promise you won't be cross with me?'

'Why? What have you done?'

'Nothing. Only . . . do you think you could take me home with you?'

'Why? What's wrong? What's the matter?'

'Absolutely nothing. It's been fine. It *is* fine. Only . . . I think I'd rather quit while I'm ahead. And, anyway, I miss you.'

She heard the sigh. 'What are you like? OK, my little

love, I'll bring you back – provided I can have a cup of tea when I get there.'

'Only, Dad . . .?'

'Yes?'

'Can you not say anything about it being a sudden decision? Make out that you knew I wanted picking up and taking home today?'

'If you want. But why didn't you tell me before?'

'Oh, I just didn't want to worry you. You'd have come down straight away because you'd have thought I was unhappy and I'm not.'

'OK, sweetheart. Look, I'll have to go now. The traffic's getting a bit clogged. You know what Exeter's like. I'll see you soon, all right?'

'Thanks, Dad. You're a wonder.'

'Aren't I just? Lots of love. 'Bye.'

Tally sat on top of her suitcase and tried to force down the lid. It would need greater pressure than her slender frame could provide. She checked the wardrobe, then the chest of drawers to make sure that she had cleared them of all her clothes. In the back left-hand corner of the top drawer she found a triangle of black silk. She looked at it for a moment, then pushed it among the other clothes in the case, and went in search of Alex for a bit of muscle power.

David Blane-Pfitzer had returned late the night before, when the rest of the household was in bed. Now he was down in the kitchen with his family – Helen washing up at the sink, Henry complaining of a lack of milk for his cereal, and Alex staring vacantly out of the window. 'You ready for the off?' asked David, as Tally came in.

'Almost. Just need a strong arm on my case.'

'That'll be you, then, Alex.'

Alex looked up. His father smiled at him and nodded at Tally. 'Yes. Yes, of course. Sorry, miles away.'

He tramped up the stairs after her and along the landing to her room. It took only a few seconds to fasten down the lid.

'You look a bit sad,' said Tally.

'Aren't you?'

'Yes.'

'Sure you won't stay?'

She nodded. 'Can I ask you something?'

He looked up.

'This is really none of my business, and I shouldn't be interfering. You'll probably think I'm stupid . . .'

'What is it?'

'Your dad.'

'What about him?'

'Would you ask him to go sailing with you? In the little boat?'

'What on earth for?'

'Oh . . . I just think he might like to.'

He shook his head and smiled. 'I shall miss you . . . Tal.'

'And you. More than you know.' She leaned over and gently kissed him. He smelt of . . . Alex.

Within the hour, her father had arrived, drunk the promised cup of tea and thanked the Blane-Pfitzers for looking after his daughter. He was sorry she had to leave after just a week, but there were things that had to be attended to at home. He hoped they wouldn't mind. Tally looked anxious, Alex and his father smiled under-standingly. Mrs Blane-Pfitzer confiscated the Gameboy from Henry and told him to go and play quietly in the garden instead of making a nuisance of himself.

While the families exchanged pleasantries and promises of doing this again some time – 'She's been no trouble, we've hardly seen her' – Tally said goodbye to Alex at the bottom of the garden, by the summerhouse.

They kissed tenderly. 'It's a bit like a dream, really. I didn't know it could be like this. Thought you only read about it in books. Do you think I'm soft?'

'No.' She felt a rising sense of panic now that it was time to go. 'You do understand why I'm going, don't you?'

'I think so.'

'You will ring me?' She squeezed his hand and looked at him searchingly. 'Promise you'll ring me.'

'Yes. Every day.'

'Well, text me at least.'

'At least.'

She let go of his hand, feeling her reluctance to be parted from him more keenly than ever, and began to walk up the garden, then stopped, turned to face him once more and fixed his eyes with hers. '*Arrivederci, amore mio.*'

He smiled at her, sighed and said, very slowly, '*Guardati a dietro.*'

Her heart missed a beat. 'How did you know . . .?'

Alex shrugged. 'Granny lives in Florence.'

The journey home was uncharacteristically quiet. Tom was keen to find out all about her week away, but he soon realized that now was not the time to ask. He caught glimpses of Tally from time to time, looking out of the window, a million miles away. Just once she slipped her hand into his and squeezed it, then carefully withdrew it and laid it in her lap.

It wasn't until they were home and she was unpacking that he felt able to enquire how the week had gone.

'It was lovely.'

'But you came home?'

'Yes.'

'I see.'

Tally realized that some sort of explanation was only fair. She flopped on the edge of the bed and looked up at him. 'It was so good I didn't want to spoil it. We got on really well. I didn't want to risk it all going wrong.'

'Simple as that?'

'Simple as that.'

'And I needn't worry.'

'No. He's lovely and . . . I'm very fond of him.'

'Good. And the rest of the family . . . were they OK?'

'Yes. Surprisingly. I hardly saw anything of his mum or Henry, but I had a chat with his dad.'

'You said.' Tom was leaning in the doorway, trying to appear casual.

'Da-a-ad?'

The three-note dad: the precursor to a tricky question.

'Mmm?'

'Do you think there's a difference between being a father to a girl and being a father to a boy?'

'Yes. Tons. Why?'

'What sort of difference?'

'Where do you want to start?'

Tally leaned back on her pillow. 'Anywhere.'

'How long have you got?'

'As long as it takes.'

'Well, I suppose it's all to do with the future, really. And rivalry.'

328

'Rivalry?'

'Yes. I think with fathers and sons there's always that undercurrent of . . . succession, I suppose you might call it. The leader of the tribe knows that one day he'll be knocked off his perch by a young upstart.'

Tally propped herself up on her elbows. 'But that's primitive. I've seen it on nature programmes on TV – lions and tigers – but not still with fathers and sons, surely?'

'Oh, I think it's there, buried deep down – instinctive rather than conscious. Then you have all that stuff about a son carrying on the family name, achieving his father's unfulfilled ambitions, the father not wanting to lose face in front of his son, the son not wanting to let his father down. It's a heck of a lot of baggage when you think about it.'

'Do you think some fathers are better with daughters than sons?'

'Most, I should think. Most men relate better to women than to other men. Why should it be different within a family?'

'Because some men are better with women than others.'

'You think so?'

'I know so. Just before I went on holiday, you asked me about my time of the month.'

'Well? I thought it was important.'

'Some fathers couldn't have done that – not like you did, so matter-of-fact. They'd be embarrassed even to admit it existed.'

'Probably, but maybe it's not that straightforward. I guess it's all a matter of aptitude. There are different problems in being a father to a daughter.'

'What sort of problems?'

'I think by now, my little love, you probably know every last one of them.'

He turned to leave. 'Oh, by the way. Did you wear that little triangular thing? The one made of black silky stuff.'

'No.'

'Oh. Good.'

And then, under her breath as he walked away down the landing, 'I didn't need to.'

Chapter 29

Alex was true to his word. He called her every day and texted her morning and evening. She felt wanted, cared for, loved in a way she had not experienced before, yet there was an awareness about her of the fragility of any relationship. She helped her father move some of his study furniture down into the shed, which she liked: it looked out over the herb garden and smelt of fresh timber. Wendy liked it, too, and made it clear that she had taken up residence there.

Tom tapped away daily at his laptop, and Tally read, dared to dream, and even started to pull a few weeds from among the mint and the parsley, conscious of its importance to her father. She realized, now, why he had cared for it so assiduously. It was another way of showing that he cared for her mum.

She still watched him carefully, but tried to ease away a little, to find her own feet, ever conscious that he should not think she was shutting him out. He seemed happier now that he was writing somewhere other than in his study, happier that he had started a second novel. But there was still an air of preoccupation about him.

She thought how best to cheer him up. She considered it a lot. What he really needed was company – new company. Tally sometimes let herself think about the prospect of him finding someone else. It was not easy. She had read how some children fall out with a widowed parent when another partner appears on the scene. She determined to ready herself for events that would be likely to happen one day, but not just yet.

It was during a trip to Axbury, when she picked up her holiday snaps, that she thought about Janie and remembered her father's rather pathetic excuse for not being able to get hold of her.

She sat on a bench in the shadow of the Minster and rang Janie on her mobile.

'Giorgioni,' came the reply.

'Janie? It's Tally.'

'Sweetheart, how on earth are you?'

Tally explained about the holiday, with Janie anxious for details about 'that man'. 'I was wondering if you would come for supper. We haven't seen you for ages and I think Dad could do with cheering up.'

'Have you asked him?'

Tally wanted nothing more than to make Janie welcome. 'Of course.'

'And he doesn't mind?'

'Of course he doesn't.'

If Tally had said, 'Why should he mind?' Janie might have suspected that she had not asked him. As it was, she assumed that Tom had been consulted and had agreed.

'Well, only if you're sure your dad's happy with that.'

'Perfectly. I know he's dying to see you.'

A date was fixed for two nights hence and Tally rang off, feeling pleased with herself. Then she met Emma for a teacake and Coke. It was not the happy reunion she had expected.

Emma sat across the table, looking haunted.

'What on earth's the matter?'

Emma bit her lip.

Tally recognized the problem. 'Did you . . .?'

Emma cast her eyes down.

'Oh, God!' Then, after a pause, 'Not very good?'

'Awful.'

Tally put her hand across the table and laid it on top of Emma's. Their Cokes and teacakes came. Tally began to eat, but Emma was gazing out of the window into the distance.

'Want to talk about it?'

'Not really. Just wish I could go back and start again.'

Tally sat quietly and listened.

'I was pretty sure I didn't want to, but we had a few drinks. It didn't seem so important then. Just like fun, really.'

'Did he . . . you know . . . was he wearing . . .'

'Oh, yes. That made it worse in a way. I mean, I wouldn't have, without it, but it just made it so . . . basic, really. I felt as though it ought to be special, tender. But it was all so . . . quick. It was over before I knew it, and there he was, sort of panting. I felt used. As though I wasn't really a part of it.' She sat with her hands in her lap.

'Oh, Em!'

'I know. Stupid me. Can't go back now. Lost it and will never find it again.' Her eyes filled with tears.

'Hey, come on. It's not the end of the world.'

'Pretty much.' Emma blew her nose and changed the subject. 'How did you get on?'

Tally looked apologetic. 'Fine. It was lovely.'

'And he didn't try it on?'

'A bit.'

'But you . . .?'

'No. I was tempted, though.'

'You've got more sense.'

'Not really. Just more scared.'

'Well, you keep being scared. It's a good defence mechanism.' Emma slurped at her Coke, and attempted to cut up her teacake. 'When will you see him again?'

'I don't know. We haven't decided yet. He's still down in Devon.'

'Why didn't you stay?'

'Because I didn't want to spoil it. I wanted it to be special.'

Emma looked disbelieving. 'But if it was so good, how could you bear it to end?'

'I don't know, really. I just know it was right to come away. I want to love him . . . I do love him . . . but I've got exams and he's going to uni in Edinburgh, and then when will we see each other?'

'So Little Miss Sensible walked away?'

'No. I'm just terrified of getting hurt, if you want the truth. I've had enough hurt to last me for a long time.'

'Me, too.'

'You've done what?'

'Asked her to supper. We haven't seen her for ages and I thought you needed taking out of yourself.'

Her father looked irritated. 'You should have asked me.'

Tally looked surprised, and a little hurt. 'I thought you'd be pleased.'

Tom was aware that he would seem to be making a

mountain out of a molehill, but he needed to find an excuse not to meet Janie. 'What about food and stuff?'

'Dad, that's pathetic. I can do the shopping if you're busy writing. Don't you want to see Janie?'

'Yes, yes, of course I do . . . It's just that . . .' He knew he had his back to the wall. There was nothing he could do without drawing attention to the situation and making Tally suspicious.

'Look, Dad, I think you need a bit of female company.'

Her candour surprised him. 'I've got female company. You.'

'That's different.'

'In any case, why Janie?'

'You get on so well together. And she makes you laugh.'

He wondered if somehow she knew. Perhaps she was paving the way for . . . what? No. He tried to put the thought out of his head. And yet she seemed insistent that Janie should come. Maybe she was trying to make it easier for him. Dear old Tal, doing her best to sort her dad out. But he still felt uncomfortable, and wondered how Janie would feel.

'Did she seem happy to come?'

'Of course.'

'Right. Will you do the shopping?'

'I'll do the cooking, if you like. My treat.'

This was all a bit unnerving, but he said, 'Great, I'll leave it to you, then.'

That evening Tom was still recovering from the Janie revelation when the phone rang. It was Kate Lundy: 'Just to say that my solicitor is ready to exchange contracts and he'll be talking to your solicitor in the morning, if that's OK?'

'Fine.'

'Look, are you in for half an hour?'

'Yes.'

'Would you mind if I came round? It's just that there's something I want to talk over with you.'

'I'll be here.'

He hoped she would not ask him to have some involvement in the Pelican. He was looking forward to a new start now, to leaving that bit of his past behind.

Tally was upstairs in her room when Kate arrived – Tom had said he needed half an hour to discuss business – but that did not stop her peeping round her curtains to take a look at the woman who would be taking on the Pelican. She was not at all as Tally had imagined her but instead was petite and pretty.

Tom let Kate in and returned her kiss on the cheek.

'How are you getting on?' he asked.

'Very well.' She looked a little uneasy. Embarrassed, even.

337

'Are you sure?'

'Yes.'

He tried to make her feel more at home. 'Glass of wine?'

'No. No, thanks, I won't. It's just that I wanted to tell you before you heard it anywhere else . . . It's just that Pete and I . . .'

Tom felt a rising sense of panic. 'What's gone wrong?' he asked cautiously.

'Nothing.' She smiled. 'We're moving in together.'

Tom could not help but look surprised. 'I see.'

'Oh, I know I've only just got divorced – you'd think I'd have learned, wouldn't you? But, well, there we are. We just found that we like being together.'

'I see. Er . . . how long?'

'Oh, the break-up with Rachel came before . . . you know. I mean, the chemistry was there, I think we both knew that, but we didn't do anything about it.'

'Where are you, er . . . ?'

'At my place for now, but we're going to buy a flat in Axbury somewhere near the Pelican.'

Tom half laughed. 'This is all so sudden.'

'Oh, it's quite mad. I must be barmy. But you don't meet someone you get on with like a house on fire every day, do you? Got to take your chances while you can, I suppose. And I've been hurt once, so I'm going into it with my eyes open. Pete, too. He knows as well as I do that it might not work, but we both want to give it a bash. Just don't want to waste time. When you like being with someone it's wrong not to be with them just because of . . . customs, I suppose. Respectable intervals and all that sort of thing. Who does that please? Only the gossips.'

'I suppose so.'

'Anyway, I won't hold you up. I just wanted you to know from me rather than from those gossips.'

'That's very kind. Thanks.'

'Are you managing OK?'

'Oh, yes, I'm being well looked after.' He raised his eyes in the direction of Tally's bedroom. 'Too well looked after, probably.'

'Don't get used to it. She'll have flown the nest before you know where you are, if not for a while yet.'

'I hope not. Look, are you sure you won't have a glass of wine?'

'I'd love one. I wasn't sure how you'd take it about me and Pete. I thought you might think me a bit of a schemer.'

'Oh, I'm past making judgements. Lost any appetite for it.' He opened a bottle and poured two glasses of white wine. 'Well, here's to you and Pete.'

She smiled, rather guiltily. 'Cheers.' She took a gulp of the chilled wine. 'I needed that. You've no idea how nervous I was coming here and telling you.'

'Am I such an ogre?'

'No, not at all. It's just . . . well . . . circumstances, I suppose.'

'Oh, I shouldn't worry about those. Can't be helped.' He hoped she might change the subject. His luck was out.

'Tom?' She seemed unsure how to proceed.

'Yes?'

'I'm not sure how to ask this . . .'

'What?'

'Do you . . . I mean would you be interested . . . I have a friend who's on her own. Another divorcee.'

Tom fumbled for a way out. 'Oh, I'm OK at the moment.'

'Too soon?'

He sighed. 'Yes. Well, no, I suppose not. I don't know, Kate. There is somebody, but I'm not sure . . .'

'Tom, don't feel bad.'

'But I do.'

'There's no need. It happens.'

'Yes, but . . .'

'Have you heard that theory . . .'

'I've heard quite a lot of theories recently. Which one?'

'Sorry. Only they do say that the more someone loved the partner they have lost, the more likely they are to fall in love again.'

340

'Well, that's convenient.'

'I think it's true. If you've loved a lot you don't suddenly stop having all that love inside you.'

'Maybe it just gets transferred in another direction,' Tom mused.

'You mean Tally?'

He nodded.

'It's not the same kind of love.'

'You mean that's fatherly love and the other kind isn't?'

'You know it isn't.'

'Yes. But why should a person expect to find someone else they can love when they've already found one person? Love doesn't always mean happy-ever-after, you know.'

'Tell me about it. I was in love with someone who didn't love me as much as I loved him. Now, that's the hard bit. It seems to me that holding back when you know that your love is returned is wasteful. And that's putting it mildly.'

'Especially if the reason you're holding back is respectability?'

'And misplaced guilt, yes.'

Tom took another sip. 'You've really thought this through, haven't you?'

'I've had plenty of time. I just think it's wrong not to love someone else because it seems disrespectful to the memory of the person you've lost. That's such a waste.'

'Well, thanks for your concern.'

'I've spoken out of turn. I'm sorry.'

'No, not at all. It's good to talk it through. But I seem to have advice coming out of my ears right now.'

Kate turned in the doorway. 'You deserve happiness, Tom, not advice. You're a good man. Nobody will begrudge you a bit of company.'

She got into her car and motored off down the drive. It was a battered old Volkswagen Golf.

The following day Tom could settle to nothing. He tried to write but the words came out in a childish jumble. He made a sortie into the herb garden, but the coriander and parsley were running to seed and the mint was making a takeover bid for the marjoram. The battle for male supremacy was lost. Pippa would have fared much better.

He listened to Tally in the kitchen, singing as she prepared the supper for three. He had not heard her sing for a long time. Half of him was longing to see Janie, the other half was apprehensive. Would she be standoffish? No. Standoffish was not what Janie did. Maybe she would surround herself with the armoury of mock abuse she had once reserved especially for him – until that morning when she had opened up. Should he have been more receptive? It must have taken courage for her to admit her feelings, and he had brushed them off. Now she figured largely in his dreams. And still he felt riddled with guilt.

At six he bathed, put on smart chinos and a clean shirt, then paced up and down the sitting room. It was too cold to dine outdoors, so Tally had laid the kitchen table and beavered away preparing her salad and smoked-salmon starter.

When the sound of car wheels crunched up the drive, Tom felt as nervous as a schoolboy outside the headmaster's study. He took a deep breath, and went to the door to greet her. The battered Golf GTi had been replaced with a newer model, but it was still liberally garnished with dust and grime. Janie stepped out on to the drive, her dark hair shining, her skin more than usually tanned, her figure slender in navy blue pants and a white shirt. She closed the car door and said, 'Hello, you.'

'Hello, you, too,' he replied. She walked up to greet him, kissed his cheek and squeezed his arm. 'Nice to see you,' he said.

'And you.'

He waited for the sobriquet, but it never came. There was no 'old sod' or 'bastard', just a simple 'And you'.

Tally came racing out of the front door. 'Janie! *Come stai?*'

'*Molto bene, grazie.*'

'Now, look, if you two are going to *parlare Italiano* all evening I shall feel out in the cold.'

Tally grinned. 'It's just nice to get a bit of practice.'

'Hello, my little angel, how've you been?'

'Very well.'

'And what about your pa?' Janie enquired.

'Getting better. Still room for improvement. I thought you could help.'

At the kitchen table, decorated with fat, stubby candles that cast an orange glow over their faces, the three talked about Tally's holiday, Tom's shed and the general state of the nation. Both Tom and Janie became more relaxed, even cast each other knowing glances during the meal, while Tally served up the smoked salmon, then pasta with bacon and herbs, and finally raspberries and cream. There was even a brief moment when Tom laid his hand over Janie's and smiled into her eyes. She returned his smile, then slid her hand away when Tally returned with coffee.

'Well, I have to say, miss,' said Janie, 'that was the best meal I've had in ages.'

'Glad you came?' asked Tom.

'Very glad.'

Maybe he was reading too much into things, but she seemed to say it with more feeling than he had expected.

'So what are you doing?' Tom asked over coffee.

'This and that. A bit slack at the moment. How's the writing?'

'OK, now that I've got my shed.'

Tally rose from the table. 'Back in a minute. Just going upstairs.'

Tom waited until she was out of earshot, then said softly, 'How have you really been?'

'Pretty grim. How about you?'

'The same. I'm sorry. It all came as a bit of a surprise.'

'To me, too.'

'I thought you might be upset. About my reaction, I mean. I wasn't exactly encouraging, was I?'

'No.' She smiled ruefully. 'But, then, it was my fault, really.'

'You were only being honest.'

'Always my problem.'

He hesitated. 'I wanted to say – needed to say . . . Well, I don't want you to think that I don't feel . . . well . . .'

'It's OK. Really it is. Do you think Tally . . .?'

'I'm not sure.'

They heard her coming downstairs and turned as she came into the kitchen.

She had her hands behind her back and spoke to her father. 'I've got something for you.'

'What sort of something?'

'Promise you won't be upset?'

'Why should I be upset?'

'Well, because you might. Only I thought you'd like to have it.'

'Have what?'

'This.' She pulled her arm from behind her back and handed him a single photograph. It was of him and Pippa lying side by side on sunbeds, with their eyes closed, holding hands.

Tally went to bed at eleven, leaving Tom and Janie sitting either side of the kitchen table.

'Shit,' said Janie. 'Shit, shit, shit.'

Tom leaned back in his chair. 'Timing.'

'Impeccable.' Janie looked thoughtful. 'Do you think it was a warning shot?'

'The photo?'

She nodded.

'No. No way. That's not Tally's style at all. She'd suddenly have remembered getting it from Boots and knew I'd love it and acted on impulse.'

'Nothing else?'

'Nothing. Whatever else Tally may be she's not calculating – not in that way. And she's not cruel, either.'

'I suppose.'

'You know, there are two ways of looking at this.'

'That's one more than I can see.' Janie took a large sip of wine.

'Either we go back to where we were, and I start trying to climb the ladder again, or we grit our teeth and get on with it from where we are now.'

Janie put down her glass. 'What?'

'I can't work magic, Janie, but I don't want to lose you.'

'You won't lose me. I'll always be your friend.'

'I was thinking of rather more than that.'

'Don't. I'd rather you didn't say things when you've had a few glasses then regret them in the morning.'

Tom pointed to his wineglass. It was full. Then he raised a glass of water. 'Wanted to keep a clear head.'

Janie ran a hand through her hair. 'What are you trying to say, Tom? And please be bloody careful how you answer.'

'I'm trying to say rather a lot of things and they might not come out in the right order.'

Janie stared at him. He had never seen her look scared before.

'You think far too much when you've been through what I have. There are days when you'd give anything just to stop thinking. Your mind goes over and over and over the same things, and you end up exactly where you started. But you can't stop. It's some kind of rite of passage, something you have to go through – like going to church and reciting a million Hail Marys as a kind of penance. There seems no earthly point in it, yet you do it because you know you *have* to do it, even though there's no end in sight.'

Janie was listening attentively, unsure where he was going.

'It's even harder when the faintest glimmer of hope appears, because then you tell yourself you're giving way, losing your resolve. What you've been doing to get yourself through it all suddenly becomes a way of life in itself. You've clung on to it so hard and for so long that now you can't see a way forward without it. The grief, in its way, is your only source of comfort.' He paused. 'Is this making sense, or does it sound absolute cock?'

She spoke steadily. 'Go on.'

'Letting go of misery is scary, because at least it's constant. You can't believe or trust in happiness ever again.'

'But that's wrong.'

'I can see it is now, but it's taken me so long to get there and I'm not confident of never having a relapse.'

'But you won't have a relapse, provided that the source of the happiness doesn't let you down.'

'Yes, but what about other things? Outside agencies.'

'Death, you mean?'

'Yes.'

'You can't legislate for that one, Tom. That's the risk you take.'

'I know. I took it.'

'And you don't want to take it again?'

'I'd be mad to take it again.'

'So?'

'Can I plead insanity?'

'What are you saying?'

'I guess I'm asking you how serious you are.'

Janie looked at him and said nothing for a few moments. Then, very softly, her voice lacking any drama, she said, 'I've never been more serious in my life.'

Tom sighed. 'Isn't that a bit frightening?'

'Scares the shit out of me.'

'Me, too.'

'But you seemed so surprised . . . when I said.'

'I was. Too frightened to admit it to myself.'

Janie leaned back in her chair. 'Well, what a night this has turned out to be.'

'Yes. Do you think I could have a glass of wine now?'

'As long as I can have a brandy. Look!' She held up her hand. It was shaking.

'Come here.' He stood up and held out his arms.

She got up and walked towards him. 'This is so silly.'

'What?'

'Feel.' She took his right hand and laid it on her left

breast. He could feel the thumping of her heart through the white linen of her shirt. He felt the soft warmth of her breast, and bent down to kiss her. When he broke off and looked into her eyes, he saw they were glistening with tears.

'I think I understand,' she whispered.

'Mmm?' He was stroking her hair.

'You know what you were saying about how frightening happiness can be? I think I see what you mean.'

They kissed goodnight in the kitchen and Janie spent the night in the spare room. For hours neither slept, both staring at the ceiling, separated by a wall. All Tom could think of was how to break the news to Tally. All Janie could think of was how Tom would break the news to Tally.

They were both downstairs and dressed by seven. There was no sign of Tally. Tom had been making coffee when he heard Janie's footsteps coming towards the kitchen. Anxiously he looked round: would she look worried, would she have changed her mind, decided that it was all too much, too soon?

She seemed anxious, too. He feared the worst. 'Are you OK?'

'Yes. Are you?'

'I mean really OK?'

She smiled. 'Yes. As long as you haven't changed your mind.'

'Thank God for that.' He walked over to her and gave her a hug. 'I was so worried that I'd wake up this morning and find you gone.'

'No chance.'

They kissed tenderly and his heart beat faster. 'Oh, you feel so good,' he whispered.

'And you. Oh, and you.'

'You mean I'm not an old sod or an old bastard any more?'

'Oh, you'll always be an old bastard to me,' she said.

'That's all right, then.'

He held her silently for a few moments. 'Which leaves us with . . .'

'Yes.'

'Any suggestions?'

'Absolutely none.'

'So we can either go on pretending nothing has happened, or broach the subject gently and see what her reaction is.'

'Oh, shit! Is that coffee ready yet?'

'Why don't we just wait for a while? I mean, nothing's happened yet. Well, you know what I mean . . .'

'Yes. Sadly. Mind you, I don't know how long I can keep my hands off you.'

A flicker of a smile crossed Tom's face. 'Nor me.'

The discussion was interrupted by the sound of Tally's bedroom door opening. Tom and Janie stared at each other as she came down the stairs.

'Morning!'

Tom busied himself with coffee-making. 'Hello, sweetheart. Sleep well?'

'Not really. Too many things to think about.'

'What sort of things?' asked Janie.

'Oh, you know. This 'n' that.'

'Coffee?'

'No, just cereal, thanks.'

Janie watched as Tally, wearing a baggy white T-shirt emblazoned with the legend 'Does Not Mix Well With Others', poured milk over her cornflakes.

As she spooned up her cereal she asked, 'And what are you two doing today?'

Janie and Tom spoke in unison. 'What do you mean?'

Tally laughed at their chorus. 'I mean, what are you doing? It's Saturday. Start of the weekend, you know? Time off!'

'Oh, hadn't thought,' blustered Tom.

Janie shrugged. 'Dunno.'

'Oh. Well, I thought I'd go out for the day with Emma. She needs cheering up.'

Tom did his best to sound casual. 'OK.'

'Da-a-ad?'

'Yes?'

'Would it be all right if I stayed the night?'

'Er, yes. I suppose so.'

'Fine.' She finished her cereal and began to climb the stairs. 'Only I don't want to cramp your style.'

'Can I just ask you something?' Tom was driving Tally into Axbury.

'Of course.'

'Last night, when you gave me that picture . . .'

'Yes. I'm sorry. It was wrong of me.'

'How can it have been wrong of you?'

'Because the timing was wrong. I realized the moment I'd done it. I felt so stupid.'

'But it was a lovely picture.'

'I know. But I should have kept it for later.'

'So this morning, when you said . . .'

'Yes?'

'What did you mean?'

'Oh, I think you know.'

'I don't!'

'Dad, I can see it even if you can't.'

'What?'

'You and Janie, you're good together.'

'Yes, but . . .'

'Mum?'

'Yes.'

She looked across at him. 'You're too good to waste, Dad.'

He pulled up at the side of the road. 'But what about you?'

'I'm your daughter.'

'That's what I mean.'

She leaned across and kissed him lightly on the cheek. 'And I'll always be your daughter.'

Tom put his arm around her shoulders and pulled her close to him. He took a deep breath, then sniffed loudly.

'But only on one condition,' said Tally.

'What's that?'

'That you'll always be my dad.'

Chapter 30

There are things you ought to know about Tom Drummond. For a start, he knew that living with a daughter was never going to be a soft option. But he battles on. Janie stays with him every weekend – but Tom is still wary of expecting too much, too soon. The finished novel, *Making Waves*, has not yet lived up to its title. He is collecting a file of rejection slips with growing resignation, but next week he has an appointment to see a literary agent. This will make sure at least that his manuscript gets read before it is returned.

He is on the fifteenth chapter of the new book. It's called *Reasonable Behaviour*.

Janie remains as ebullient as ever. Almost. Her

language is not quite as colourful as it was. She is conscious of not setting a bad example to Tally, though she is loath to admit it. But she does seem more relaxed than she used to, and she has learned to be patient. It's all in a good cause.

Maisie has given up gardening, having decided that wild flowers are more beautiful. Her wardrobe continues to amaze. She has still not confessed to Tom that the letter she found in her kitchen drawer had been given to her by Janie. But Maisie was always good at keeping secrets. She remains a colourful but shadowy figure in their lives.

The Pelican continues to serve good food, but some say the service has gone off a bit. Kate and Peter move in and out of each other's flats with a regularity bordering on tedium but, then, two culinary temperaments under one roof was always going to give rise to fireworks. Rachel has reputedly found another man. A bank manager.

And Tally? She passed her A levels – a B in English, a C in General Studies, and an A in Italian. She is now taking a gap year and thinking of spending some time in Florence.

Alex remains the love of her life, and they meet as often as they can, but Edinburgh is a long way from Sussex, and there are the obvious distractions. Tally is steeling herself for the inevitable – not that it makes it much easier. At the time of writing, the two are determined not to lose touch. One can only hope.

Today Tally sits at her bedroom window and looks out over the Downs, remembering the shopping expeditions with her mum and the holiday in Devon. She's come to terms with Janie's relationship with her father, though at times it can be hard. But, then, having been in love herself she can recognize it in others. She tries hard not to worry about her dad, but he remains a bit of a trial to her. Perhaps one day he'll fully admit to his feelings and be happy. Until he does, she'll be there whenever he needs her.

Oh, and Wendy had kittens. Tom does not know who the father is, but he's making enquiries.

If you liked *Only Dad*
don't miss

Mr. MacGregor

by
Alan Titchmarsh

Chapter 1

"Counting out: ten, nine, eight, seven . . ." The voice in Rob MacGregor's earpiece seeped into the back of his mind while his lips continued to deliver words unrelated to those he was hearing. The bright lights of the television studio shone on him from above and three large grey cameras stared at him – one on a wide angle, another on a mid-shot and the third on close-ups of the lily bulbs he was planting in a terracotta pot on the bench in front of him.

Over his shoulder were mock-ups of a potting-shed interior, a pastoral backdrop of an English country garden and a pale blue cyclorama of a summer's afternoon, although it was February. Beneath his welly-booted feet the wooden shed floor was laid over plastic grass.

"And when they've been potted up like that, water them in and stand them outside by the house wall . . ."

"Six, five, run VT," came the count in his ear.

". . . so that they're protected from the worst of the winter weather. It's as easy as that."

"Four, three, two, one . . . and cue the trail . . ."

Computer graphics whirled brilliant pictures of verdant lawns, bright flowers, lawn-mowers and garden views on to the monitor suspended from the lighting gallery above him as Rob went into the voice-over: "Next week I'll be showing you how to make a new lawn from turf, finding this year's best new seed varieties, looking for the kindest cut of all when it comes to lawn-mowers, and paying a visit to Pencarrick in Cornwall, a place where spring always comes early."

"Just loike Mr MacGregor," said a rustic voice off-screen. For a moment Rob froze, then turned to see the portly man with sandy-coloured hair advancing towards him. Bertie Lightfoot was wearing yellow corduroy trousers, a green waistcoat over a check shirt, and a scarlet handkerchief around his neck. The ruddiness of his cheeks was due more to Max Factor than Jack Frost. He smiled deviously at Rob, then sweetly at the camera, his gold filling (third on the right in the top set) twinkling in the bright light.

"Goodbye, all, and just remember that what goes in must come up," said Bertie, in his Somerset burr, looking at Rob then touching his forelock and winking at the viewers.

"Er, yes, until next week," said Rob, and then, recovering himself and smiling at the camera, "From Bertie and me, goodbye."

The upbeat signature tune for *Mr MacGregor's Garden* started, while the animated cartoon credits of Rob pushing a wheelbarrow appeared on the monitor, names flashing up in time with the music until the cartoon gardener closed the garden gate behind him and the producer's name came to rest on the watering-can.

"Thank you, studio." The voice of the floor manager cut through the final bars of the music and he wove among the cameras towards Rob before he had a chance to say anything to his portly co-presenter. "Thanks, Rob. See you again next week. Oh, and I'll bring you my fern. It's got brown fronds."

"Don't bring it in," said Rob, casting a nervous glance towards Bertie. "Just water it, and stand it on a tray of damp gravel so that it has a moist atmosphere around it — it's dry air that's burning it up. Your central heating's probably on full blast."

"Oh, I never thought of that. Simple when you know, isn't it?"

"Oh, yes, dear, a piece of cake . . . when you know," said Bertie. His Somerset burr had been replaced by camp, flattened Yorkshire vowels and a sour expression had taken the place of the smile that, moments ago, had creased his ruddy cheeks. He grunted, cast a sideways look at Rob, then turned on his heel and minced off into the shadows towards the distant yapping of a small dog.

Rob sighed distractedly, wiped his hands clean of compost and walked off in the opposite direction. Once through the hefty double doors of the studio, he went into Makeup, grabbed a handful of baby wipes from the plastic drum in front of the brightly lit mirror, smiled at the girl doing her best to pacify a neurotic newsreader, whose bald patch was taking more than the usual amount of black pancake to make it invisible, then wandered along the corridor to find his producer.

It was a strange environment for a lad who had begun his working life as a gardener in the Yorkshire Dales, but one in which Rob had always felt comfortable – at least, until Bertie had started being a problem. His first call to the studio had come out of the blue one summer three years ago. Greenfly had invaded gardens in their millions, blown over the North Sea and the English Channel by warm winds from Europe. Painters in coastal resorts had found thousands of fat little bodies stuck to their non-drip gloss. The newsroom of Northcountry Television, like those all over Britain, was peopled by eagle-eyed hacks who knew a quirky story when they saw one and they needed an 'expert' to tell gardeners what to do. Their resident gardening man, Bertie Lightfoot, was then on holiday in Tenerife, so an alternative had to be found at short notice. One of the news editors came across Rob's column in his local paper and put in a call, expecting some horny-handed old son of the soil to turn up. Instead, a man in his early twenties had put his head round the newsroom door, a man whose looks and build would have been perfectly at home modelling rugged outdoor wear in a Racing Green catalogue.

When he'd turned up at the studio, Rob's mind was whirling with information and excitement and he was fighting the desire to be sick.

"Don't panic," he'd said to himself. "You know the answers, it's your job. Just be bright and pleasant and try not to speak too fast."

The producer of the early-evening news programme had been very encouraging. "Don't worry," he'd said to Rob. "Be yourself and try to relax. The interviewer will ask all the right questions. He's handled people far more nervous than you are. Enjoy yourself!"

He'd felt as though he was on the threshold of something new that day. He wondered what his dad would make of it. He was anxious not to let him down. If he did a bad job it would reflect on Jock MacGregor and on the nursery where a father had taught his son all he knew about plants and gardening. He didn't want that. He knew his mum would think he was wonderful whatever he did, but if the old man grunted that he'd not done too badly then he'd be well pleased.

Jock had worried about a son learning his trade at the hands of his father. He needn't have done. Rob had the sense and the patience to make allowances for his dad, and for old Harry Hotchkiss who'd helped Jock since before Rob had been born.

Rob's five-year apprenticeship of boiler-stoking, pot-washing, cutting-taking and shrub-growing with his father was boosted by day-release classes at the tech in Bradford – a place as foreign to Rob as if it had been on the other side of the world, but by the time he came to the end of his indentures he was itching to get away. He left for York, for a year's full-time training at the county agricultural college, and then to the Royal Botanic Garden, Edinburgh, for three years, which made his Scottish father almost burst with pride.

Rob did well. He'd grown into a good-looking lad with a passion for gardening and an infectious enthusiasm for passing on his skills. Now a six-footer, he had green eyes and a mop of untameable curly brown hair that framed a face which, more often than not, sported a crooked grin. And Edinburgh had opened his eyes. There was the entertainment and culture provided by the Festival, and the entertainment and culture provided by the women. Leaving at the end of the three-year diploma course had been a bit of a wrench, for one girl in particular.

He'd come back to the nursery for a few months but was soon restless. Gardening and selling plants were no longer enough for him: he really wanted to pass on his passion.

He rang up the local paper, the *Nesfield Gazette*, and spoke to the editor – a young raven-haired beauty, Katherine Page. She called him in, looked him up and down, asked him a few tricky questions then took him on, first as a columnist and then as a boyfriend. She was sparky and opinionated, and gave Rob a good run for his money both professionally and personally. His column caught on quickly: he had a flair for turning out copy that came to life on the page.

Which was exactly what had caught the eye of the man in the newsroom at Northcountry Television. His first appearance, when he waxed lyrical about greenfly, had gone down well. He could remember that first moment of live television even now: the countdown on the hushed studio floor; the red light and the wave of the floor manager's arm that indicated they were on air; the thrill, the dryness in the mouth, the fluttering in the stomach and the strange sensation that the sensible words coming out of his mouth didn't belong to him. It was all over before it had begun and they were patting him on the back and saying, "You must come back, you must do more."

He'd left the studio light-headed, and come home with his feet barely touching the ground. He *wanted* to do more. This was what he had been born to – communicating his passion for gardening to a huge audience. Then he watched the video recording his parents had made and for the rest of the week he didn't want to think about television again. What a let-down. His voice sounded strangled. Why hadn't he known what to do with his hands? Why had he kept looking at the wrong camera?

But they did ask him back. Would he stand by if Bertie couldn't make it? There were several occasions when Bertie couldn't make it – due to gippy tummy, said Bertie (due to Johnnie Walker, said the newsroom).

Slowly but surely his camera technique improved, he gained confidence and began to present his own pieces. 'I don't think you need me any more,' said the interviewer, good-naturedly. By now he knew what to do with his hands: if he carried something they looked natural. He knew that the camera to look at was the one with the red light, and if ever you wanted to change cameras, look down or look away first and then come back to the new camera whose light would already be on. Simple when you knew how. He could even carry on talking when the voice of the production assistant was counting down the minutes and the seconds in his ear, though for the first few times he felt his eyes glazing over as he listened to her too intently. It was, he decided, a matter of practice and aptitude. If you had both, the technique would become secondary and you could concentrate on your style and the content of the programme.

Some time later Rob was given a short programme of his own, regional at first. It captured people's imagination, and just a year later it was expanded to half an hour and screened live right across the country – most other gardening programmes were recorded. Their viewers, so used to staid, sober television gardening, or Bertie's phoney Mummerset, had shown their approval by making *Mr MacGregor's Garden* one of the most popular programmes on the network, and almost before he knew it – if, indeed, he ever believed it – Rob MacGregor was a star, especially with the female viewers who found his drop-dead good looks and slightly off-hand charm irresistible.

His friends had teased him mercilessly and Katherine had refused to take his new status seriously and persisted in making him push the trolley whenever they shopped together in the supermarket. When people asked for his autograph, she would stand behind them while he signed, making faces at him over their shoulders.

Rob wouldn't have known how to be starstruck. He'd dealt with customers in the nursery since he was a boy, and this was just the same. Be nice, smile and answer questions. There was nothing insincere about his manner: he was open and at ease in company. It was only when female fans flattered him too much about his looks and his flower-bedside manner, or asked if they could see if his fingers were really green, that he coloured and fumbled for words. One woman who bumped into him at the nursery even went so far as to try to roll up the leg of his jeans, saying, "Ooh, Mr MacGregor, you've got the sexiest legs on the box." Katherine had had silent hysterics behind a very large hanging basket.

Rubbing off the last of his makeup with the baby wipe, Rob pushed open the wood-veneered door to the office at the end of the corridor and walked in. There were around twenty desks in this open-plan area, and he threaded his way between them. At each sat a man or a woman, gazing at a computer screen, and, more often than not, remonstrating with some caller on the phone. His own producer, Steve Taylor, was no exception.

Fresh out of the studio gallery, glasses on the end of his nose, lank black hair pushed back and the sleeves of his white shirt rolled back, he waved at Rob and raised his eyebrows as he continued his conversation. "Yes, I understand that but, you see, he gets so many requests like this . . . I know, I know . . . Yes, you're right, it *is* a good cause. I will put it to him. But if you could just send him a note." A flailing arm motioned Rob to sit on a tubular steel chair next to the desk. "Yes, that would be lovely. Thank you. Yes. OK. Goodbye." He dropped the receiver into its cradle and slumped back into his chair. "Aaah! Why did they put her through to me? I hope your ears are burning."

"Why?" asked Rob.

"I'm getting fed up of acting as your secretary. When are you going to get one?"

"When you give me one."

"Steady! The budget for your programme's large enough already."

"What! I did all that stuff at Pencarrick last week as a single camera shoot, and now I'm doing winter programmes on a studio set that looks as though it's been designed by Walt Disney."

"Oh, God, prima-donna temperament already and you've only been on telly for a couple of years."

"No, not really. It's just . . . Well . . ." He sighed a long sigh, looked out of the window at the dark February sky, then back at Steve. "It's Bertie."

"Tell me about it." Steve leaned back in his chair, pulled off his glasses and rubbed his eyes. "'What goes in must come up'? I ask you."

When Rob had been given his own programme Bertie Lightfoot's nose had been put well out of joint. *Mr MacGregor's Garden* had replaced *Bertie's Beds and Borders*, and Bertie, yet again, had seen his career on the skids. Once a variety artiste – 'Bertie Lightfoot, a song, a dance and a merry quip' – Bertie had found his work on the boards diminishing and decided he needed to branch out to survive. His hobby had always been gardening, and his garden, in Myddleton-in-Wharfedale where he lived with his partner Terry and two King Charles Cavalier spaniels, was regularly open to the public and had given him something of a reputation as a green-fingered thespian.

He'd written occasional articles for glossy magazines, and eventually been given his own television programme, for which he had adopted a stage accent more suited to Shakespearean mechanicals or rustics in Restoration comedy than to a twentieth-century gardener.

"Makes the advice sound more authentic, dear," he'd said to Rob, off camera on their first meeting.

Eventually Bertie's television programme had been considered past its sell-by date, and his bulbous nose too purple to cover up with concealing cream. The up-and-coming Rob MacGregor had been earmarked as a suitable replacement.

At first, Bertie had decided that he'd go quietly, with just the odd tart retort aimed in the direction of the young up-and-coming star. It had all been made easier in that his usurper was a friendly sort with no overblown ego, and Steve had suggested that the old stager should have a small slot in *Mr MacGregor's Garden* each week as a kind of sop.

Rob had foreseen no difficulties with this, and for a time the two had rubbed along fine. But lately Bertie had been getting just a touch more venomous towards his successor, and Rob had felt uncomfortable. The once-witty asides were now verging on animosity, which was not lost on Steve Taylor.

"Look, I'm sorry, old son. I know it's a problem – I can see it is. The trouble is, he's got friends upstairs."

"I can believe it," said Rob.

"Now, don't be unkind."

"Oh, but come on, Steve. I hate making a fuss about this. It's not that I haven't got a sense of humour, it's just that it's getting so embarrassing."

"Leave it with me. I'll see what I can do."

"I don't know what the solution is," said Rob. "I don't want to see the old bugger pensioned off. It'd break his heart, even if it is pickled. Perhaps I'd better try and sort it out for myself. Look, don't say anything. I'll have a word with him."

"You know, sometimes I think you really are a star," said Steve, with a relieved smile. "I'll see if I can't get you a bit of help with your secretarial work. Perhaps Lottie could take you on. Only part-time, mind. She's got her work cut out with me, so don't get excited about it."

"Thanks, Steve. You're a star yourself. Anyway, I'd better dash. I'm off to see a lady about a garden."

"Oh-ho-ho."

"No, she's old enough to be my mother." A shadow crossed Rob's face and his words hung in the air.

"Well, just watch out. I've seen how these old biddies look at you."

Rob recovered himself. "Oh, not you as well! Why does everybody seem to think that every single woman over the age of thirty is about to pounce on me?"

"It's not just the single ones."

"Thank you! Even Katherine's got this bee in her bonnet that I'm easy prey for vultures."

"And are you?"

"I think I'd better go. This conversation's getting far too personal." He laughed.

"Cheers, then – and good luck with the old son of the soil."

"I'll need it!" Rob lobbed the now salmon-coloured wipe into Steve's waste-bin, went back through the desks towards the door and, as he pushed it open, almost bowled over a devastating blonde. "Sorry!" he stammered.

"Don't be," replied Lisa Drake, giving him a look of amused admiration. She and Rob had never met before, although they were two of Northcountry Television's most popular figures. Rob was regarded as the rustic hunk, but as the station's main newsreader, Lisa's reputation was anything but that of a blonde bimbo. Politicians took this girl seriously.

"I'm in a bit of a rush I'm afraid."

"Evidently." Perfectly enunciated by glossed lips, set off by the wide smile of even teeth. The two-piece navy blue suit, with a white silk blouse beneath it, was the ultimate in soft-edged power dressing.

Rob took her in at a glance. Rather too long a glance.

She tucked the script she was carrying under her arm and offered her hand. "I'm Lisa Drake." She looked him straight in the eye. The handshake was firm and sure. "You're Rob MacGregor, aren't you? I can't think why we haven't bumped into each other before."

"Nor me. Funny, really."

"Your programme's going really well. You must be pleased?" She leaned on the door frame, legs crossed, sizing him up.

Rob felt as though he were about to be given the sort of grilling that Lisa normally reserved for cabinet ministers. "Er, yes, very pleased. Lucky really."

"Oh, I don't think it's luck. You're very good. You must be. I've never watched a gardening programme before in my life but I try to catch yours. It's fun."

Rob looked at the floor, then became aware that Lisa might think he was looking at her legs, which were certainly worth looking at, so he lifted his eyes again, in time to see her flash a final smile, glance at her watch and say, "I must dash. I've a bulletin in a couple of minutes. Great to meet you, I'll see you again some time."

And she was gone. Only a whiff of Chanel remained.

The bonfire crackled and a plume of amber sparks spiralled upwards into the lowering February sky as Jock MacGregor, his flat cap protecting his watering eyes from the heat, hurled another young tree into the centre of the blaze. Through the shimmering haze above the flames he saw the youth retreating towards the nursery gate, his khaki lunch-bag slung over his shoulder and a young pot-grown tree in each hand.

"Oi!"

The lad stopped dead in his tracks and looked around sheepishly, the whites of his eyes almost luminous against his black skin.

"Where do you think you're going?"

"Home," said the lad.

"Not with those you're not," said the old man. "They're for the bonfire."

"Aw, go on. If they're going to be burned I might as well take 'em 'ome." He stood near the old wrought-iron gate, embarrassed at being caught out.

"And where will you say they came from?"

"From work."

"Oh, yes? And what will folk think of this nursery then? If the lad who works here takes home shapeless trees with half their branches missing, what kind of advert is that for a business?" Jock beckoned the lad over. "Do you really want two trees?"

"No, not really. One'd be enough. It's for the old lady's garden – you know, the one I do of a weekend."

The old man looked at the youth. His tightly curled hair was close-clipped into a spiral pattern above his wide, honest face, and three rings were spaced around his left ear. Not the way apprentice gardeners had looked in Jock MacGregor's day. Then they had worn green baize aprons, clogs and corduroy trousers, rather than the baggy jeans, gaping trainers and sloppy sweaters that oozed out from beneath Wayne Dibley's slogan-painted donkey-jacket.

"Get yourself over there." The old man pointed to the standing ground where container-grown maples and birches, rowans and limes stood in neat rows, their vigorous young trunks strapped to stout horizontal wires to stop them blowing over in the wind. "If you want a tree for your old lady take a decent one."

He shuffled back to the bonfire, poked it with his long-handled fork and sent another fountain of sparks dancing upwards into the darkening sky.

"Thanks," said the lad, his eyes widening. "Can I have a birch? They've got dead cool bark. She'll be chuffed wi' that."

The faintest glimmer of a smile came to the old man's lips, then he was serious again. "Just remember," he said, "it takes years to build up a reputation and seconds to destroy it. Folk come here for quality plants and I don't like them to be disappointed at what we turn out."

"Sorry. I didn't mean to -"

Jock MacGregor cut him short. "Go on. Get off home. I'll see you in the morning."

The old man watched him go, a spring in his step and a tree in his hand, whistling some God-awful tune. He looked up at the sky, now a dark blue-grey, and then back at the dying fire. He prodded again at the bright embers that lit his craggy old face with an orange glow. A sad face. The face of a man once happy with his lot but which now reflected a hollowness inside.

Wayne Dibley, for all his unruly appearance, was, Jock thought, a good lad. Jock had thought he was joking when he had arrived there a fortnight ago, looking like a refugee in his ill-fitting clothes. But something about his persistence had told the old man that he might be worth taking on. Harry Hotchkiss was approaching eighty and his muscle power was worth next to nothing. Jock could do with a couple of strong arms about the place, provided they didn't cost too much.

"I don't mind 'ard work," the youth had said.

"I should 'ope you don't," said Harry. "There's plenty of it 'ere."

The irony of Harry's response was not lost on Jock, an early riser who unlocked the nursery gates to let himself in at seven thirty every morning. Harry, with good luck and a following wind, could usually drag himself in by a quarter to nine, and would then sit in an old armchair in the corner of the dusty potting shed, downing sugary dark-brown tea from a stained pint pot. He had a smoker's cough that could rattle the roof tiles, and spent a good half-hour every morning ensconced in the toilet with a Capstan Full Strength hanging off his lower lip and a copy of the *Sun* on his lap. Jock made sure that he was watering in the greenhouses while Harry's routine was in full swing. Yes, he could do with some fresh company as well as fresh muscle power. It might help to take him out of himself.

Jock perched on the side of the wooden cart that held the trees he considered too inferior for his customers. The lad had thought him barmy for not selling them. Maybe he was. But his own training had left him with a carefulness that he recognized as truly Scots. How far away it all seemed now. Like another world. Another life.

Young Murgatroyd MacGregor – he'd been happy to let folk call him Jock – had left school in Perth at fourteen and gone straight into service like his parents before him. He'd never shone at school – for him the three Rs meant rambling, rabbiting and ratting – but give him a plant in a pot or let him loose in a garden and he felt instantly at home. He'd tried to work out why and had decided that quite simply you were born with an affinity to nature; it was not something you could acquire.

Looking at the nursery now, even in the dim twilight, Jock could see why he and Madge had known that this was their rightful place. It was a picturesque spot: the beer-coloured river flowed by at the bottom of a steep grassy bank. When Jock and Madge had come to view it on that warm May day it had been swathed in cow parsley and red campion. It was only a couple of acres, but lapped by the river on one side, and with the moorland rising above the small town of Nesfield behind it, it had seemed like a patch of paradise to the young couple.

On the opposite bank of the river, crossed by a small, hump-backed stone footbridge, was the nursery cottage, a simple affair of local sandstone with a purple slate roof and small sash windows. It was surrounded by its own garden and enclosed by a drystone wall. Over the wall leaned a green sign with gold lettering, though when Jock and Madge had come here its message had been faded and peeling: "Wharfeside Nursery. Prop: F. Armitage", it had said, with an arrow pointing across the river.

Fred Armitage, the bespectacled old Yorkshire nurseryman had quietly impressed on Jock the need to keep down weeds and produce good-quality stock, and asked if it would be possible for his "lad", Harry, to remain with the business. Harry had been in his thirties then, and willing to work, if a little slow. Gradually Jock turned round the flagging nursery and built up the business, with Harry doing the labouring, and Madge keeping the books and looking after the boy.

All things considered, he couldn't have wished for a better son. And now they called him a star. One newspaper had even dubbed him 'The King of Spades'.

Jock couldn't have been happier. And then it had happened. For a month or two Madge had not been feeling herself. Just dizzy spells, she had said, no point in seeing the doctor. Until Jock returned home from the nursery one night and found her on the kitchen floor. There had been no time to take it in; no chance to help her. She had waved him goodbye from the doorstep in the morning when he'd walked over the bridge to the nursery, and when he returned that evening she was lying dead by the kitchen table. A brain haemorrhage, the doctor had said. Instant and painless. But not for Jock. The loss was agonizing, bewildering. What was the point in going on?

He watched the embers of the bonfire turn from bright orange to dull red, and felt a tear trickle down his stubbly chin. It was six months since Madge had died and the fire had gone out in his heart. He turned towards the wrought-iron gate, walked through it, secured the padlock, pocketed the key and crossed the bridge for home.

POCKET
BOOKS

This book and other Alan Titchmarsh **Pocket Books** titles
are available from your local bookshop or can be ordered
direct from the publisher.